Ancient Enemy

Ancients Rising Series

KATIE REUS

Cover Art by Sweet 'N Spicy Designs
Editor: Julia Ganis
Author Website: https://katiereus.com

Publisher's Note: This is a work of fiction. Names, characters, places, and incidents are either the products of the author's imagination or used fictitiously, and any resemblance to actual persons, living or dead, or business establishments, organizations or locales is completely coincidental.

Ancient Enemy/Katie Reus.—1st ed.

ISBN-13: 9781635561470

eISBN: 9781635561463

For Kaylea Cross. Thank you for everything.

"I just can't get enough of these sexy, growly, dragons and the women who are strong enough to put up with them." —Edgy Reviews

"Katie Reus pulls the reader into a story line of second chances, betrayal, and the truth about forgotten lives and hidden pasts."
—The Reading Café

"Nonstop action, a solid plot, good pacing, and riveting suspense."
—RT Book Reviews

"Enough sexual tension to set the pages on fire."
—*New York Times* bestselling author, Alexandra Ivy

"...a wild hot ride for readers. The story grabs you and doesn't let go."
—*New York Times* bestselling author, Cynthia Eden

"Has all the right ingredients: a hot couple, evil villains, and a killer action-filled plot. . . . [The] Moon Shifter series is what I call Grade-A entertainment!" —Joyfully Reviewed

"*Avenger's Heat* hits the ground running...This is a story of strength, of partnership and healing, and it does it brilliantly."
—Vampire Book Club

"*Mating Instinct* was a great read with complex characters, serious political issues and a world I am looking forward to coming back to."
—All Things Urban Fantasy

CHAPTER 1

Rhys stepped up to the nondescript door of the warehouse building in Biloxi, Mississippi, where a big male was standing guard. It was amazing that this place was standing at all, but most of the Gulf Coast had fared well even after The Fall seven weeks ago.

The Fall, aka when a bunch of asshole dragons had decided to nearly burn the world down so they could take over. Things hadn't worked out the way they'd planned, but supernaturals were out to the world, a lot of people were dead, and nearly everywhere was rebuilding.

As a dragon shifter himself, he wanted to hunt down and destroy those monsters for the death and destruction they'd committed. Many, but not all, were dead at least. And the newly created supernatural territories, which had replaced all human governments, seemed to have things well in hand. They were taking out those dragons one by one.

Which was good, since his mission in life—the one that had been driving him for as long as he could remember; the one that had forced him into Hibernation thousands of years ago—was still riding him hard.

That same mission was the reason he was standing outside a nightclub owned by a half-demon he'd never met so he could get some information. The club itself wasn't open anymore, or at least not right now, but the male had agreed to meet Rhys here.

"I'm here to see Bo. My name's Rhys," he said to the male who was watching him cautiously.

The broad-shouldered, muscled guy nodded once and Rhys wasn't sure what kind of being he was. He smelled a bit like a vampire but not quite. "He's expecting you," he said as he opened the door.

Rhys was aware of video cameras aimed at his face as he stepped inside.

The place was expansive, and he imagined that when the world wasn't turned upside down, this place probably stayed busy. A supernatural-only club was fairly rare and his kind often needed the chance to unwind without prying human eyes. Not that it really mattered anymore since they were out to humans.

It was easy to find Bo Broussard, even if he hadn't known what the male looked like, thanks to his intel.

The only person visible was a male with light brown skin standing behind a huge bar, pulling out various bottles. Subtle waves of power rolled off him, though whether intentional or unintentional, Rhys wasn't certain. Some supernaturals couldn't contain their power—he was one of those as well.

"Bo Broussard?" Rhys asked as he approached, scanning the entire place. Empty dance floors, high-top tables with chairs stacked on them, clean floors. There were a few doors that he guessed led to a kitchen and maybe bedrooms, if the rumors he'd heard of the place were true.

The male gave him a quick sweep and nodded once. "That's me. And you are?"

He knew the male was expecting him, but he still needed to introduce himself properly. "Rhys of the Donnachaidh clan from northern Scotland." Though his home hadn't been called Scotland back when he'd gone into Hibernation. He missed his homeland but nothing felt like home anymore. Not even the place with fields so green men wrote poetry about them. "Thank you for meeting with me. I know times are tough right now."

The male simply snorted. "I needed to go through some stuff anyway. Why don't you have a Scottish accent?"

"Ah…" He hadn't been expecting that question.

The male paused when Rhys did, pinning him with an electric amber stare.

"What do you know of my kind?"

The male's mouth curved up in a sort of knowing grin. "More than most."

Rhys wasn't sure what to make of that. But he knew he needed this male's knowledge so he was honest. "Do you know what Hibernation is for our kind?"

"I do."

"All right, then. I just woke up from one about a year ago and I've been living here in the States ever since then." He'd been told that he didn't have any discernible regional dialect—and he liked it that way. His access to and ability to converse in modern language was another thing in itself—through magic mainly. As of now, he spoke a few languages thanks to an old friend who'd helped him get acquainted with this modern world.

"Tell me why you're here."

"I'm hunting a witch named Catta. I have no idea what name she goes by now, but it's the one I knew her by thousands of years ago."

The male stopped what he was doing and leaned against the back of the bar, crossing his arms over his chest. "So why are you here talking to me?"

"Your name came up a couple times as the male who knows all sorts of things."

"Why are you hunting her?" Bo watched Rhys with bright eyes and Rhys was under the impression that the answer mattered.

He could've lied but what would be the point? He wasn't sure how accurate the half-demon's sense of smell was, but it didn't matter. He had no reason to lie. "Because she killed my baby sister. She tortured her and stole her blood in exchange for immortality. Because I'm going to kill her. I won't rest until she's dead. So let there be no doubt, if you give me information on this female, I plan to kill her." Slowly, painfully.

Bo's jaw clenched once and Rhys knew that he had a sister of his own. "You're sure she got immortality?"

"I…" He knew he would sound mad if he told the male the truth. That he could sense his sister's blood flowing through the witch, that the female was out there. Nearby, if he had to guess. "I'm very certain."

"I don't know the name Catta, but I'll ask around for you. There are a couple powerful covens in New Orleans. They gravitated that way after The Fall. If she isn't there, chances are they will know of a witch who killed a dragon for immortality. Killing one of your kind is…"

"Difficult."

"That it is. Go ahead and sit down," Bo said motioning to one of the stools in front of the bar as he resumed organizing bottles. "Your hovering is annoying."

Even though he preferred to stand, especially with all the energy humming through him, Rhys sat, his gaze flicking to the muted TV screen above the mirror and shelves filled with bottles. He froze as he saw a recording unfolding on the screen.

"That's crazy, right?" Bo said after glancing at the screen once before dismissing it. As if he'd seen it before.

"When did this happen?" It couldn't be live because it was still daylight out in the video. But it was close to nine o'clock in the evening now. And from the architecture on the feed, he knew the events taking place on the screen were in New Orleans.

He stared in horror and fascination as his big brother—in dragon form—was blasting away at other dragons, fighting side by side with... *Holy shit.* He hadn't even known phoenixes existed anymore. Apparently they did, and on the screen they were having a savage battle with a bunch of dragons in a still-rebuilding New Orleans.

"That happened two days ago. Do you know them?"

"I know the male."

Bo just stared at him, clearly waiting for him to continue.

"The huge male is my brother." And he hadn't contacted Lachlan since his brother had woken up from Hibernation. He'd been in contact with Cody, their younger brother, and as far as he knew Cody had kept Rhys's secret that he was awake. He'd woken before Lachlan so his brother hadn't felt his awakening.

Shame spiraled through him that he hadn't contacted Lachlan, but he knew his brother would try to stop him from getting vengeance.

Rhys knew he was on a dark, self-destructive path and he didn't want to bring his oldest brother down with him. Because Lachlan would feel the need to swoop in and help. And they'd done that dance before. Lachlan, Cody and Rhys had all lost their sister, but it was clear that Cody and Lachlan had made lives for themselves. And as he watched the events unfold on-screen, he realized that his brother was mated. Or close to being mated, given the protective way he was fighting alongside the phoenix.

Holy shit, he needed to call Cody.

"They're still in New Orleans, if you want to see your brother."

"How do you even know that?"

The male simply grinned at him. "I know a lot of things. But my sister is friends with your brother's new mate."

So Lachlan and the female were mated. "That female looks familiar," he murmured as a new image flashed on the screen. It was a picture of the female—not in phoenix form—taken as if from afar. Kind of like a tabloid-type image.

Bo threw his head back and laughed. "That's the understatement of the decade."

Frowning even deeper, Rhys looked at the screen again, but without the volume and no closed caption, he had no clue what was being said. "Why is that funny? Who is she?"

"Before The Fall she was one of the biggest superstars on the planet. Turns out she's a goddamn phoenix."

"Oh hell." She was *Star*. Famous singer who'd taken the world by storm not long after he'd woken from his Hibernation. *Holy. Shit.* No wonder she looked familiar. He'd seen her face online, seen her on television advertising random things and in magazines. "Look, thank you for meeting with me." He needed to go though. That familiar hum in his blood was pushing him west. Even if the witch wasn't in New Orleans, he needed to head in that direction.

The male simply lifted a shoulder and put the last of the bottles away. "I'm gonna put out some feelers for this Catta, but I need to know how old she is. You can give me a description, but if she killed a dragon for immortality, then she's powerful. She's probably changed her appearance who knows how many times. Hell, she might even have a glamour spell in place."

He nodded because he already knew that. "I know what she smells like. No matter what magic she uses, she can't hide that."

The half-demon shrugged. "Maybe, maybe not. Don't underestimate your opponent."

He didn't need advice, but he nodded anyway. "Fair enough."

"How long have you been hunting her?"

"A long time...thousands of years." Technically he'd been asleep for the last few thousands of years, but even in his sleep he'd never been able to fully rest, never been able to stop wishing for her death. He didn't think Bo wanted the specifics, however.

Bo gave him a long, hard look. Then he nodded, as if coming to a decision. "I'm going to put you in contact with my sister. She can get you settled in New Orleans. Even if the witch you're hunting isn't there—and the chances are slim given how big the world is—there's still a good chance of someone knowing where she's located. Covens around the world are well connected. Too bad for you, they very rarely talk to outsiders. You're going to need an in, and New Orleans is the place to start."

"I've tried talking to witches," he snarled, the tether on his rage pulling taut. "I haven't been able to get a single witch to help me."

The male snorted. "It's no wonder. You carry your disdain for their kind around you like a cloak."

"They're witches," he muttered.

The male's eyes narrowed. "Yeah and I'm a half-demon. I've been judged for what I am most of my life simply because of the blood that runs through my veins."

"I'm sorry. I just want to find my sister's killer. She needs to pay for what she did." It was the only way Rhys could get any peace. Even if he died, as long as he took Catta out, he didn't care.

"Will you hurt any innocents in the process?"

"Never." That was one line he wouldn't cross. Because if he did, his sister would be ashamed. And he never wanted to hurt others the way his family had been.

"All right, then." Bo pulled out his phone and his fingers flew across the screen. "I just texted you my sister's information. You're going to have to get the okay from King, the Alpha of that region, but you shouldn't have a problem gaining entrance."

He nodded because he understood what the guy meant. He was Alpha in nature but he wasn't an Alpha. He wasn't looking to take over territory. It was pretty damn hard to take care of anyone else when he could barely take care of himself. That driving need for revenge was the only thing he cared about. "Thank you for this. You have no reason to help me." And Rhys was curious why the male was. "I owe you."

The male just watched him for a moment. "I hope you find peace."

He would only find peace when the female he was after was dead. When her body was completely incinerated to ash from dragon fire and scattered on the four winds.

Maybe then he could get some peace.

Once he was outside, Rhys pulled out his cell phone and called Cody as he strode across the empty gravel parking lot toward his SUV.

"Hey man, hold on." There was a shuffling sound and then his brother said, "I'll be back in a minute," to someone. In the background Rhys heard laughter and music and then the ambient noise suddenly dimmed. "Is everything okay?" Cody asked.

"Yeah. Lachlan's mated?" He wasn't sure why he phrased it as a question.

There was a long beat of silence. "I'm guessing you saw the news."

"I did. Why didn't you tell me?"

"The thing with them happened really fast and I haven't talked to you in a couple weeks." There was no recrimination in Cody's voice. Never was.

He rubbed a hand over his face and slid behind the wheel, but didn't turn the ignition on. "I'm happy for him," he said quietly, meaning it with every fiber of his being. Both his brothers deserved happiness and he hoped Cody found someone too.

"We head home tomorrow. Come home with us," his brother said, sadness in his voice.

"Not yet, but soon." He heard the lie, but it didn't matter. Rhys had a feeling he wasn't walking out of this alive. That when he killed Catta, he would die too. And that was okay.

Cody let out a long sigh. "You can let it go. You can have a life. You're putting yourself through this purgatory or whatever torture you're determined to suffer through, but you don't have to!"

He clenched his fist into a tight ball, forcing himself to breathe in and out. "I respect your life choices. Respect mine."

"So respect your need for revenge? Respect the fact that this is going to kill you?"

"It's my life. Hibernation did nothing to quell this driving need. I will find her and I will kill her." End of story. He couldn't function until she was gone from this plane.

"Where are you?"

"I'm on the East Coast. I actually am heading to New Orleans soon but I won't make it before you guys leave." A lie, since he could make it there in less than two hours. Sooner if he simply flew in dragon form.

"Do you need a place to stay? Lachlan's mate has family here. They would be more than happy to give you shelter. In fact, I think you'll actually like it here with them."

His first instinct was to say no, but he actually could use a place to stay. And since he wanted to get the Alpha of the territory to okay letting him live there temporarily, it wouldn't hurt if he already had a home lined up. And allies who could vouch for him. "Thank you, I appreciate it."

"I'll discuss it with them and make sure it's okay, but I know it will be. You'll need to talk to King first, but we can wait to leave if—"

"No. Lachlan's been away from the clan for too long. He needs to go home." His brother was linked to their homeland in a way Rhys wasn't. For Lachlan, the land was part of his soul. Unfortunately Rhys was pretty sure he'd lost his soul long ago.

Cody shoved out a breath. "You're right. I wish you could meet Star."

"I never thought he would mate, not after what happened before." Lachlan had been just as broken as Rhys had been, maybe even more so because he'd lost a female he loved in addition to their sister.

His brother was silent for a long moment.

Rhys glanced at his phone to make sure they were still connected. "What?"

Cody cleared his throat. "Nothing. I just miss you, that's all. Once we make it back to Scotland, I'm telling Lachlan you're awake. I can't keep this from him any longer. Especially if I ask his mate's family to take you in."

He nodded even though his brother couldn't see him, and scrubbed a hand over his face again. An old habit. "Thank you for keeping my secret for so long. I'm close to finding her. I can feel it in my bones. In my blood." It was true. The farther he'd flown west, the more he'd felt a thrumming beat in his blood. Like something calling him, drawing him to it. He was so damn close to finding that evil monster. So close to ending this.

"I hope you find what you're looking for. I hope you get some peace."

It was an echo of what the half-demon had just said to him. But he shook off his brother's words. Peace was an illusion for now. A far distant hope. "I'll have peace when she's gone." Then he hung up, unable to say another word to his brother as his throat closed up with emotion. He'd avoided seeing his family since he'd woken from Hibernation because deep down he knew they were the only people who might be able to convince him to stop this descent into madness.

CHAPTER 2

"I can't believe you've trained her to water your fields," Hazel said as she approached Dallas.

Glancing over her shoulder at her neighbor and friend, Dallas smiled before turning back to watch her pet dragon Willow—who was roughly the size of a rhinoceros. Her big gray wings were just a little too big for her growing body so she swooped and wobbled when she flew. She was so dang cute, it made Dallas's heart happy to watch her randomly spray water from her mouth all over one side of the garden. "I didn't teach her to do this. She watched the sprinkler for days and then decided she could do a better job."

Hazel's pretty blue eyes widened. She was a shifter of some kind, though Dallas wasn't sure what exactly. "Are you kidding me?"

"Nope. Willow has a mind of her own." Which was why the big baby slept with her head through Dallas's bedroom window most nights because she couldn't stand to be separated.

Willow flew off again and then gathered water from the nearby pond before she wobbled back and sprayed it all over Dallas's rows of tomatoes, cabbage, and peppers. Next her dragon would water the growing flowers and herbs.

"For the record, this is a weird conversation to be having," Hazel said through laughter, her dark curls bouncing.

"Trust me, I know." Roughly two months ago the world had basically imploded and now shifters were out to the world. Well, shifters and other supernatural creatures.

Dallas was a witch, and her kind had always been pariahs in the supernatural world, so she kept her distance from most supernaturals.

Not all, however, because people like Hazel, who were part of their farmers co-op for all shifters, had not only been accepting of Dallas, they'd simply made her feel welcome. Like family. And they hadn't made her feel like they were doing her a favor by being friends with her. More than all of that, they'd kept her not-so-little secret about Willow. When the world had been literally set on fire, dragon shifters had used real dragons—like Willow—to help destroy everything. Most people thought they were mindless, violent beasts. Maybe they were, but Willow wasn't. And Dallas wasn't letting anyone take her pet.

"So what's going on? Everything okay on your farm?" Because it wasn't like Hazel to stop by unannounced.

Hazel grew corn, beans and broccoli, among other things. She also had a bunch of chickens. In the area—which was about thirty minutes outside New Orleans proper—there were six farms with their lands all connected, and over four years they'd created their own co-op. They provided vegetables and other things like eggs, cheese, oils and soaps for local farmers markets. After The Fall, they'd gotten even more organized and were working with the Alpha of New Orleans on providing much needed locally grown food to the community.

"I heard from Naomi that a group of shifters stopped by her farm."

Dallas straightened slightly. "And?"

"They're from King's pack. They're just making the rounds and checking in with everyone. But I figure your farm is going to be last on their list and I know you'd want to hide Willow. So I hurried over here since you didn't answer your phone. I called you like six times."

She winced, even as her heart rate kicked up. "Sorry, I'm so bad about that." She knew she needed to be better about keeping her phone on her because she lived out here alone. And she liked it that way. No one from her former coven to deal with. But she did have a lot of human friends, and to her surprise she found that they'd been more accepting of who she was than supernaturals for as long as she could remember.

Nothing else mattered right now, however. Because she needed to get Willow out of here. There was no telling what would happen if King or his people discovered that she had a pet dragon. Because Willow was *not* a shifter, she was just an adorable baby dragonling that Dallas had found two months ago and taken in. She'd found an egg that Willow had to have hatched from, but there had been no sign of her parents. It was as if she'd just appeared.

She was growing so quickly and had stolen her way into Dallas's heart. She even tried to herd Dallas's goats. It was ridiculous and adorable at the same time the way she mothered them. But dragons had helped destroy the world and Dallas knew more than most how cruel supernaturals could be to creatures they deemed to be a threat. How they could judge and act without thinking first. They would kill Willow without even giving her a chance. "I'll get her out of here now."

"Good. Grab your phone and call me once you've gotten her to safety. I suggest heading to Naomi's, since they've already been there. It's not like they'll go back tonight."

"I will." Turning, she whistled and Willow angled toward her, hovering over her stretch of roses.

Sneezing, the little dragon expelled all the water she was carrying in a gigantic, wild arc, sending it spraying everywhere.

Next to her Hazel covered her mouth. "I kind of want to kidnap her. She's too precious for words."

Laughing, Dallas waved Willow over and her dragon immediately flew toward her, all happy and eager.

"Oh no. I think it's too late," Hazel murmured, glancing over her shoulder.

"What?" Dallas turned around and saw her house in the distance, and the rolling green fields of her land stretching out in all directions.

"They're almost here," Hazel whispered, fear lacing her words.

Iciness slid through her veins, freezing her in place for a moment. She couldn't smell or see anything out of the ordinary. Dallas didn't have the same supernatural senses that shifters did, but she trusted Hazel's.

"Get out of here now," Hazel snapped suddenly.

She nodded and turned toward Willow. But a huge dragon appeared out of nowhere, as if he'd dropped an invisible camouflage. He swooped down and headed directly for them. His indigo and violet wings glittered underneath the setting sun, creating a sparkling display that could be considered art.

Behind her, now on the ground, Willow made nervous snuffling sounds as she inched closer to Dallas.

Dallas reached back and petted her snout. "Stay calm," she murmured. Whether the command was for Willow or herself, she wasn't sure.

"If you have to, just fly her out of here," Hazel said so quietly that Dallas almost didn't hear her.

"I'm not leaving you."

"These are King's people. They won't hurt me. But they might hurt sweet Willow. Get her out of here. I'm not worried about myself."

Yeah, well, Dallas was worried. Heart racing, she stood nervously as the dragon landed about twenty-five yards away, shaking his wings out. Then three male wolves emerged from the woods, racing across one of her fields on nimble paws. She wasn't even sure how she knew they were males but some intrinsic thing told her they were.

The dragon shifted to human, sparks of magic bursting into the air before the most beautiful male she had ever seen stood twenty yards in front of her. Dark hair, broad shoulders, bronzed skin, bright blue eyes she could see even from a distance.

Moments later the three wolves had shifted to human form and she'd been right. They were all males.

It was far too late to fly away now. She needed to be calm, to keep a level head and act like having a pet dragon was no big deal. If only she could get her heart to stop racing.

"Step away from the dragonling," the big dragon called out, stalking toward them even as the wolves quickly pulled on clothes. Apparently he wasn't going to bother with clothing.

"Who are you, and what are you doing on my land?" she snapped back, tension stretching inside her bowstring tight. King's people might have a right to check in, but they should have called first. So much for staying calm. She could barely keep a lid on her fear as it bubbled out and over, spilling over her in waves. But the thought of losing Willow was too much. Because Hazel was right—they wouldn't hurt her or Hazel, but Willow was a different story.

Before the male could answer, one of the wolves ran forward, his palms out in a placating gesture. "My name is Darius. I'm with King's pack. We just came out here to talk to you about something. What's going on with the dragon?"

She sniffed slightly. "Willow is my pet."

They all stopped and stared at her, looking between each other in confusion before looking back at her.

"You can't have a pet dragon," the dragon shifter finally snarled. "They're dangerous."

She snorted. "Dragon *shifters* are dangerous, in case you haven't been around the last couple months. And it's a good thing I didn't ask for your opinion—jackass."

Behind her she heard Willow whining softly, clearly not liking the tension buzzing in the air. Dallas reached back again and patted her gently.

"Look, Ms. Kinley, I'm going to have to ask you to step away from the dragonling," the wolf named Darius said quietly and calmly, as if he was completely reasonable.

"And I'm going to have to ask you to get the hell off my land. I have no problem providing food for the city, but that doesn't give you the right to show up and steal my pet."

"Ms. Kinley, that dragonling isn't—"

"The dragonling has a name. It's Willow."

The wolf's eyebrows raised slightly, and she was vaguely aware of the other two wolves slowly moving outward from their partners—as if they wanted to surround her, Hazel and Willow.

Oh, hell no. She wasn't going to give them the chance.

Without waiting another second to let them dare try to hurt or take Willow, Dallas crouched down, shoving her fingers straight into the rich soil of her land. Then she softly chanted a spell before raising her hands above her head and tossing a ball of wild magic at the wolves and dragon.

She moved so quickly they didn't have time to react.

Except for the dragon. He started forward, smoke coming out of his nose. "What the hell—"

Hundreds of lavender plants rained down from the sky onto their heads. *Take that!*

"Holy shit," Hazel murmured as Dallas grabbed her hand and tugged her toward a softly whining Willow.

"Hold on tight," she ordered as they both jumped on Willow's back. Leaning forward, she held on to her dragonling and ordered, "Fly!"

Hazel let out a yelp as she grabbed onto Dallas's waist from behind.

They rose into the sky in jerky, quick movements as Willow frantically flapped away. It was like riding on a broken tilt-a-whirl, but she was able to keep a solid grip on Willow's neck, keeping her footing.

She glanced over her shoulder, knowing they wouldn't be able to outrun the others forever. The big dragon hadn't shifted yet because he was still fighting through all that lavender. She knew the male could follow them, but if he tried, she'd toss another spell at him.

For now, she was going to hide her dragon away and then come back and talk to them. She wasn't exactly sure what King's wolves would do to her but at this point she didn't care. If they wanted to arrest her or whatever it was they did, then fine.

She wasn't going to let them kill her pet.

She'd lost so much. She wasn't losing Willow too.

CHAPTER 3

Rhys watched as the little dragonling flew awkwardly into the sky, the two females hanging on tight. As he batted away the ridiculous amount of lavender covering his face, he looked over at King's wolves, who were doing the same.

"Damn it," Darius said as he managed to swim out of the mountain of flowers.

"Could've been worse," one of the other wolves said. "Could've been a swarm of bees. Now we just smell good."

Darius's jaw tightened. "She obviously wasn't trying to hurt us. She's just really protective of the dragon. How the hell does she actually have a dragon as a pet?" Even though it came out as a question, it was pretty clear the male wasn't looking for an answer. Grumbling, Darius rubbed a hand over his face and grabbed his phone out of his pocket before calling King.

Rhys was quiet as he watched the little gray dragon fly over the treetops and disappear. He wanted to race after them, but unfortunately he followed King's orders right now, and would as long as he lived in the Alpha's territory.

Not that he was actually living here in the permanent sense. He'd been here almost two weeks and all he wanted to do was hunt down and destroy Catta. King didn't actually know his purpose for being here, however. He just knew that Rhys was here while he worked on "something." And as payment for him being allowed to live here, he got to help out in any way King saw fit. Unfortunately that cut into his hunting time, but he knew he was supposed to be in New Orleans. Could feel it in his blood.

"King says to bring them in," Darius finally said as he slid his cell phone away.

Rhys nodded because he'd figured as much. He'd just been waiting for the go-ahead.

Darius gave him a hard look. "You can track them?"

He made a scoffing sound. Of course he could.

"Good. Find them, get them to sit still and wait for us. Do not harm any of them." A soft, deadly order.

Rhys narrowed his gaze. He didn't need to be told that. Somehow he bit back a sharp response. "I don't think they're going to go far. It's clear all the farmers here are pretty tight."

"I thought of that too," Darius said, pulling his cell phone out again. "I'm gonna call all the locals in the area and tell them to contact me if she stops by."

"They might not listen to you." The people who lived out here might be part of King's territory, but almost all of them lived away from the city, away from hordes of people. Because they liked the solitude, and if he had to guess, they liked making their own rules.

Another long sigh. "I know."

Rhys stalked away and let the change come over him, magic and pain bursting together in a bright display of light as he shifted to his animal form. That was why he hadn't bothered with clothing before—it would have shredded when the change happened. Without pause, he took to the skies, his wings flapping hard as he flew after the little dragon and two females.

The one that had smelled like heaven and called him a jackass was a witch. He'd known that before they'd arrived and was ashamed that he'd been ready to dislike her upon arrival. Which made him feel...petty and small and worse than the jackass she'd called him.

His dragon had immediately liked the look of her, and okay, he could admit that she was *very* attractive. Her eyes were a pale gray that had seemed to see straight to his soul. And her scent reminded him of moonlit nights and gentle spring air.

He inhaled deeply, following her distinctive scent and the sharp fear scent of the dragon as it zigzagged across the sky in random patterns.

The sun was setting as he trailed after them, and twenty minutes later he found himself back at the first farm they'd visited. It didn't matter that it was now dark out, there were solar string lights stationed everywhere, lighting up the place for half a mile in each direction around the house and farm. Not that it mattered, because they were definitely hiding. He couldn't see the dragon or females anywhere but he could smell them very clearly. Especially the witch.

Dallas. He liked the sound of her name.

Find Dallas, his beast rumbled. *And don't be rude.*

Landing in the middle of the field, he shifted back to his human form, then picked up his bag of clothing. If the females and young dragon ran away again, he'd deal with it, but he figured if he wanted to convince them to stay put, he needed to be dressed. Not walking around with his dick hanging out.

Once he'd pulled on his pants and shirt, he stalked across the grass toward a huge red and white barn. There were a multitude of scents here now, not just a dragon and Dallas. He scented the one called Naomi and the other one with dark, curly hair, Hazel. And…at least eight other individuals. He couldn't sift through all of them so there might actually be more.

He couldn't see any threat so he stalked straight to the barn. As he reached the set of doors, they slid open and Naomi and Dallas stepped out.

"What are you doing here?" the petite Naomi asked, her eyes narrowed. This was her land so it made sense she was out here demanding answers.

His gaze flicked to Dallas and he found he couldn't tear it away from her. She watched him warily, her hands balled into fists at her side. "You can't take my dragon!" she suddenly shouted.

Naomi winced and rubbed her temples with her hands. "Dallas, you've got to chill for a minute."

"She's never hurt anybody!" the female with the long, dark hair shot through with strands of red shouted again as if her friend hadn't said a thing. "She's the sweetest thing ever. And you're a monster if you hurt her!"

"I'm not going to hurt your pet," he snapped out. He was a lot of things, but he wasn't going to hurt a little dragonling unprovoked. Not even if King ordered him to.

The witch's shoulders seemed to ease a little bit as she watched him. "Swear it?" she demanded.

"I swear on the name of the Donnachaidh clan—my clan—that I will not hurt your dragon unless it attempts to hurt me or any other beings."

She nodded once, the mistrust in her gaze easing back a little more. Not by much, but it was something. It was a little ironic that a witch was trusting him, when he'd all but loathed witches for ages.

"I'm pulling my phone out of my pocket," he said, holding his hand out to make it clear he wasn't reaching for a weapon. Not that he actually needed one, but he wanted her calm. "I have to call Darius and tell him where I am."

He could hear murmuring inside the barn as well as the whining dragon when Dallas spoke again. "You think we're going to wait around for him to get here?"

"Look, I can track you all night. Your dragon is *not* a very skilled flyer. She's small and young. You're not going to get far, which means the only thing you're going to do is tire her and yourself out. And likely annoy King's wolves. King wants to bring you in to talk to you about something—it's part of the reason we were out here today visiting everyone."

Her face paled at his words and for the first time in a very long time, guilt punched through him. He didn't know this female. The only thing he knew was that she smelled liked heaven, cared for a dragon and…was a witch.

"He's not going to hurt your dragon," he continued. Inside, his own dragon agreed. King was a fair Alpha. Young, but fair.

"You can't know that."

"Fine, *I'm* not going to let anyone hurt that damn dragon," he snapped in exasperation. "King simply wants to see you."

"About what?"

"I don't actually know. I'm not part of King's pack."

"Then you can get off my property right now," Naomi said, stepping forward. "You have no right to be here if you're not part of his pack."

That was…actually true. *Damn it.* He shouldn't have said anything. Since he had already texted Darius, he shoved his phone back in his pocket and held his hands up in a placating gesture. "Why don't you just take this up with King's wolves when they get here? I might not be part of his pack, but I'm here under his orders."

Naomi bit her bottom lip and looked at Dallas, who appeared just as worried.

Every farmer they'd met today had been a shifter of the peaceful variety. He was pretty sure Naomi was a deer shifter. He wasn't sure what Hazel was, but she'd seemed so peaceful that he wouldn't be surprised if she was something along the same lines as Naomi.

"Okay, fine. I'll go with you, but I'm not bringing Willow," Dallas said.

"That's not my choice." Frustrated, Rhys rubbed his hands over his face and stepped back. That wasn't his call to make and he didn't even want to be here—didn't want to be tangled up with a bunch of random farmers and a random witch who made him uncomfortable. He wanted to be out hunting down Catta.

Just then the barn doors opened and a dozen people strode out, mostly females. But there were two male children as well. None of them looked happy as they watched him with mistrustful gazes.

"You big bully, you think you can come and take our sweet Willow," one of the females he didn't know accused. She had to be pushing sixty and was definitely human. Her white curls bounced wildly as she strode forward. "You listen to me—"

"Listen, ladies, calm down—" The second the words "calm down" were out, he knew that he'd made a huge mistake.

The tension in the air ratcheted up as they all continued to glare daggers at him.

"I mean… Dammit, can we just wait for King's wolves to get here? No one will hurt the dragon," he insisted for what felt like the tenth time.

Dallas turned away from him then and he felt the loss of her gray gaze on him as she looked back at Willow, who was cowering at the back of the barn, her wings covering her face.

Oh, hell. Poor thing really was scared. Not a vicious beast at all. He stepped forward slightly, only stopping when the other shifters seemed startled by his movement. "Dallas," Rhys said quietly, even though they hadn't been formally introduced.

Startled, she turned to look at him.

"I truly swear, on my honor as a dragon, that I will keep Willow safe," he told her. He wasn't sure why he wanted her to trust him. It didn't make sense, but it was clear that she cared about the little beast. And it was hard not to like that.

She stared at him with those piercing gray eyes for a long moment and finally nodded as if she approved of what she saw.

He hadn't felt very good about himself in a long time, but when she looked at him like that, as if she actually might trust him, he realized he didn't want to let her down. Which was…disconcerting to say the least.

At that moment, he heard the gentle sound of the wolves' paws against grass in the distance. They would be here soon.

Less than five minutes later, he was proved right when Darius and the other two strode out of the darkness, in human form and fully dressed. The wolves looked surprised to see all of the farmers outside the barn and glaring at them.

For a moment, as all the farmers stared at them with mistrust in their gazes, including Dallas, he was struck by the reality that he'd mistrusted all witches for so long. Even if he hadn't known them. That was…not a good feeling. The mistrust that rolled off them right now scraped against his senses, making his dragon edgy.

"I'm sorry you felt the need to run from us," Darius said as he approached Dallas.

"Are you really surprised? When four warrior males show up on my land and try to take my dragon away?"

He paused. "Fair enough. Look, King wants to talk to you about setting up some greenhouses, food plots and mini-forests in the city. He knows how talented you are with natural magic and basically growing things. He wants your help. The dragon surprised us, that's all."

"Willow. Her name is Willow," she snapped, all fire and attitude.

"Ah, yes, *Willow* surprised us. You can bring her into the city with you. Nothing will happen to her and I swear she'll be under King's protection."

Dallas looked over at Rhys then, eyebrows raised.

He nodded, and the fact that she actually trusted him felt strange. She didn't even know his name.

"Okay," she finally said. "But first I need to go talk with the others to make sure my goats and crops will be tended to. And I need to get my sprinklers set up so everything is watered."

Hazel strode up then, a couple inches taller than Dallas, and wrapped an arm around her shoulders. "Don't worry about anything. We'll take care of everything. Just make sure you take your damn phone and I'll keep you updated. Stay as long as you need."

Dallas turned and gave Hazel a big hug. "Thank you."

Rhys had the strange thought that he wished she was wrapping her arms around him.

"I guarantee if any of you hurt Dallas or Willow, you're going to answer to all of us," Hazel said matter-of-factly as she looked Darius in the eye. "You won't like what happens if you screw up."

Rhys blinked in surprise because it was clear that Hazel was a peaceful shifter. There were no waves of aggression rolling off her and she didn't carry herself in the way apex predators did. But he could also see the electricity spark between her and Darius.

Darius cleared his throat, and there was almost a hint of amusement in the wolf's gaze as he nodded in agreement—as if he didn't take her seriously.

Rhys kind of figured that he should, because this whole group of pissed-off females could probably wreak havoc if they chose to. It didn't matter if they were apex predators or not.

"I will bring your friend and dragon back in one piece, unharmed and happy," Darius said quietly, watching Hazel with a whole lot of male interest.

Hazel sniffed once. "Good."

"How long will I be in the city?" Dallas asked Darius.

A deep, completely uncivilized part of Rhys wanted to demand that she look at him, and only him. Which was ridiculous. But there it was. His libido had been dead for…as long as he could remember. But one sniff of this beautiful female—this witch—and something had awoken inside him. He didn't like it at all.

"A week, maybe. But I can't say for certain. We've got a place for you to stay, though we didn't realize you had a pet," Darius said, looking past her at the still cowering Willow, who was watching them with her wings lifted just enough to show her eyes. "She really is cute," Darius murmured.

Dallas sniffed as if to say "duh."

"How do you think she'll do around a bunch of wolves?" Dallas asked, biting her bottom lip.

"She can stay with me," Rhys said before Darius could answer.

They both turned to look at him then. He lifted a shoulder. "What? You know who I live with. Almost all females." He was staying in a mansion owned by his oldest brother's mate and a random group of shifters—avian shifters, a phoenix, a couple tigers, and a lazy male lion. It was a misfit crew to be sure, but he had a feeling Willow would be at ease with the females. They would probably fawn all over her and spoil her.

"We'll talk more about it once we get back to the city," Darius said instead of answering one way or the other. He turned back to Dallas. "First, let's head back to your place so you can pack a bag and then we'll head out. Will Willow be okay flying to the city?"

She nodded. "She's a little wobbly but she can do long-distance fine."

"Okay then, let's go."

Rhys scented the subtle pop of fear rolling off Dallas and he couldn't blame her. She was going to be heading into the city with him, her treasured pet, and three other warrior males.

In that moment he vowed to make sure she felt secure during the trip as much as he could. His mistrust of witches might run deep, but right now she was a female who needed protection. And he would keep her and her dragon safe.

CHAPTER 4

Dallas couldn't remember ever being so scared in her life. Not even when she'd defied her coven and left them decades ago. The only silver lining tonight was that for some inexplicable reason she intrinsically trusted the giant dragon, flying in front of her and Willow, to keep his word.

She was really good at judging people, and while she didn't think she could trust him a hundred percent, he'd given his word and named his dragon clan. That was *serious* business where dragons were concerned. Especially since he'd made it a thing about "honor."

So here she was, flying into the city with a trembling Willow and a glittering dragon escort who could breathe fire at any moment if he chose. As the wind rolled over her, she realized that the huge dragon was angling himself so that they were protected from the full force of the wind. If it was intentional, it was actually pretty sweet.

Willow was still nervous, her big body tense underneath Dallas as they swooped over the sprawling oak treetops throughout the city, but as they followed after the dragon some of Willow's tension seemed to ease. Willow almost seemed to be…mirroring his movements. Anytime he dipped downward, so did she. Anytime he banked left, she did the same. Yep, she was definitely copying him.

The moonlight and city lights guided their way, making the flight easy enough. However, she was nervous how Willow would react to being around so many people. Maybe she should have left her with Hazel. Willow might be large, but she was only around three months old if Dallas had to guess. And Dallas wasn't sure how dragons aged in relation to other animals. Unfortunately she didn't have a way to look up the information either.

The big dragon—she really needed to learn that male's name!—circled what appeared to be a huge walled-in compound and landed on a grassy patch in the back.

Dallas could see plenty of wolves trotting around inside the walls and outside as well, either patrolling or just out for a stroll. With the exception of her former coven and her current neighbors, she didn't have much experience with other supernaturals. Well, not good experiences anyway. She knew the basics of how packs worked, but that was about it.

Willow circled in the air, making little crying sounds and refusing to touch down—probably because of all the wolves milling about. *Crap.* Dallas had no idea what to do now. She made little soothing sounds, trying to convince Willow to land, but it was no use.

Finally the male dragon lifted his head and let out some kind of call. Whatever it was, Willow dove straight down for him, forcing Dallas to hold on tight as Willow basically crash-landed next to him, sending dirt and patches of grass flying up everywhere. Dallas tossed out a small spell to cushion her landing as she was thrown off into the grass.

Willow made a happy chirping sound and flapped her wings out, definitely showing off for the other dragon.

The male shifted to his human form and Dallas looked away automatically, not wanting to stare at all that expanse of bare skin. Especially at what was between his legs, because after the little glimpses she'd had... Well, it was impressive. Something she was most *definitely* not thinking about. *Nope. Not gonna think about it at all.*

"I'm dressed," he said a few moments later, clearly having understood why she'd turned away.

She turned back to face him to find that he was indeed dressed, though he didn't have on socks or shoes. In faded jeans and a body-hugging T-shirt, he looked rugged and had a natural, earthy scent to him that appealed to all of her most feminine senses. His dark hair was cropped close, showing off a strong jaw and sharp cheekbones she was a teeny bit jealous of. She had a feeling the reason he kept his hair cut so short was more for efficiency than anything else. He seemed very no-nonsense. His shoulders were broad and that freaking T-shirt was leaving little to the imagination. Not that it mattered since she'd seen him without his shirt. Sure, she'd been scared on her farm, but she'd still seen all those muscles and hard striations. Kinda hard to miss. If she had to guess, she'd say he was about six feet four inches. She was five feet nine, and he still towered over her. Which was kind of hot.

Nope. Stop that train of thought right now, she ordered herself. "I still don't know your name," she said as she kept her hand on Willow's head. It seemed to calm her dragon down.

"Rhys," he said simply, pinning her with those dark blue eyes before he turned away and began scanning the yard, his body language alert, as if he was preparing for danger.

And that was when she realized a handful of wolves had trotted over toward them, some in human form, others in wolf form.

Next to her Willow was trembling, letting out little whimpering sounds at all the new animals. Dallas wanted to tell her that she was a dragon, that she could fly away from them or at least do some damage if someone attacked her. But Willow didn't seem to have any idea what she was, except a pet.

"Back up!" Rhys snapped at the others, his voice commanding and oh so deep.

Dallas felt a shiver of awareness spiral through her at the sound of that voice.

He'd clearly surprised them because one of the wolves held up her hands. "Chill, dragon. We're just curious."

"Well, Willow here is clearly nervous, so I think it might be better if you guys give her some space." His tone made it clear it wasn't a suggestion.

The female nodded once then held up a hand, motioning for everyone else to move back. The wolves all obeyed instantly.

She turned to Dallas then and smiled. "My name's Cat, and you must be Dallas."

Dallas nodded, smiling back at the woman with dark brown skin and tight-braided hair. "I am, nice to meet you."

The woman's smile remained in place. "King told us you guys were on the way. It was honestly hard to believe that someone has a pet dragon. She's so cute," Cat added, her gaze straying back to Willow. "Is she hungry? What does she like to eat?"

"Grass mainly. And she'll chew on bamboo, but she loves berries and bananas more than anything."

"Seriously?"

She nodded. So far Willow hadn't eaten any sort of meat, which had surprised Dallas because she'd thought Willow would try to eat her goats. Instead, she'd tried to mother them.

A female who she recognized as Delphine strode across the yard, her steps sure. "Dallas, good to see you. King is ready when you are. Cat, get out of here. You're supposed to be working the other perimeter."

Cat whined a little before waving at Willow, as if to say goodbye.

In that moment Dallas realized that she would have to go inside and leave Willow behind. Outside, with a bunch of wolves nearby. *Oh, no.*

She shifted from foot to foot, not sure what to do. King was Alpha; she couldn't very well demand that he meet her outside. Sure, the guy was nice enough, but she understood how hierarchies worked.

"Do you think that King would mind coming out here?" Rhys asked Delphine.

Hell, maybe he really was a mind reader. Surprised and grateful, Dallas looked over at him.

Delphine glanced between the two of them. "Why?"

"Because I don't want to leave Willow alone," Dallas said. At that moment Willow covered her face with her wings and crouched down, as if trying to hide from everyone.

The female's hard expression softened, basically turning to mush. "All right, just give me a second." Turning away from them, she spoke quietly into her cell phone for a few moments before she tucked it away. "Come on. Let's head to the pool area. It's being cleared out so you can talk to King."

She was surprised that Rhys was walking with her and she was also curious what his whole role in King's pack was, because he'd made it clear that he wasn't part of the actual pack. No, he was part of a dragon clan. One that seemed to matter to him, if the way he'd spoken about honor was any indication. But he was silent as he strode alongside her, a steady presence that smelled like the earth and made her a little light-headed.

Willow raced after him on all fours instead of flying, taking in everything with wide blue eyes, her wings dragging behind her. Though she didn't stray more than a foot from Dallas's side as they headed across the lawn and around the mansion. As they rounded the back of the house, an Olympic-size pool with lights strung up over it came into view.

Everything was all stone and brick and had clearly cost a fortune. There was a built-in bar area separate from the house, complete with an economy-sized refrigerator and a bar that would put some clubs to shame. Nearby was an oversized fire pit, and a bunch of seating surrounded the pool—lounge chairs, bar-top tables and chairs, two hammocks, and tanning chairs in the actual pool. And a volleyball net was strung tight across it. The thing must be heated—probably with the huge solar panels set up on top of the roof and in the yard—because there were balls and toys gently floating across the lit-up blue water, indicating someone had been in it recently.

Delphine simply nodded at Dallas once and left her and Rhys on the patio as King strode outside with a dark-haired female.

She blinked once when she realized that this female was definitely *not* a wolf. She was a phoenix, a rare creature Dallas hadn't even realized existed anymore. She'd thought they had all died out thousands of years ago. But a news broadcast a while ago had shown the world that nope, phoenixes were real.

"Thank you for meeting me here," King said, flicking a curious glance at Willow, who was tentatively dipping her nose into the pool, making a snuffling sound, probably unsure of the scent of the chlorine.

"Pretty sure I didn't have a choice," she murmured as he motioned for them to sit around a glass-topped table.

To her surprise, King's mouth kicked up as he sat across from them. He was young for an Alpha, maybe a hundred or two hundred years old. Though to look at him, he appeared to be in his twenties, maybe early thirties. With brown skin, ice-blue eyes, a fit body and a fair, if deadly reputation, she could feel the subtle waves of power rolling off him.

"I'm Aurora," the phoenix said, holding out a delicate hand splattered with flecks of paint and a big sunny smile on her face. Her eyes appeared almost brown, but under the hanging lights they glinted a dark violet.

Immediately she put Dallas at ease. "I'm Dallas. I saw that video feed of you a couple weeks ago with your sister." One of the only silver linings of those dragons who'd tried to destroy the world—they'd made it a point not to take out satellites or cell phone towers. So communication around the world was fairly decent. "It was pretty incredible. I mean...*you* were incredible." The female had battled midair over downtown New Orleans, bright blue wings of fire keeping her afloat as she shot bolts of fire at her enemies. Destroying them with a savage ease that was frankly a bit terrifying, if amazing.

Under the Edison-style lights, the female's cheeks flushed pink as she brushed off the compliment with a wave of her hand.

"I asked you here because I wanted to talk about setting up gardens and greenhouses throughout the city," King said, pulling the focus back to the purpose of this meeting.

"Of course. I have no problem with that." Dallas would do everything she could to help people get back on their feet, to get everything running smoothly. Being able to grow their own food was a major step toward security. And because she was a witch, she'd created a sort of bubble around her farm and neighboring ones, allowing them to grow crops now, months earlier than they should have been able to under normal circumstances. She resisted the weird urge to look over at Rhys, who was a silent presence next to her. "What about the current ones in the city?" Because there were a few around New Orleans proper. Not like hers. They were all very small, regenerative farms in the city limits working together within their own communities. "I know Golden Root Farms is okay but I wondered if any others were destroyed."

"Three were destroyed, but the majority are doing well. All human run and all thriving within each small neighborhood or community." He paused slightly.

"But?"

King half-smiled and the tension that had been in his shoulders eased slightly. "I need you to take over planning new small food plots and farms around the city. I'd also like to work on planting mini-forests around the city as well, but the food plots take priority. What the humans are doing is great, but I need a witch right now. I need someone with your skills to handle new regenerative farms because I need them up and running much quicker than humans or shifters can handle. I don't want to have a food shortage problem. So far we're on track to be okay given our current population, but I want to be overprepared. We have a lot to talk about, but Aurora is going to basically be your liaison from this point forward. She's been working with various communities around the city over the last few weeks and everyone likes dealing with her a hell of a lot better than me."

Next to him, Aurora snickered slightly but didn't deny it, and smiled at Dallas again. "I just have better people skills than the Big Bad Wolf here. And according to everyone I've spoken to, you grow some of the best crops. Though I completely admit I now want to know everything about that cute girl of yours."

Dallas glanced over her shoulder to where Willow was now making a giant mess and tossing water everywhere as she attempted to get into the pool. Her wings flapped wildly and she kept sneezing out water as she tried to gain her balance on the steps. And...she popped one of the beach balls when she hit it too hard.

Wincing, Dallas looked at King. "I'm sorry about that."

"My own pack sets things on fire at an alarming rate. Trust me, this is nothing. Though we do need to talk about how you came to own an actual dragon?"

"I found her two months ago. Simple as that. She was sleeping under some Virginia Willow bushes, which is why I named her Willow. I had no idea what to do with her and she decided to come home with me. She's been living with me since The Fall. She's sweet and kind and gentle with my goats. She treats them like her children even though she's a baby herself. I don't know if there's any truth to the nature versus nurture thing, but she's shown absolutely no aptitude for violence. She doesn't even eat meat so I don't know if she's a carnivore. Not yet anyway, but that could change. I've still got a lot to learn about her, but what I know without a doubt is that she's sweet and loyal."

The words all came out in a rush, along with the fear she'd been bottling up inside. It didn't matter what Rhys had said. King was Alpha and he made the rules. If he decided that Willow was a threat... She fought back a shudder, not wanting to go there. On instinct she flicked a glance at Rhys, who simply gave her a subtle nod. Maybe as a way to reassure her that he still had Willow's back?

King looked over at Willow again, his mouth twitching ever so slightly before focusing back on Dallas. "No sign of her parents? Or a parent?"

"I found an egg that most definitely was hers. I...saved the shell in case we ever needed it for something."

King looked at Rhys then. "What do you know about dragons?"

He shrugged. "She's correct, real dragons hatch from an egg. Unlike *most* dragon shifters, which are born. Though some of the very, *very* old dragon shifters were hatched as well."

"Hmm."

"Maybe some of the dragons that destroyed the city laid an egg—or eggs—before they were unleashed on everyone," Aurora said quietly.

That tension inside Dallas tightened until King simply let out a sigh.

"Okay. She's fine for now," he said. "But if you discover more about her, I'll need to know. I'm going to need you to stay in the city for a couple weeks at least while we figure out the schematics for setting up gardens. It's my understanding that your neighbors have no problem taking care of your land, right?"

She nodded once.

"Good. Then I've got a couple options for where you can stay while you're here."

Rhys cleared his throat next to her. "I suggested to Darius that she stay at our compound," he said, looking at Aurora as he spoke.

Our? Was the big male next to her mated to Aurora? And why did that bother Dallas? She had no claim on him. He was sexy as hell—of course he wasn't lacking for any sort of company.

"That's a great idea," Aurora said, her smile growing. "We have so much room there and the girls—and Axel—will be so excited with the addition of Willow," she said laughingly.

"Aurora's sister is mated to my brother," Rhys said to Dallas. "They're allowing me to live with them while I'm in the city."

So that just added even more questions to Dallas's growing list about this male. At least he didn't seem to be mated to or taken with Aurora. Which...Dallas wasn't even sure why she cared. She was being ridiculous, in fact. It wasn't like she wanted a relationship or sex or anything with anyone. She was alone and she liked it that way.

"That will make my life a lot easier," King added. "I know you guys will be safe there. And it's even better because Rhys here is going to be your guard over the next couple weeks."

"Guard?" Rhys demanded, straightening suddenly.

"She's a witch," King said bluntly. "I don't want her getting hassled by anyone, so yes, you are going to keep an eye on her as she visits all the plots I've got lined up for her. I need to know she's with someone trustworthy, and Lachlan assured me you're the male for this job. Is he wrong?"

A beat of silence stretched between them, making Dallas shift uncomfortably in her seat. She was under the impression that she was missing something. It was clear that Rhys didn't want to guard her. And that was...oddly disappointing.

"Of course not," Rhys finally said through a tight jaw.

A weird, heavy sensation settled in her belly. So what if he didn't want to babysit her? If she was in his shoes, she probably wouldn't want to either.

Still...it bothered her that she was so fascinated by him and he couldn't seem to get away from her fast enough.

"Good. It's settled, then." King turned back to Dallas. "Once you've visited all the plots and got a feel for the city, Aurora will take over and work with you in regards to the others."

She simply nodded, feeling out of her depth and wishing desperately she was back at home on her farm, away from all these strangers.

CHAPTER 5

"Aurora isn't coming with us?" Dallas asked as they headed down the street, her sweet lavender and spring scent teasing him.

Rhys had opted to walk back to the mansion in human form and Willow was flying above them, making pleased little sounds every time she ducked underneath a tree branch. He'd only ever battled full-grown dragons millennia ago. He'd never seen a dragonling before, had never imagined they could be so innocent and peaceful.

He noticed that Dallas looked up every now and then at her dragon, making sure that Willow was okay. And yeah, he liked that she was so concerned about her pet. She was nothing like he assumed she would be. He was...annoyed that he liked her so much.

"She'll be back later. She helps King out with a lot of stuff." Rhys wasn't exactly sure of the relationship between Aurora and King, but he knew it was a recent one. Not sexual or anything, though he was pretty sure they also wanted it to be that. But according to his brother, Aurora had recently taken over liaising with vampire covens, witch covens and shifter packs or prides who lived in the territory. There were no dragon clans in the territory, just a few random dragons who had given their loyalty to King.

"I'm surprised he doesn't have a wolf doing that. I thought wolf packs were fairly insular about things," Dallas said with no judgment in her voice, just curiosity.

"They can be. But I think King is trying to take a different approach to running New Orleans." Rhys also figured that since Aurora was new to the city and had no preconceived opinions about anyone here, it might make it easier for people to talk to her. Plus she was unique, which made her a curiosity to supernaturals. And long-lived supernaturals tended to be drawn to all things rare.

He wasn't sure of the politics on her new position and they didn't really concern him. He only had one goal, which unfortunately now was going to be detoured yet again. But he'd agreed to live and work in King's city on the understanding that he would help out when needed. Which was why he'd gone with King's wolves today to talk to a bunch of random farmers about their crops.

And met Dallas.

"I'm sorry you're stuck babysitting me," Dallas said as she shoved her hands into the pockets of faded jeans that molded to her curves. She'd changed from her dress earlier into jeans and a zip-up hoodie that made her appear young. Even though she had some height on her, she looked small and nervous as they headed down the street. Her long braid hung down her back, and under the streetlights the glints of red and gold peeked through. Not for the first time he wondered if her hair was as soft as it looked.

He didn't like the sharp, nervous scent that rolled off her. "It's fine."

She snorted softly. "Trust me, I don't want a babysitter, so if you want to say you came with me, that's fine. But you don't really have to."

He made a scoffing sound. "King gave me an order, and while he's not technically my Alpha, I am living in his territory." Which meant he would respect the Alpha's rules.

"Maybe they can get someone else to come with me."

"Seriously, it's fine. Unless…you don't want me going with you?" For some reason that thought bothered him a whole lot more than it should. He had one goal. One focus. And she was trying to let him off the hook. He should take it and run. But…he found that he wanted to be around her and her pet dragon, which made no sense. His annoyance at himself rose up again. He'd never thought with his dick and he didn't plan to start now. Except…

"Your reaction to King's order was pretty clear. I get it, I'm a witch," she muttered, and there was a note of sadness in her voice.

He didn't like *that* at all either. His dragon snarled at him, swiping angrily and telling him to fix this. Rhys resisted the urge to reach out and comfort her. He didn't have that right. And he shouldn't want it. Witches had been his sworn enemy for thousands of years. "It's not that, I swear. I just...I'm working on something right now. And I want to give it all my attention." That was vague enough without giving any pertinent details.

She didn't respond, simply followed him when they made a left at the next street. "How long have you been in New Orleans?" she asked as they continued walking.

Even though it was late, there were a few people out jogging, and others who were clearly headed to a local bar or watering hole. Even with The Fall, some things hadn't changed.

Willow got a few surprised looks but mostly people went about their business and simply gave the swooping and chirping dragon plenty of space. "A few weeks."

She shot him a surprised look. "Oh, I guess I assumed you'd lived here a while."

"Nope. I'm just here until I take care of my business."

"Then you're heading home?"

He didn't have a home anymore. At least it didn't feel like it. "Hopefully." That was vague enough as well. And somewhere deep inside him, he acknowledged that he wasn't going to come out of this alive. A witch powerful enough to bring down a dragon—and who now had dragon blood in her—was a foe he wouldn't underestimate. He would eventually kill her, but that didn't mean he would come out of the battle alive. And if he had to die too, then so be it. It was why he never let himself imagine going home. Never allowed himself to imagine a life, a family. Those things weren't for him.

"Where is home, exactly?"

"Ah...Scotland."

She shot him another surprised look and nearly tripped on a jutting tree root that had upended the sidewalk.

He steadied her, grasping onto her forearm, though he wasn't sure she needed the help at all. Still, he liked touching her, liked the feel of her soft skin under his fingertips. And just this bare touch sent a rush of heat to...a place that he wasn't going to focus on. "Why the surprise?"

"You don't sound Scottish."

His lips kicked up. "My homeland has many names, and if I'd woken from my Hibernation there, perhaps I would sound like…" He'd been about to say his brothers, but held off. The more he talked about his family, about his people, the more he would open himself up to her. He couldn't be foolish. "I woke up in the wilds of what is now called Wyoming, and when I started hun—" He cleared his throat. He wasn't very well going to tell her that he was hunting down one of her kind. "It was easier to pick up a local accent while living here." There, that was simple enough.

"Hmm." She sidestepped another protruding root and ran her fingers along a bunch of multicolored beads strung up on a wrought iron fence. They made a little rustling sound as they fell back into place. "So…what are you taking care of while you're in town?" she asked.

He lifted a shoulder, not wanting to talk about it. And strangely, he also didn't want to lie to her.

"Oh, sorry for prying. I'm just sort of nosy by nature."

"It's not worth talking about."

She simply nodded before looking up at Willow again.

"This is us," he said in relief as they reached a wrought iron gate that was open.

"Wow, no wonder Aurora said I can stay here. This place is massive."

A purple and yellow three-story mansion that looked whimsical and inviting loomed in front of them. There were a few stained glass windows in the third story and she imagined they looked pretty during the day. As they stepped through the gates, he immediately spotted Harlow and Brielle patrolling the outer perimeter in human form. They'd recently installed cameras and sensors so it wasn't strictly necessary for the tiger twins to even be patrolling.

Brielle waved from her perch on the wall and he nodded back at her.

Harlow, however, jumped off her perch farther down the wall and jogged toward them, her gaze on Willow still above them. "I thought Aurora was joking when she sent me a text about a dragon," Harlow said animatedly, which was out of character for the normally quiet tiger. "Hey, I'm Harlow," she said to Dallas.

"Dallas. And this is Willow." Her full lips curved upward as she talked about her pet.

Rhys wondered how she'd taste, if she'd be playful if he kissed her, or if things would be intense and—

"She's just the cutest thing!" Harlow's voice broke through his thoughts.

Brielle jogged up a few moments later. "This is what it takes to get you to start talking?" she asked her sister, laughing. Then she introduced herself to Dallas, continuing, "Everyone's in the back if you guys want to head that way."

Dallas looked up at him and he nodded. So instead of heading through the front door, they looped around the back of the mansion where the others were indeed talking and laughing around the big patio table. Edison-style lights hung throughout the pergola and over the patio and wove through the trees. The place was full of lush greenery, including a greenhouse. A bunch of chickens normally roamed around the yard but they must be hiding from Willow.

"Everyone, this is Dallas," he announced, then pointed to Willow, who had landed on wobbly legs on a nearby patch of grass. "And that's Willow." The dragon covered her face again with her wings but slowly slid them down and peeked out at everyone with wide blue eyes. At first glance he'd thought Willow's scales were pure gray, but under the manufactured lights he saw little streaks of the faintest red shooting through her scales.

Everyone stared, smiles on their faces. In that moment, he could sense the tension leave Dallas as the others looked on in curiosity more than anything.

"It's really nice to meet you," Bella said as she stood, her long, jet-black hair pulled back in a ponytail. "Aurora said that you'd be staying with us for a little while. I hear you run a huge farm outside town."

Dallas nodded, still looking a little nervous. "I do. And full disclosure, I'm a witch," she blurted, watching them as if she expected their rejection.

In that moment Rhys felt like the biggest asshole on the planet. Because he *had* judged all witches based on a horrific experience with *one*. But it was so damn clear that Dallas wasn't like that, yet was used to being rejected for who she was. And he hated that he fell into that category.

"I'm a snow leopard," Bella said without missing a beat. "And it's pretty cool that you're a witch. I don't want to make assumptions, but do you happen to have any types of remedies for upset stomachs? Poor Axel must have eaten something earlier and our lion has been struggling."

Rhys had wondered where the lion was and had assumed the male was sleeping.

Dallas seemed surprised, but nodded, her expression softening a bit. "Yeah, I can whip something up, depending upon what you have in stock. But I can add a little extra to it," she said, wiggling her fingers lightly. "As long as he doesn't mind drinking something that's spelled. I don't ever give anyone anything without their knowledge, so I'll need his consent."

Rhys heard the truth in her words and felt even smaller.

"Great, I'll show you what we've got in the pantry."

Dallas glanced over at Willow, who was lying on her back on the grass with her wings spread out, eyes half closed in bliss as she got her tummy rubbed by Harlow.

The others were laughing lightly at their antics. And Brielle was just staring in surprise at her twin sister, who was normally beyond quiet.

Instead of heading inside, Dallas shifted on her feet almost nervously. "Generally I don't leave her for very long. Also, by chance do you guys happen to have an unused bedroom on the first floor? She normally sticks her head through my window at night because she doesn't like to be separated. I'm worried about how she's going to handle sleeping apart from me."

Bella's expression melted. "That's the cutest thing I've heard. There aren't any bedrooms on the first floor but there is an office with French doors. We can set up a cot or something in there and leave the doors open if that works?"

She nodded, looking relieved. "Thank you for being so accommodating. And thank you for letting me stay here."

The petite snow leopard shot a knowing look at Rhys. "I heard you didn't have much of a choice."

Rhys simply snorted in agreement and Dallas laughed lightly. The action completely changed her countenance, the sight of the pleasure in her expression like a punch to all of his senses.

Everything about her was stunning—beautiful. And he hated that he was thinking about running his hands through her dark hair, hated that he even noticed the bright red and gold strands woven throughout.

Something told him they weren't dyed either.

"I have to go out for a bit," he said abruptly, needing to put distance between himself and the sensual Dallas. She was a witch, here to help King. He was in the city for revenge. Something he'd never had to remind himself of before.

Bella simply nodded and Dallas gave him a half-smile.

Without another word he stalked off. The farther he got away from Dallas, the easier he found it to breathe. As he made it to the edge of the house, Willow let out a sharp cry.

Surprised at the sound, he turned and saw her flying toward him. What the heck was she doing? The little dragon barely stopped herself from crashing into him.

Oh, hell. She hovered in midair, watching him closely, getting up in his personal space, and chirped animatedly at him as if demanding to know where he was going.

"What's wrong?" he murmured.

As if she understood, she chirped even louder, nearly headbutting him. *Oooohh.* She needed reassurance from an Alpha. Sighing, he held out a hand, smoothed it over her face and pressed his forehead to hers. The action seemed to soothe her because she stopped making the distressed sounds and basically started purring.

"I'll be back, I promise," he murmured. She really was the sweetest little thing. "You need to stay put."

He wasn't sure that she understood his words, but she must have understood his meaning, because she let out a loud chirping sound and flew back to the others.

He caught Dallas's gaze from across the yard, and when he saw her soft, open expression he forced himself to turn away again. This female was threatening to undo him.

Yep, he needed distance from her. Fast.

CHAPTER 6

Two hours after he'd left for his own sanity, Rhys returned to the mansion with no new information and a strange sort of anxiety buzzing through him at the need to see Dallas again. What the hell was wrong with him?

He rolled his shoulders as he quietly slipped in through the front door. He needed to get his shit together, needed to stop thinking about Dallas. Although that was going to be pretty damn difficult, considering he'd been ordered to be her shadow the next couple weeks.

As he started to head up the stairs, he paused as he heard voices trailing from somewhere in the house. A very distinctive male voice—Axel's—followed by Dallas's laughter. Rhys straightened and instead of heading upstairs to his bedroom where he should be going, he hurried as casually as possible through the house to where the voices were coming from.

"I swear, you are magic," Axel said, practically purring.

Damn lion.

"I'm just glad the tea worked," Dallas murmured.

Rhys stepped into the kitchen to find the two of them sitting across from each other at the white granite center island, Axel holding a mug of tea that smelled like peppermint and something else Rhys couldn't quite figure out. Only the small pendant light over the sink and some of the under-cabinet lights were on, giving the whole room a sort of…romantic feel. Rhys didn't like this at all.

"Rhys, my man." Axel smiled in that genial way of his, as if he didn't have a care in the world. "Dallas here is a goddess. Whatever she gave me, I feel a hundred times better."

Rhys clenched his jaw and actually had to bite back a growl at this male praising her. It was clear that Axel wasn't hitting on her, just complimenting her. But his dragon wanted to rip Axel's face off nonetheless. Then burn him to a crisp. And maybe eat him for a midnight snack.

Whatever expression was on his face, it made Axel frown at him. "Everything all right?"

He cleared his throat and realized that Dallas was watching him warily as well. "Yeah, I just had an unsuccessful night, that's all." And he did *not* want to care about the witch in front of him. Or the fact that he was beyond annoyed that Axel seemed so enamored by her.

Axel pushed up from his chair and took his mug to the sink. "Maybe if you ask nicely, Dallas will make you some tea as well." Then the big lion kissed her on top of her head and said, "Welcome to the house. If you need anything, my bedroom is on the second floor."

Rhys couldn't tell if the male was flirting with her or just trying to be helpful, but he felt his dragon in his eyes so he turned away until he was able to get himself under control.

Dallas murmured a generic thanks as the lion strode from the room. Then she smiled at Rhys. "I'm sorry you had a bad night. Did you want some tea?" Her voice was like sunshine, bathing him in its warmth. "He's had like two pots of this stuff."

"I don't want you to go to any trouble." He didn't want any tea, but he also didn't want to go to bed. He just wanted to be around Dallas for a few more minutes, to extend their time together as long as possible. Something about her presence soothed something deep inside him. Which made no sense.

"It's really no trouble," she said, glancing out the kitchen window. "Poor Willow, she can't seem to get settled. I was hoping she would calm down a little bit as it got later." Moving around the kitchen with ease, she pulled out another mug. "Oh, it looks like there's enough, so I don't even have to make any more," she said as she poured him a full mug.

"Thank you." He took it, careful not to brush his fingers against hers. Then he motioned that he was going outside.

She followed after him and he could see what she'd meant because Willow was pacing, her little wings flapping up and down as she tried to get settled on a soft patch of grass next to the open French doors that must lead to Dallas's room.

Willow let out a little snort of happiness when she saw Dallas and nearly stumbled over a lawn chair in her quest to get to her.

I understand the feeling, he thought.

"Hey, sweet girl," Dallas said as Willow met her halfway on the lawn. The dragonling put her face against Dallas and Dallas kissed her cheek.

The little dragon made another snuffling sound that was a mix between a sneeze and a cough before she looked over at him and made a happy chirping greeting as she raced toward him.

His heart thawed a bit as she practically headbutted him in her attempt to get close. Laughing despite his mood, he petted her head, right behind her ear where she seemed to like it, if her purrs were any indication. "I can sleep out here with her." The words were out before Rhys realized what he'd been about to say.

Dallas stared at him in surprise, her pale gray eyes wide. "What?"

"I'll just stay out here in my dragon form. I like sleeping that way anyway. I can stretch my wings and it should settle her." The dragonling was far from home and needed some comfort. He understood that on a bone-deep level. And who was he kidding? He simply felt protective of her. And Dallas.

"Seriously?"

"Yeah, it's a nice night." It was chilly and overcast since the clouds had moved over the bright moon, but he didn't care.

"They put me right over here." She pointed to the already open French doors on the east side of the house and strode toward them, Willow right on her heels.

He'd been in the room before and it was an office/library, but they'd set a little foldout bed in there for her.

"I was just thinking that Willow could stick her head in here while I sleep. I don't plan on being here too long, so I think she'll be okay for a week or two."

Some part of him didn't like the thought of Dallas sleeping with the doors open, even with Willow as a guard and with the security cameras and sensors—and two shifters on patrol. It seemed too exposed. His dragon wanted to guard her.

He lifted a big shoulder, as if he didn't care one way or another, even as his dragon insisted they protect her. "Look, I'm going to sleep out here no matter what."

"Okay then…would you mind hanging out here with her for a little bit while I get changed?"

"Of course not." He wasn't going anywhere.

Even though Dallas stepped inside and shut the door behind her, Willow didn't whine. Instead, she butted her head up against Rhys's hand and he realized that she wanted to be petted again. Laughing, he set the tea down on the ground and rubbed her head with both hands.

She closed her eyes and snuggled up against him, perfectly at peace.

As she started to calm down and finally curl up into a little ball, he quickly stripped and put some distance between them so he could shift. Once he was in his dragon form, she slowly inched her way toward him until she crawled up right under his chest. She let out a sigh of happiness, curled back up and fell into a fast sleep.

Oh sweet goddess, this dragon was too much.

He heard the French doors open, and then a little gasp of surprise from Dallas. When he looked over, she had on yellow lounge pants and a formfitting T-shirt that outlined every curve of her very full breasts. He shouldn't be noticing, but his beast called him a fool for trying to ignore her.

She lifted a hand as if checking in with him.

He simply lifted one of his wings, which seemed to satisfy Dallas. For Willow's part, she hadn't even moved. She stayed tight against him, breathing in and out in a steady rhythm.

Closing his own eyes, he wrapped his wings around her and tried to get some sleep.

And tried *not* to think about the sexy female a few yards away from him.

CHAPTER 7

Dallas opened her eyes with a start, then settled when she remembered where she was. Faint daylight streamed in her open French doors. The thick cream and white silk curtains covering the windows on another wall barely stirred with the light breeze. Sitting up on the cot, she saw that Willow and Rhys weren't sleeping where she could see them, but she heard female voices outside.

Standing, she stretched, curling her toes into the thick multicolored Persian rug. Then she grabbed a robe and tugged it on before hurrying out the doors. As soon as she stepped into the backyard, she blinked to see Willow pouncing on Rhys, who was still in his huge—gorgeous—dragon form, barely moving as Willow "attacked." Her sweet girl was clearly playing with him as a baby tiger might play with its mama.

She spotted some of the women from yesterday sitting around the long patio table, watching the show. And she was pretty sure she spotted coffee. While she preferred tea, she could admit she was a sucker for bean juice too. She hurried over to the table. "Got any extra coffee?"

"Take whatever you like," Brielle said as she moved the carafe toward her. She was already dressed in what looked like tactical clothing—cargo pants, a tight black T-shirt. She had a couple weapons strapped to her legs, and her hair was pulled back into a neat ponytail. "We've got creamer and sugar inside."

She sank down into one of the chairs and poured herself a mug. The hazelnut blend teased her nose before she took a sip. Yep, she was definitely going to need some sugar but she wanted to watch the show for a while. "How long have they been doing this?"

"About twenty minutes."

She let out a startled laugh as Willow pounced on Rhys's head, covering his eyes with her wings before she suddenly let go and rolled off him in a free fall.

Moving lightning quick, Rhys scooped her up with his massive indigo and purple wing before she hit the ground, then gently set her on a patch of grass. Willow let out a little shrieking sound of pure happiness that Dallas had never heard before. Then she flew right back upward and pounced on his head again. Acting as if she actually was a toddler, she did the same thing again and "accidentally" fell off, tumbling toward the grass. Once again, Rhys caught her and she made the same shrieking sound of joy.

Dallas's heart squeezed as she watched the two of them. This big, kinda grumpy dragon apparently had a marshmallow inside. At least where Willow was concerned. And that…was pretty damn hard to resist. Not to mention he was stunning in this form, like a piece of art. She wanted to take a picture of him, to capture his beauty, but didn't think it would do him justice. She couldn't even begin to guess how huge he was— if he stood up fully, his head would top the nearby oak tree. But it was his scales that drew all her attention; the blues and purples seemed to flow and shift when he did, glittering prettily underneath the rising sun.

"This level of cuteness should be outlawed," Bella said as she joined them in a robe and pajamas covered in dancing cats.

At least Dallas wasn't the only one still in PJs. It was kind of weird to be around other people, especially in the morning. Normally she liked her quiet, her routine, but she could admit this was nice too. It was the company that made the difference, however. So far everyone who lived here was warm and welcoming.

"How long have you had her?" Harlow asked, plopping down next to her twin, fully dressed as well as she munched on an apple.

"Not long. I found her a couple months ago."

"Crap, we'll need to get her food, won't we?" Harlow said, shifting in her seat as if she was about to run out and do just that.

Yeah, she'd thought about that this morning as well. "I can take care of it. There are some pear trees on the west side of the yard that likely won't bloom for another four to six months. But I can change that—does anyone mind if I inject a little magic into the trees to get some more fruit for her?" She could make the fruit grow to proportions perfect for Willow.

"Please go for it," Bella said. "Hey, can you make our chickens turn into, like, mutant chickens? Have them produce giant eggs?"

Brielle shot her a horrified look but Dallas snickered and shook her head. "No. I mean I guess technically I could, but that's weird and I'm not going to attempt it."

"What's it like being a witch?" Bella asked.

"I don't know, what's it like being able to turn into a snow leopard?"

Bella sighed happily. "The most awesome thing in the world."

She laughed lightly at the woman's answer. "I don't really know how to answer, honestly. It's just who I am, I've had my powers since I was born."

The females at the table stared at her and she squirmed slightly under their scrutiny. Because yeah, she knew that she was different. Most witches came into their power in their teens or sometimes even in their twenties or thirties, but she'd just been born this way. The magic was always there for those who didn't come into their powers until later. Usually an event triggered the awakening, but for her, she was who she was.

She knew it made her rarer than most of her kind. She also didn't mess around with blood magic, because that shit was dark. She tried to respect everything around her, especially nature. And despite what some human scientists were still trying to grasp, science and magic worked beautifully together. So when witches injected natural magic into crops, it wasn't remotely the same as using pesticides or hormones.

"That's pretty cool," Brielle finally said, turning back to watch the dragon show.

She heard the truth in the woman's voice and the band clenched tight around her chest eased. Maybe...she could be friends with these shifters. "Thanks. I think being able to turn into an animal is pretty cool too."

"There really is nothing else like it." Brielle stretched out her long legs and took a sip of her coffee.

"I swear if I found that male attractive, this whole scene would get my ovaries going," Bella murmured, making the others snicker.

Dallas wasn't sure why Bella didn't find Rhys attractive, because that male was the sexiest she'd ever met. Like, *ever*. He was walking, talking, panty-melting hotness. So clearly something was wrong with Bella's eyesight.

Axel approached the table with two canisters in hand. "I don't know how you guys drink this stuff without sugar or cream. You're barbarians."

"Thank you," she said, reaching for the one marked *sugar*.

"So what's on your agenda today?" he asked as he sat next to her, stretching out in that languid, feline way. His long hair was pulled up into a bun and his bronze skin seemed to practically glow, as if he'd just spent the day tanning outdoors.

Before she could answer, she was aware of Rhys suddenly shifting to his human form and heading toward them—sans pants.

She felt her cheeks turn red, even though the others didn't seem at all bothered by the display of nudity. She'd forgotten that shifters could be so blasé about any sort of nakedness, but she was a witch and her kind did *not* go around taking off their clothes at random intervals. Witches had that in common with humans for sure.

"Good morning, Dallas," Rhys said in that deep, delicious voice as he sat in the chair across from her. Somehow, he'd found pants on the walk over here when she'd been turned away. Though it did seem a bit of a shame to cover up all that glorious skin. And...other stuff. But this was much better for her sanity. At least he didn't have a shirt on. Instead he was displaying all those ridiculous muscles, which were really, really hard to ignore. Somehow she forced her gaze to remain on his face.

She loved the way he said her name but reminded herself that she had to keep her emotions on lockdown because if she allowed herself to get turned on or anything, he would definitely smell it. They all would. And that was just plain embarrassing.

"Good morning," she murmured, glancing at him and then Willow over his shoulder, who was currently doing midair dive-bombs toward the ground then basically cackling to herself when she swooped up at the last minute before crash-landing. "What have you done to my dragon? I've never seen her like this."

"She's a playful little thing," was all he said.

"She didn't bother you last night?"

He simply snorted softly. "She slept like the dead. Then the chickens woke her up so she tried to play with them, but I could tell that was going to end poorly, so we had a bit of fun in the yard. She's a fast learner."

"Thank you," she said, meaning it. He didn't have to be so sweet to Willow, and the way he was acting brought up far too many maternal instincts inside her. Instincts she hadn't even realized she had. She'd never once thought about how a past lover might be as a father, but with Rhys, it was easy to imagine different scenarios where he was one. And that…that was not good. For too many reasons.

She realized that Axel was watching the two of them, his interest in their conversation clear. She frowned at the lion, who looked far too smug. She couldn't imagine why he was smug, however. Maybe it was just a feline thing?

"What time would you like to get started today?" Rhys asked, drawing her attention back to him.

"Yes, what time?" Axel asked. "I would *love* to join the two of you."

"Your help is not needed, cat," Rhys snarled.

She blinked, looking between the two of them, and she realized that the female shifters were all smirking into their mugs. What was wrong with everyone this morning? Grabbing her coffee, she stood, feeling awkward. This was why she liked her solitude. At least then she always knew where she stood and there was never any weirdness. "I just need to grab a quick shower, then I'll be ready to head out. King sent over a list of places and I'm not completely sure which ones would be better to go to first. We can come up with a game plan before we head out though."

"I've got a great working knowledge of the city." Smiling, Axel crossed one ankle over the other as he watched her. "I think I would be a great asset to you guys."

She nodded, ready to tell him that of course he could come with them, but Rhys abruptly stood. "King does not want you with us." *And neither do I* seemed to be the unspoken words.

She looked over at Bella, who simply shook her head. "Willow will be fine with us while you're gone," she said, reading Dallas's mind.

"Thanks. I might bring her with us though, if you don't think it would be a problem in the city?" She probably should've asked King about that, but last night had been so hectic. She hadn't expected them to discover her dragon or to be called into the city on a sudden job. She liked her routine and now everything was in disarray.

"Whatever's easiest for you, but we really don't mind. Lola will be home soon too and she'll be excited to meet Willow."

Dallas hadn't met Lola yet, but had been informed by Axel that she was a badass hacker. "Okay, if you guys really are fine with her..."

"We are, promise." Bella's smile was warm, real.

Axel, still grinning, cleared his throat. "I'm going to call King and—"

Rhys clasped Axel on the back of the neck. "We're good." His words were gritted out.

Okay, something weird was going on between the males, but she wasn't going to worry about it. She didn't have enough understanding of shifter hierarchies to understand the dynamics between dragons and lions. Instead she hurried over to give Willow kisses before she headed inside and jumped in the shower.

The guest bathroom was small but must have been remodeled before The Fall. The shower tile was a gorgeous white stone material that seemed to sparkle as water hit it. The floor tile was an intricate-looking basket weave of mostly white with black squares woven throughout it. The seamless look extended to the rest of the small room, tying everything together nicely.

She paid attention to aesthetics and this little bathroom had a peaceful feel to it. While she shampooed her hair in said bathroom, she forced herself not to think about Rhys—or his broad shoulders, plethora of muscles, the sweet way he played with Willow...all those damn muscles. How he'd looked like an avenging warrior as he'd stalked across the grass naked this morning. *Gah!*

Scrubbing at her hair way too hard, she decided that another pep talk was in order. She only had two weeks at most to be stuck here in the city.

Then she was heading back to her farm, back to her quiet life, her goats and her home. Far, far away from the brooding dragon shifter with the dark blue, haunting eyes.

CHAPTER 8

Dallas and Rhys didn't have to walk far to look at their first designated garden plot. It only took twenty minutes on foot to make it to the neighborhood. Rhys had offered to fly them to the rest of the potential plots around the city, but Dallas wasn't sure how comfortable she felt with that. Riding on a dragon—who was not her pet—was a big deal in the supernatural world. It surprised her that he'd offered at all. Still, it made her feel uncomfortable and she wasn't sure why.

That wasn't true. Maybe it was because there was underlying weirdness between them. She could tell he didn't trust her so the fact that he'd offered to let her ride him was, well, weird. Maybe it had to do with more of those shifter things she didn't understand. He might have offered because King had ordered him to.

"This place is fantastic," she murmured as they stepped through open gates into a huge yard that surrounded a mansion very similar to the one they were staying in. "Who lives here?"

"A vampire coven *used* to live here," he said shortly, his gaze tracking over all the overgrown foliage.

She barely glanced at the huge mansion, not really concerned with it, not when there was so much lush greenery here. There was enough room for a decent-sized greenhouse and open areas of lawn where she could plant a bundle of trees. If she used her magic, the trees and other plants would be able to grow at a rapid rate and start producing earlier than normal. It often took a few years for fruit trees to even bloom or produce, but she'd always adhered to her own gardening rules. She'd been born with the gift of helping things thrive and grow, so she used it and injected all the kindness and happiness into her projects that she could.

Next to her Rhys was a statue, his body still in that way shifters could be.

"Is everything okay?" she asked.

"Yes. Why?" He didn't look at her, just continued scanning as if there was a threat behind the walls of the mansion. Maybe he sensed something she didn't.

She lifted a shoulder as they walked through the calf-high grass. "You and Axel were kind of weird with each other this morning." Though for all Dallas knew that was normal behavior for the two of them. She really didn't have much of an example to go on since she'd only seen their interaction once before.

Rhys snorted, the sound kind of at odds with the serious dragon shifter. "Axel's a jackass."

"I don't know, he seems pretty nice to me."

He shot her an annoyed look, his gaze landing on her mouth for a moment before he quickly looked away.

She blinked, wondering if that little spark she'd seen had been her imagination. "Are dragons and lions at odds with each other?"

"Nope. Just me and Axel."

Huh. Okay, then. Clearly he wasn't going to give her more, so she let the subject drop. She had no interest in shifter politics...or whatever was going on between them.

As they reached an area where a cluster of hydrangea shrubs circled a huge oak tree, she reached down and slid her fingers into the soil. Sending out a tiny pulse of magic, she felt how rich this area was. Yes, they could grow a *lot* here and in the surrounding areas.

On impulse, she sent out another burst of magic over the shrubs and gorgeous hydrangeas blossomed, purple flowers covering the previously green leaves. The burst of color surrounding the tree stood out against the green backdrop of the yard and just the sight of it made her heart smile. This would only last twenty-four hours, then they would recede and only come out in a few months when they were supposed to. For now, however, they got to shine.

"What kind of magic are you using?" Rhys snapped suddenly, making her jerk.

Startled, she realized he was glaring down at her.

Withdrawing her hand from the dirt, she wiped her hands off on her jeans and stood, looking up at him, a thread of worry winding its way through her blood. "What do you mean?"

"Nothing," he muttered before stalking away, quickly putting distance between them.

Dallas wasn't going to deal with some weird hot-and-cold attitude. Instead of letting him walk away, she hurried after him and grabbed his forearm. "Seriously, what's going on? Don't say nothing, because that insults me and it's just plain annoying. I'm only doing what was asked of me. If you're going to act like this, then I'm going to request that someone else escort me around the city. I'm sure Axel won't mind." He'd seemed eager to come out with them today and right about now she wished she had a buffer in the form of a friendly lion shifter.

Rhys turned to her and didn't pull away from her hold. "You're a witch," he finally said, each word clipped.

She let her hand drop at the way he said the word *witch*, because she realized he was just like everyone else. "Oh, I see. You just judge me for what I am. I get it. *Trust* me." She was unable to keep the bitterness out of her voice. Normally she could go full-on neutral and pretend she didn't care what others thought of her. Because she'd convinced herself that she didn't. That it didn't hurt every single time she thought she'd found a friend, only to have them decide she wasn't worth it once they discovered she was a witch. It was why she now told people what she was up front— saved her a lot of heartache.

Turned out he was just another asshole. It shouldn't hurt, but for some reason it punched deep. Probably because she was attracted to him, so that just made his judgment and rejection all the more upsetting.

Not wanting him to see how much he'd hurt her, she turned away and closed her eyes. Then she took a deep, steadying breath to center herself. When she opened her eyes he was standing in front of her. Dallas took a startled step back then, surprised by how quietly he moved.

"I'm sorry," he said. "Being around you...made me realize that...I have made some inaccurate judgments."

"Whatever," she muttered. "I'm going to ask King to assign someone else to me."

"A witch killed my sister," he suddenly blurted.

Surprise punched through her. "What?"

He shoved his hands in his pockets but held her gaze. "A long time ago, thousands of years, in fact, a witch murdered my sister. She entrapped her, using their friendship, then drained her blood for immortality. She tortured her and didn't stop until my sister was nothing but bones."

"Blood magic," Dallas whispered, suddenly cold inside. She abhorred blood magic. It could actually be used by humans as well as natural witches. It was dark, unsavory, and very, *very* dangerous. It could open dangerous doors or portals to Hell realms, even to Hell itself. And...other places. For a witch to be able to ensnare a dragon...she must be powerful.

Jaw tight, he nodded.

"I'm sorry about your sister." No wonder he didn't like witches.

"I am too. Her name was Eilidh... I'm still hunting for her killer."

Understanding dawned inside her. "Is that why you're here in New Orleans?" Because she'd been wondering why he was away from his whole family, in the city, under an Alpha who was not his own. It didn't make sense. Not when such clear power rolled off him in waves. This male could easily run his own territory if he chose. Not that he seemed to have any inclination to do so, but still.

"Yes. Though King doesn't actually know that. He never outright asked me, so I never told him. My brother informed him that I would obey any rules while I was in his city and help out where needed, so King gave me passage."

"Exactly how long ago was she killed?"

"Long before you were born, little witch." The last two words, which could have sounded condescending, just came out exhausted. "Thousands and thousands of years ago. So long I can't give an exact date. I went into Hibernation when I couldn't find her killer. I stopped sensing her, I guess, is the only way to put it. It was like she winked out of existence, sort of like dragons do when they go into Hibernation. Once I couldn't sense that monster anymore, everything seemed pointless. But since I've woken from my Hibernation, I know she's out there. I can *feel* her."

She nodded once. "If she killed your sister for her blood, then it stands to reason you're sensing your sister's blood in her veins."

"I know. The witch's name was Catta."

Dallas went stock-still, unable to hide her reaction.

Rhys's dark blue eyes narrowed on her as everything between them faded away. His stare was heavy, almost accusing. "You know her?"

"I know—or knew—a witch who went by the name long before I was born. It might not be the same witch, however." Though something told Dallas that it was. Because Catta was an evil monster. She was part of the reason Dallas had run from her very first coven over two decades ago. She'd started to see the truth behind the curtain of lies Catta had erected.

He stared down at her long and hard. "Where is she now?"

"I honestly don't know." And he would be able to scent the truth on her. "I left her coven long ago."

His eyes widened slightly. "You were part of her coven?"

"I was. I left when I realized how evil she was." More truth.

"I need details about her," he snapped out, his muscles pulled taut.

She wrapped her arms around herself, suddenly unsure. "What will you do when you find her?" She already knew the answer, but wanted it confirmed.

"Kill her." Two simple words, spoken with lifetimes of rage and pain.

Dallas had never been a violent person but she actually found herself nodding as if to say she understood. Because she did. Catta was true evil—though she masked it, making everyone think she was all light and sunshine, that she cared about the world. She'd pretty much written the book on how to gaslight. Dallas wondered if she even bothered to hide her true self anymore. When she'd escaped her coven, the members had all been turning dark—assuming their worst selves. If that was true now, then Catta had no reason to hide who she was.

Dallas turned away from him, scanning the yard again as thoughts turned over in her mind. "I'll help you find her," she finally said. She shouldn't help him—Catta was too powerful, too old. Goddess, she was ancient, just like this male in front of her. But what Catta had done was evil and wrong. Rhys and his family had suffered a horrific, senseless loss. They deserved justice. And peace. So did all of Catta's victims.

Next to her Rhys sucked in a breath. "Seriously?" There was so much hope in his voice it sliced at her.

She didn't turn to look up at him, however. But she felt his gaze on her face as she continued. "As soon as I'm done helping King, yes. I don't know how much help I can be. I left her coven decades ago. Out in Washington. I have no idea if they're still around or if they disbanded. I never kept tabs on her, so I can't give you details. But I can put out some feelers and see what I get back." Though it scared her to ask about Catta, Dallas would do it. When she'd run, she'd cut all ties.

His big, callused fingers skated down her arm gently for the briefest of moments, just a barely there touch that sent a cascade of sparks bursting inside her. "Thank you," he rasped out.

She took a step away from him, even though her instinct was to comfort him, to ease his suffering. That was just the healer part of her nature. But he didn't care for her kind and she wasn't helping him for any reason other than it was the right thing to do. "We need to finish scouting the rest of the areas King wants me to look at. Then I need to go see someone downtown. You don't need to come with me."

"Who?"

"A human named Thurman. But most people just call him the Magic Man."

"I'm going with you."

She wanted to tell him not to bother but instead pulled out her notepad and made some notes about this area and the many things that King could do with it. When she was working on something, she was able to compartmentalize. Right now she needed to not think about Catta or even the sexy, angry male who was standing right next to her.

Ignoring him, she made a note to question whether or not King was going to tear down the mansion, but she hoped he didn't. The place was gorgeous and it was another area for people to live. Safe housing was in short supply since so many had been displaced after The Fall.

"Dallas," Rhys said gently, pulling her from her note-taking.

She looked up at him and saw a myriad of emotions in his gaze. "What?"

"I didn't mean to insult you before. And I am sorry for... I'm just sorry. For my anger. For...everything," he rasped out, anguish in his eyes. "I've been angry and bitter for a long time."

An image of him playing with Willow in the yard that morning was the only thing that dispelled some of the anger—and hurt—inside her. He'd been hurt by a witch, deeply and in such a way that it had changed the entire trajectory of his life. If his sister had been murdered thousands of years ago, then he'd been carrying that rage for a very long time. Even into his Hibernation, it seemed. Something like that could change a person, reshape them. Still, it didn't make it right for him to judge an entire group of people based on the actions of one.

She simply nodded. "Okay." That was all she had to say for now.

Especially since she had another secret—one she wasn't sure how he'd handle if he found out about it. She didn't trust him enough to tell him the truth yet.

Didn't trust him not to use the knowledge against her if he found out that the witch he wanted to kill was her mother.

CHAPTER 9

"Thank you for coming with me," King said as they entered the formal parlor of the Cheval coven. This was one of the last places he wanted to be, but duty called.

Aurora snorted softly. "Well, Ingrid did ask me to tag along."

"She didn't actually use the words 'tag along,' did she?" he asked dryly.

Aurora snickered and shook her head as she perched on the edge of a tufted yellow loveseat. "No. But I was under the impression that it would go better for *you* if I was here."

King simply snorted and didn't bother sitting. He wasn't sure how it had happened, but in the last few weeks Aurora had become his liaison, more or less, between him and...many other species. After the display from that news feed of her destroying dragons along with her sister and her sister's mate—and King as well—the city was very curious about "Aurora the phoenix." Not that he blamed them, because he was curious about her as well. What he did know, he liked.

More than liked.

Not that he had the luxury of indulging in anything right now. He was the Alpha of a rebuilding city and his people came first. Even people who did not like him. Such was the mantle of responsibility, his mother had once told him. And he was a fool for having not quite believed her.

Damn, if she was still alive, he would tell her that she was right. Then she would simply say "I know, sweet boy, I am always right." God, he missed his mom.

Shaking off those thoughts, he turned at the sound of heels clicking over polished wood. A moment later, Ingrid, current leader of the Cheval vampire coven, stood in the doorway, holding her hands out for a grand entrance.

He kept his annoyance in check. She'd called him here, had made it sound like a demand, which rankled his wolf on every level.

Her long, caramel-colored hair had been pulled up into a twisted crown at the back of her head. He wasn't sure how old she was, a couple hundred years maybe, and he believed she was originally from Portugal. But he knew that her given name wasn't Ingrid, that was just what she called herself now. Such was the way with supernaturals. Always changing, always reinventing themselves. Though that might slow down now since they were all out to humans.

"King, Aurora," she said, rolling the R's in Aurora's name and focusing on her just a little bit too long, a hungry glint in her dark brown eyes.

Now *that* definitely annoyed King. He didn't like anyone looking at what was his. But Aurora wasn't his no matter how much he wanted her. No matter how much she filled his dreams. No matter how much his obsession grew. No matter how much he and his wolf were in agreement that she was perfection. They were friends. Plain and simple. It was all he could handle right now. And she hadn't given him any signal that she wanted anything more, regardless.

"Thank you for inviting me," Aurora said with a sunny smile.

Ingrid returned the smile as she strode farther into the room and sat directly across from Aurora, crossing her long legs, flashing all the way up to mid-thigh. "Why don't you sit, King?" she asked without looking at him.

"I'm good, thanks." Instead of sitting, he stood behind Aurora so they could both face the vampire. He knew he could take on Ingrid if it came down to a fight, but he wasn't foolish enough to give her his back. He would never underestimate an opponent. That was something he'd learned young. "Why am I here?"

Ingrid sniffed haughtily. "I forget how rude you can be," she pouted in a way she likely thought was charming.

"Ingrid," he growled out.

"Some of my people are missing," she suddenly snapped, her body straightening into pure Alpha mode as she spoke, truth in every word.

"Missing?" Aurora asked before he could, concern punching off her in soft waves. She definitely had a gentle touch and something about her simply drew others in. He wondered if it was part of her phoenix heritage, because she often seemed to have a literal glow about her. Like she was this bright beacon.

Ingrid nodded, focusing on Aurora now. "Yes. Half a dozen of my people so far. And I've heard rumors that humans are going missing as well. No shifters, however," she growled, her fangs dropping as she looked at King.

He growled low in his throat, his beast right at the forefront, though he didn't release his canines. No one challenged him and got away with it. It was always a balance, deciding when someone was actually challenging him or just putting on a show. And he almost always went with his instinct, let his wolf decide. Because his animal side was usually right.

Ingrid's fangs withdrew almost immediately, as if she'd read his mind. He would take on Ingrid right here, right now. And win.

"I'm not challenging you," she snapped. "I'm angry and worried for my people. I'm worried for my kind. Because no one is looking for them except us!"

"This is the first I'm hearing about vampires or humans going missing," he snarled back. "Now tell me what's going on."

"Why don't you tell me why there's a freaking dragon in our city, because I just heard a rumor that one has been flying around all day. An actual dragon, not a shifter! It seems as if you've completely lost control of New Orleans!"

He got whiplash at the direction the conversation was heading and forced himself to take a breath. It was clear she was worried about her people so he was giving her a little slack.

Before he could speak, Aurora shifted slightly in her seat. "Ingrid, there *is* a dragon in the city right now. She's a dragonling, barely three months old. If that's the rumor you're hearing, then yes it's true, but she's someone's pet and she's actually staying with me right now. She's harmless and adorable, nothing like the monsters who attacked our city. She won't be setting random things on fire."

Ingrid shifted, surprise clear on her face. "Really? She's staying with you?"

"Yes. Really. She doesn't even eat meat. And it's clear that you're not really concerned about her. So let's focus on the real problem. Talk to us."

Ingrid's slender shoulders slumped. "The youngest members of my coven went out to a club a few nights ago and never came back. They never actually made it to the club, from what I've been told, but I haven't corroborated that. You truly haven't heard about it?"

"King has been busy today saving a smaller coven in the bayou from being systematically harassed by some rogue shifters. It's the only reason he hasn't heard about your missing vampires. I haven't either, or I'd tell you." Aurora's voice was a soothing balm.

Surprise rolled off Ingrid as she flicked a glance up to him, her icy expression thawing slightly. "I heard about that. The Guillory coven, right?"

"Yes. Those shifters won't be a problem anymore—for anyone," he said.

She watched him for a long moment. "Fine, I'll tell you what I know." She launched into a ten-minute diatribe, listing the names and descriptions of her missing coven members, when they'd gone missing, who they had relationships with, and their favorite haunts.

When she was done, he said, "I assume you have all of this written down?" He would remember it all, but she didn't need to know that he had an eidetic memory. Some things he kept to himself.

She nodded. "I've already started a file."

"Just send it to me," Aurora said as she stood and joined King, her shoulder gently touching him.

It didn't matter that they weren't actually a unit, that they weren't a mated couple. It felt right to have Aurora next to him. It was where she belonged. And this showed everyone that she was more than his liaison; she had his back and was an important part of his pack. Not officially yet, but he was going to make the offer. He still couldn't believe how quickly she'd fallen into this role but when he'd asked her to come with him on a call to see someone—at their request—she'd readily agreed. And she'd been coming with him ever since. It had to be the phoenix part of her, drawing people in.

"It will be in your inbox before you reach the end of the walkway." Ingrid stood as well, more composed now. "And you and I need to plan a girls' night where we get to know one another better," she said, eyeing Aurora with a whole lot of interest. "Once all this mess is cleared up, of course."

"I'll get back to you," Aurora said noncommittally, which just made Ingrid grin even wider.

Once King and Aurora were outside, he finally let some of his guard down. It seemed she was one of the few people he allowed himself to be free around. It was strange because he'd only known her for a short time, but the second time they'd spoken, she'd told him her deepest secret—that she was a phoenix. It was before she'd come out to the world.

The amount of trust that she'd placed in him with that secret was something he would never forget. He felt so damn honored that she'd let him into her life like that. And he would do anything to protect this brave, skilled fighter. "Why did I ever think I want to be Alpha?" he grumbled, acting a bit like a whiny pup instead of the Alpha he was. Running his pack was far different than running a whole city full of different types of species.

She laughed, the sound rich and throaty as she bumped him with her hip. "You're good at it, even if everyone drives you crazy."

"Lately I'm questioning my sanity."

"Sometimes you let them push your buttons...intentionally, I think." She shot him a sideways glance.

He snorted as they stepped out onto the sidewalk. This neighborhood had fared well during The Fall. Most of the damage had been contained to pockets of areas. Here historic homes—mostly owned and lived in by supernaturals—had large lawns, an overabundance of trees, and off-street parking. Not that it mattered too much since people weren't driving nearly as much. "I don't let them do anything. They just do it. I swear the supernaturals in the city are like children most of the time. I used to think we were so evolved compared to humans, but now I'm starting to question that too."

Next to him she snickered again, the sound music to his ears. "I'm not going to argue with you. Not when I live with a bunch of grown-ass shifters who act like nine-year-olds on their best days."

"So how are things at the house? How are things with Dallas and the dragon?"

"Oh, you know, it's always a wild time." Her tone was dry. "But Willow is great. She's having a good time, I believe. She's been making the chickens crazy all day from what I hear. Apparently she keeps trying to herd them, as if they're sheep, I guess, and they just want to mind their own business and do whatever it is chickens do. She's making them peckish. Pun intended."

He laughed at the thought of that. "This I have to see."

"Well, you know you're always welcome at our place."

He *did* know that. She'd told him on more than one occasion that he could drop by whenever he wanted. Since he was Alpha, he could always drop by. But she was letting him know that he could as a friend. He tried not to go over there too often; he didn't want his enemies to know what she meant to him. For now, she was acting as his liaison, so it was obvious why they spent time together.

But it might be inevitable that sooner or later someone was going to realize she was more than just a packmate to him.

He'd deal with that day when it came. For now, he needed to keep his city from devolving into chaos—and find those missing vampires and humans before the powder keg that was New Orleans exploded.

CHAPTER 10

As they reached two intricately carved, oversized wooden doors in a quiet alley in the Quarter, Dallas held a hand up and Rhys swore he saw a burst of colors right before the lock snicked open.

He frowned down at her, surprised she seemed to be breaking into this place. "I thought we were meeting your friend." Some *male*. Rhys didn't know who this Magic Man was, but the most primitive part of him didn't like the thought of Dallas being friends with any man. Which was beyond stupid. He had no claim on her and never would. And even if he did, she was allowed to have friends of the male variety. But his beast was riding him hard right now, clawing just underneath the surface, in a rage that he'd clearly upset Dallas earlier. Something he felt bad about.

"Trust me, he doesn't mind if I do it. We have an understanding," she said as they made their way inside.

They'd only taken a few steps before they were in a courtyard that housed an oasis of colorful plants and flowers. Bursts of reds, purples, yellows and greens were everywhere, pots covering every surface. Maybe this Magic Man was a witch too, because none of these plants were in season right now. There shouldn't be this much blooming before spring.

"Dallas!" a rich, almost lyrical voice called from somewhere.

"Come on," she murmured, her boots thudding against the stone as they stepped farther into the courtyard, dodging hanging plants and planters.

As they stepped around a small, potted palm tree, Rhys stopped when he saw a tall man with dark brown skin who had to be at least seventy sitting at a table, his long legs crossed at the ankles as he lifted up a small teacup to his mouth. He was dressed elegantly in a three-piece suit that

Rhys could tell was custom-made. He also had on a wool newsboy cap that he took off as he stood and greeted Dallas.

Dallas smiled, a huge grin on her pretty face, and the first truly open and genuine one he'd seen from her. Her smile was like the sun shining.

"Thurman," she said as she closed the distance between them and pulled him into a hug. "It's so good to see you." She squeezed tight as the man hugged her back and kissed her on the top of the head in a fatherly gesture.

That eased his dragon's claws back a bit. Not completely because his dragon was in a *mood*.

"You as well. I have a treat for you." He flicked a slightly curious gaze at Rhys, but showed no more interest in him than that.

"Bourbon?" she asked as she stepped back and motioned Rhys to come closer. "This is Rhys," Dallas said as she gave him a neutral look. "And this is Thurman," she said, smiling at the other man.

His dragon crawled under the surface, swiping at him. *He* should be making her smile, and it was his own damn fault that she was now wary of him.

The man nodded at him once, a polite smile on his face. "Another dragon in the city," he said as he held out a hand.

Rhys frowned even as he took the human's hand. A pulse of power rolled through the man but he was still human, Rhys was almost sure of it. "You know what I am?"

"I do. I can see what you are underneath the surface."

Ah, a seer. They were rare, and though the man was still human, he was a little bit *more*.

"To answer your other question," Thurman said as he turned back to Dallas and motioned for them to sit, "I do have bourbon. The best money can buy. I've been saving it for your visit."

Dallas flushed a pretty shade of pink, clearly pleased as she sat down at the mosaic-topped table.

"I'm delighted you're in the city. How long has it been?" Thurman asked, sitting against his chair in a deceptively casual manner.

"Six months maybe. I'm sorry I haven't stopped by but the world went to hell and…" She shrugged.

He reached out to place a hand over hers and squeezed. "And you've been busy on that farm of yours. I hear you've been working overtime making sure everyone's crops get a little extra magic."

She blushed at his words and didn't deny them. Rhys hadn't realized she'd been doing that, because he didn't know enough about her. And watching her now, so at ease with the human, he desperately wished they had that kind of relationship, that he knew everything about her. And not just because she could help him find his sister's murderer.

"So, you're here to see me today about the dying humans?" he bluntly asked as he sat back.

Rhys straightened even as Dallas jerked slightly in her seat. "Dying humans?"

Before he could answer, a man who looked as if he could be related to Thurman—maybe a nephew—strode out with a small tray of three tumbler glasses and a bourbon bottle.

He silently poured them, and once he was done, kissed the top of Thurman's now hatless head and disappeared back through the myriad of foliage.

"A toast first," Thurman said, lifting his glass. "Then we'll talk."

Dallas lifted hers so Rhys did the same as well. He would be able to smell poison anyway.

"To friendship, new and old," the older man said, clinking his glass with Dallas's and then Rhys's—a speculative look in his eyes.

Rhys took a sip of the bourbon. Flavors exploded on his tongue—an oaky flavor, but with honey and sweetness. He found he liked it and so did his dragon, who purred in appreciation.

"Tell me about the dying humans," Dallas said as she set her glass down.

"Not just humans. Vampires as well. Some are dead, some are dying, and more will die."

She sucked in a little breath. "How? Why? By who? Where?"

He lifted a shoulder, but Rhys could tell the information bothered the man. "I just see their deaths. And blood magic. So much blood magic," he whispered the last part.

Dallas went still, the distress rolling off her potent. It was like little waves in the air.

Blood magic was mostly done by witches, though some other supernaturals and even humans engaged in it as well. It was dark, evil stuff that ate your soul.

"You're sure?" Dallas said.

"I know what I know."

"Does King know what's going on?" Dallas continued.

"I'm sure King knows a lot of things," the human said before taking a sip of his drink.

"Don't be difficult," Dallas chastised. "If you are, I won't tell you my new growing spell."

The man's dark eyes twinkled at her words and he set his glass down. "Fine, yes, King must know by now. I heard through the grapevine that he's been to talk to Ingrid and others, so she'll have told him."

Dallas frowned slightly. "The vampire?"

Rhys recognized the name because he'd made it a point to learn about the different powers in the city, and if he remembered correctly, Ingrid was leader of the Cheval vampire coven.

"Why are you telling me?" Dallas asked.

Thurman reached into his jacket pocket and Rhys instantly tensed, the warrior in him ready to defend Dallas, but the man pulled out a piece of paper and pen. Instead of answering, he silently started sketching what ended up being a crest of some sort.

He slid it across to Dallas, who simply looked at it and shrugged. "What is this?"

It was an intricately designed coat of arms with four feathers slashed across the middle of it.

"It's very clearly a crest. The humans and vampires are being held in a place with this crest branded on it."

"We need to take this to King," Rhys said. He might be on a quest for vengeance—and even now he wanted to demand that Thurman tell him everything he knew about Catta—but if people were being held and murdered, King should have enough of a pack to scour the city for this crest.

Thurman held up a hand, motioning for both of them to settle back. "Only a witch can see this crest," he said as he looked at Dallas. "It's a spelled symbol, embedded at the entrance of where the humans and vampires are being held. You'll be able to see it, not King's shifters."

"Do you know who's behind the murders?" she asked.

"Witches. But I truly don't know more than this. I've seen this in my dreams for weeks and then last night I dreamed you'd be coming here. I knew I had to tell you."

"I didn't come here about this."

He shook his head. "No, not about this. But this involves you nonetheless. That much I'm certain of."

She frowned, shifting uncomfortably in her seat. "How?"

"I don't know. I just know that it does involve you somehow—and it's linked to the reason you came here today."

Rhys was getting a headache at the human's vague words.

"I came here to ask you about—"

"About another witch," the man finished for her.

Damn, he really had been expecting them, Rhys thought.

"Yes," Dallas said simply.

The human flicked a glance between the two of them, his heavy gaze settling on Rhys for a long moment before he looked back at Dallas. "If you find this crest, you will find what you're looking for."

All the muscles in Rhys's body pulled taut. If they found the crest, they would find Catta? "You're sure?" he demanded.

The human watched him carefully. "You're seeking vengeance. If you find this crest, it will lead you to what you desire."

At that moment, Dallas's cell phone rang and she jumped a little. When she saw the screen, she gave them an apologetic look as she stood. "Let me grab this, it's one of my neighbors. I need to make sure everything's okay."

Rhys's gaze lingered on the curves of her ass as she walked away, long-dead need pushing to the surface once more.

"How do you like the bourbon?" Thurman asked Rhys, watching him with eyes that were far too old for the human male sitting in front of him. His gaze held centuries of knowledge and it was disturbing to see human eyes looking back at him with that much inside them.

"It...reminds me of my homeland."

The man half-smiled, as if he'd known that.

Which was disturbing as hell—and maybe it was the reason that the human had chosen this drink. "What can you tell me about the witch I'm hunting?" he asked, needing more information.

"I've told you everything I know." He cleared his throat, taking a sip from his glass, and Rhys had the feeling he'd been dismissed—as if he'd gotten all the information he was going to get. But then Thurman continued. "Would you like some advice from an old man?"

Rhys nodded because he had a feeling that whatever this man had to say, mattered.

"Soon you're going to have a decision to make. Make the right one, or you will lose everything that matters to you."

Vengeance was the only thing that mattered to him. Before he could respond, Dallas slid back into the seat, seeming at ease, so her land and goats must be fine.

"Is everything okay?" he asked nonetheless.

"Yes, Hazel said the goats are doing fine, but she thinks they miss Willow."

"Is Willow this pet dragon I hear you have?" Thurman asked.

"You really do know everything," she said laughingly as she stood and motioned for Rhys to do the same.

Apparently it was time to leave. He finished the bourbon, because there was no way he was letting the liquid gold go to waste.

Thurman lifted an elegant shoulder. "Now what about that spell you promised me?"

Dallas reached into her pocket and held out a folded piece of paper. "You won't be disappointed. Thank you for the information. I'll tell King everything you told me. He'll have more information than I do, and hopefully we can narrow down where to look at least."

"Stay safe," Thurman murmured, standing and pulling her into another brief hug.

"You too," she said as she stepped back. Then she cleared her throat, looking up at Thurman with curiosity. "You could have just told King all this, you know."

"I know."

She watched him a moment longer. "Why didn't you?"

"Because I told you."

She sighed and even Rhys knew they weren't getting any more from Thurman.

Rhys could barely contain himself until they'd stepped out onto the sidewalk, alone once again. "Do you think Catta is with this coven?" he asked as she shut the door behind them.

He'd tucked the piece of paper with the crest drawing into his front pants pocket, as if having it close to him could somehow help them find Catta faster.

"Maybe. But if she was in New Orleans I think I would have known by now. Thurman is almost never wrong, however. It sounds like finding this coven might bring us one step closer to who you're looking for. He knew we were coming."

"And you are clearly not surprised by that."

She snorted softly. "I'm not surprised by anything that man knows. He's better at spells than me, and he's a human. It's quite impressive."

"He's also got a few years on you if I had to guess." And he did want to know how old she was, but knew better than to ask outright.

She lifted a shoulder. "A few."

She looked to be in her mid-twenties, but witches aged much slower than humans—and faster than shifters—so she could be anywhere from thirty to a hundred and he'd have no clue.

The only thing he knew right now was that he was far closer to finding Catta than he'd been in years. He was so damn close he could taste it.

Thurman's words about having to make a choice rattled around in his head. He gave them heed, but knew that in the end if he had to die to get his vengeance, he would. If he lost his life, so be it.

CHAPTER 11

Catta looked at the photos on the cell phone screen and handed it back to Margaret before turning back to the bound vampire on the table in front of her. She dragged her blade across the writhing female's forearm, watched the blood trickle down onto the platter under her body.

"Well?" her subordinate asked, a dark eyebrow arched in question.

As if she had the standing to question Catta. "Well what?" Her tone was dry as she took her attention away from her victim.

She tossed her red hair back slightly, the action haughty. "She's here in the city. I thought you said she never left her land."

Catta lifted a shoulder, unconcerned about Dallas. The child she'd borne was weak—one of Catta's greatest disappointments. They could have ruled together, had immeasurable power. But Dallas had run away like the coward she was. "She has friends here."

"Yes, but she is with a *dragon*."

She stared at Margaret, not bothering to hide her annoyance at this line of questioning. She was beautiful and Catta had enjoyed fucking her on occasion, but couldn't this fool see that Catta was busy? "And?"

"What if she's here to disrupt our plans?"

"Please. She's a scared little bunny who wants nothing to do with me." It was a shame too, because untapped power simmered inside Dallas. But she'd never wished to open up her heart, her soul, to all of that glorious power. Instead she was so worried about doing good for others. Catta held back a snort. "How about you let me worry about her, and *you* worry about doing your damn job." Fire flickered against her fingertips as she took a step toward Margaret.

The other witch didn't step back but she shifted nervously on her feet. "I'm not challenging your authority," she said before ducking her gaze in subservience.

"Sounds like you are," she murmured, feeding on the fear that rolled off Margaret. She wouldn't kill her, not now anyway. She still needed her, needed her power reserves if necessary. And Catta was all about playing the long game. It was how she'd survived in a world where witches normally only lived a couple hundred years, max.

"It won't happen again."

Catta turned away, dismissing her. "Good. But keep an eye on Dallas—without being obvious. I don't want her or the dragon to know we're watching." Because she recognized that dragon. If he was still hunting her, he would be sorely disappointed. She'd managed to change her scent over the years. Not completely, but enough that he wouldn't know her by scent.

"Of course, mistress."

Catta dismissed her with a flick of her wrist and returned to the vampire she was currently draining of blood. She ran her fingertips over the writhing female's cuts and sucked on her blood. Like fresh candy. There was no other taste in the world like it.

And vampire blood was so much stronger than human.

But Catta wanted dragon blood. Craved it. Had been desperate for it for eons. After the last dragon she'd killed, she'd ended up in a stasis of sorts until only decades ago. The dragon's blood had been so strong it had forced Catta to go into Hibernation just like the dragons did.

She'd learned to control it since waking up, however. And now she was more powerful than ever.

Soon she would have everything she'd ever wanted. Immortality and the ultimate control over life and death.

CHAPTER 12

"I left a message with King." Rhys tucked his phone into his back pocket as they strode through the open gates toward the mansion they were staying at.

"I'm sure he's dealing with a whole lot of things at once." Dallas had been quiet on the walk back from the Quarter, seemingly lost in her own thoughts.

"Yes. My brother is the same, always putting out fires," he said, then chastised himself for opening up to her. He needed to keep his distance but it was damn near impossible at this point. He *wanted* to tell her about himself, and he'd already admitted the most painful memory from his past. Most of it anyway. And he wanted to know more about her— *everything* about her.

This sweet female with her big heart who lived by herself on the outskirts of town—on the outskirts of supernatural society.

"I can't imagine being responsible for all those people. Willow is enough for me." As if on cue, Willow flew down through the trees, letting out an excited chirp to see them.

Dallas broke away from him and raced across the front yard as her dragon landed on the grass. She threw her arms around Willow's neck, and the dragonling simply flapped her wings excitedly and nuzzled Dallas's face.

He followed after her, watching the interaction between the two of them with a weird ache in his chest. Everything about Dallas was so open and real.

"Someone has been missing you," called Aurora as she appeared from around the side of the house. She nodded once at Rhys then looked back at Dallas, who was laughing under Willow's kisses.

"I've missed her too," she said on another laugh.

As Dallas finally stood, Willow scrambled toward Rhys excitedly. Despite his intention to stay a little removed from them, it was impossible—and he found himself crouched down and scratching behind her ear as Willow kissed his face.

"We've had an eventful day," Dallas murmured, quickly launching into what they'd learned from Thurman.

Aurora listened to everything, her eyes widening only slightly, as if some of this wasn't exactly a surprise.

When Dallas was finished, Aurora spoke. "King and I were informed about some of this earlier."

Rhys straightened, but still petted Willow's head. The little dragon leaned into him and gazed up at him with adoring eyes, and damned if it didn't cause a squeezing sensation in his chest. "About the missing vampires and humans?"

"Missing vampires, at least. Humans aren't as open with King or his pack yet. They're all still adjusting to the new order of things, I think. Or maybe people without family have been taken, so no one knows they're missing. I don't want to speculate too much, but we need to figure out *where* they're being held. Come on," she said, motioning for them to follow her inside.

Dallas kissed the top of Willow's head before her dragon took to the skies and started happily flying around the yard, completely content.

"I need to know exactly what Thurman said about this," Aurora said as Rhys unfolded and laid the drawing of the crest on the kitchen countertop.

"That only witches would be able to see this crest. It's actually not all that uncommon. This kind of thing dates back centuries. My kind have been hunted for as long as we've been around." Dallas's voice was carefully neutral as she sat at the center island and she avoided looking at him. Instead she stared at the aqua-colored bowl filled with bright red apples.

A fissure started in his chest, cracking slightly at her words.

"In order to keep coven meetings secret, witches would spell certain symbols at different houses, or locations, letting other witches know that a place was safe. So while the use of this spell is common, according to

Thurman this crest will help us find the missing vampires and humans. I can do a finding spell and at least narrow down where this place is using the crest as a guide. I won't be able to find it directly because witches are notoriously tricky like that. But I should be able to get a decent radius, which will help us narrow down where we need to search. Well, where I need to search."

"I'll be going with you," he said.

She looked up at him and simply nodded, her expression still carefully neutral. She didn't trust him yet, and he wanted her to. So much it stunned him. Not that he'd done anything to earn her trust.

Aurora had her phone in hand. "I'm going to call King. What do you need for the finding spell?"

"I really just need a map of New Orleans—something physical. Thurman didn't say *where* this place was, so it might not even be in the city. If that's the case, then my spell won't do much good and we'll have to broaden our radius. But I can't imagine why he would have had a vision of something not connected to the area."

"Give me a second." Aurora hurried from the room, her phone at her ear.

"Is it difficult to do a finding spell?" He'd studied up on witches as much as he could, over the last year especially. But knowledge on their practices was secret and limited. They kept to themselves much in the way that dragons did. He didn't blame them, especially considering he'd been a judgmental asshole about witches until the other day. Until Dallas. It made sense that they protected themselves.

Dallas lifted a shoulder.

He really didn't like that neutral expression or the way she'd pulled away from him. He'd started to say something, though he wasn't sure what, when Aurora strode back into the room and unfolded a huge map, laying it across the granite countertop. "Will this do?" Her phone was still at her ear as she asked.

"Yes, it's perfect," Dallas said.

"Good. King wants to know what you need from him."

"Nothing now. Though…I don't know who he can trust other than me to look for this crest. Because if witches in the city are involved in the taking of humans and vampires, he probably shouldn't start telling other people we're looking for them."

Aurora nodded. "He said the same thing. So just do what you need to do."

She looked between the two of them and shifted nervously on her seat. "I need a little privacy for this. You guys need to wait outside."

Rhys didn't like the thought of leaving her alone, but not because he didn't trust her. "Do you want us to leave the back door open?"

She shook her head and didn't look at him.

Some deep part of him felt like a temperamental child, wanting to demand that she look at him. Instead, he strode outside with Aurora, feeling that fissure in his chest grow even wider.

* * *

Dallas moved quickly and grabbed a ceramic bowl from one of the cabinets, then plucked a knife from a drawer. Technically she didn't need to be alone for this, but she didn't like revealing any parts of her practice to others, especially not a dragon who'd made it clear he didn't trust witches and was out to kill one.

An annoyingly sexy dragon.

She didn't have her normal tools like her athame with her, but a regular fillet knife would do.

Though she *was* going to use her own blood. This wasn't actual blood magic, not in the sense that she was practicing the dark arts like some of her sisters. Blood magic was when witches or others used someone else's blood, usually without consent, and for dark purposes.

As a natural-born witch, she could use her own blood when necessary, and if it was for the greater good, there was never any bounce-back on her. Bracing herself for the pain, she wrapped her hand around the fillet knife and slid it across her palm in one quick slice.

She hissed as it dragged across her skin, but softly chanted the simple spell as she held her bleeding hand over the bowl. Her blood started to drip into the bowl but as she continued chanting, the droplets suspended in midair, twisting and turning in a delicate dance before finding their mark on the map.

Her blood swirled around and around, hovering over the map, and for a long moment she thought maybe the missing vampires and humans weren't even in the city, when suddenly the crimson drops spread out in a circle and landed on the paper below, creating a perfect oval. Her blood immediately turned a very soft blue, as if she'd drawn the line and not used part of herself.

She quickly put the bowl and knife in the sink and washed them, wanting to get rid of any traces of her blood. A witch's blood could be used against her, something she knew personally. Her mother had tried to control her once upon a time.

She winced at the pain from the cut but her skin was already knitting itself back together. Since she'd created the spell with good intentions, wanting to help, it made a huge difference in how fast she healed.

Once everything was cleaned up and only an angry red mark remained on her palm, she opened the back door to find Aurora and Rhys standing there with Willow, both cooing and petting her. Well, Rhys wasn't cooing, but he was still petting her.

Her chest tightened at the sight of the big, strong dragon being so sweet with Willow but she shut down those emotions. That male was not for her.

"I'm done," she called out, before she quickly turned away and hurried back inside. Being around him was messing with her in too many ways.

"You're sure this is it?" Aurora asked as she traced her finger around the blue oval.

"As sure as I can be. So I need to search in this radius and it's pretty damn big." Relatively speaking anyway. "I just need to grab something to eat and then we can start." It was almost dusk, but it wouldn't matter—with symbols like the crest, it would glow neon for her to see. If anything, it was almost more visible at night.

"Are you sure? You've been on your feet all day." Rhys's mouth pulled down into a frown. His concern was...sexy. Of course, everything he did was sexy. He definitely had that whole brooding, tortured male thing going on. Something she'd never thought was attractive. Until Rhys.

"I'm sure King can find someone else to come with me." Maybe he didn't want to be her babysitter anymore, and frankly, that would be easier on her.

That intense frown deepened. "Are you kidding me? That's not what I meant," he snapped. "And I'm not leaving your side."

Aurora's eyebrows simply raised as she looked between the two of them with interest.

Dallas rubbed a hand over her face, fighting a wave of exhaustion. "All I need is some food and I'll be ready to go. We can cover a lot of ground over the next few hours. At least we can eliminate some neighborhoods and then I'll start again in the morning. Unless King wants me doing something else?" He *had* called her to the city to scout out various food plots.

"No, he said this is the main priority," Aurora said. "And he's going to pull in a few more of his pack to go with you guys. Even if you're the only one who can see this crest, if these witches are kidnapping people, they're not going to like it if you find out where their victims are. You're going to need backup."

"I am a *dragon*." Rhys sounded beyond offended at the thought of taking backup.

Aurora simply snorted. And despite everything, Dallas hid a smile. Sweet goddess, dragons really were arrogant.

"Backup won't hurt," she murmured.

His frown was still in place but he moved to the refrigerator. "I'll fix you something and you will eat all of it. You look way too tired." His voice was all gruff, but she saw the worry in his eyes.

And okay, that kind of touched her. Although maybe he was just worried that if something happened to her, he wouldn't be able to find…Catta. But whatever, he was concerned and she kinda liked it. Which was probably sad, but she ignored that thought.

As Aurora took a picture of the map—likely to send to King—Dallas sat at the island top.

Rhys peered into the huge fridge. "We've got cheeses, fruits, meats—"

"How about a grilled cheese sandwich?"

"That's it?"

"And any fresh fruit you have. Strawberries or blueberries?"

He nodded and started moving around the kitchen with an

impressive efficiency. It was sexy as hell to have such a big, capable male cooking for her. Something she shouldn't care about. But again, her head and heart were not in sync.

This male had made it clear that his goal was vengeance. He wanted to use her. Not…anything else.

She would do well to remember that.

CHAPTER 13

Catta smiled at the male vampire who sat down next to her on the barstool. She sent out a little thread of magic, searching, probing his thoughts for what he liked, didn't like. When she got what she needed, pleasure punched through her. This one would be easy. No real kinks, which was surprising for a vampire.

She stood when he was looking away, then quickly mixed a confusion spell and a glamour one before settling back on the chair and into her temporary role. She and the rest of her coven had been working overtime kidnapping humans and vampires. Normally she left this duty to her coven members but the darkness inside her craved power, desperate for it. She needed the blood.

She knew it had been a risk coming to New Orleans, but so much of the world had been destroyed, including her former residence. So she and her coven had gravitated here, not telling King they'd recently settled in the city. This was an epicenter for supernaturals and she could carve out a place here. She'd been born to rule, born to be a queen. Now her time was near. There were enough covens here that she could take over all of them.

"What are you drinking?" she purred at the male who'd already half turned in his seat, the scent of his lust rolling off him in potent waves as he raked a hungry gaze over her. Right now she knew he saw her as his ideal lover—a tall, fit blonde with waist-length hair and blood-red cupid's bow lips. So prosaic.

His gaze flicked to her neck, to her pulse. He really was a fine specimen of male. Maybe she would use him later for her own pleasure. "Hopefully you," he murmured, flashing fangs at her.

Now that supernaturals were out to the world, his flash of fang didn't surprise her in this human-run bar. Because she knew better than to hit up supernatural-run bars. It seemed he had the same idea, was likely hunting for someone to feed on. "Hmm, that sounds promising."

He turned fully to face her now, reaching out a strong, muscular arm along the polished mahogany bar top toward her. With his dark hair, a huge, muscular build and a large bulge outlined in his pants, she definitely wanted to try this male before taking his blood. Her lust was real, potent, and would help her get him out of the bar.

"Have you ever been fucked by a vampire before?"

She would give him points for boldness. She made a purring sound and stroked her fingers over his forearm, injecting just a bit of her own magic onto him. The threads were nearly invisible as they started binding his powers, making him weaker. He would have no idea. "Perhaps. But it's been a long time, so maybe you should refresh my memory."

He hadn't even ordered a drink but slipped off the bar stool and took her hand in his. She didn't have the same senses as shifter supernaturals, but his lust was a wild thing she felt pulsing in the air. Her nipples tightened as she felt it.

"My place isn't far from here," he murmured as they stepped out onto the crowded street.

"What's your name?" she asked as they headed down the cobblestone path.

"Benjamin," he murmured, his gaze falling to her neck again as they passed a quiet alley.

She tossed up a blurring spell to keep the alleyway free and dragged him into it.

For a moment he seemed shocked, maybe by her strength or by the lust she was throwing off. "I'm Catta. How about you remind me what it's like to fuck a vampire right here?" she asked as she dragged him up against a brick wall.

Hunger glinted in his glowing amber eyes as he switched positions and pinned her up against the wall, his fingers digging into her hips before he shoved her dress up.

"You're bare? That's so hot," he growled, crushing his mouth to hers.

As they kissed, it didn't take her long to free his cock. Just as it didn't take long to wrap her legs around his hips and guide his hard length inside her.

The male was so damn thick, pumping into her like an animal as he finally broke the skin of her neck with his fangs, drawing on her blood.

He sucked hard at first, in tune with his thrusts. She reached between their bodies and stroked her clit, wanting an immediate release. Because soon he would be passed out on the dirty ground. And she was getting hers before that happened.

Her climax hit almost immediately, the pulls from his fangs ratcheting up her pleasure sharp and fast. Waves and waves of pleasure rolled through her as she threw her head back. As her climax subsided, little tingles still surging through her, she dropped her legs from around him.

"What…" He frowned slightly, confused as she lifted off him, taking away what he wanted. He was still rock-hard, his cock throbbing with the need for release.

She dropped her glamour spell and smiled at him, a real one. She shoved her dress down and adjusted it into place.

He swallowed hard, blinked as he stumbled back, neither his brain nor body understanding what was happening. Her blood had put him into a state of paralysis. *Foolish, foolish male.*

"Sorry, love, it's not personal. You drank my blood and now you're mine," she whispered. She thought about jerking him off so he at least got to finish before he died, but then dismissed the thought as soon as it entered her mind. But maybe she'd screw him later once she had him back in her coven's dungeon.

As he fell to the ground, his eyes wide with horror when he realized he couldn't move, two of her coven members entered the alley on silent feet. "Take him to the van. I'm going to head back to the club. I should be able to get a couple others tonight. How is everyone else doing?"

"Very well," Margaret said, a smile on her face as she threw a cloaking spell over the fallen vampire. "He makes fifteen."

"Good." It wasn't enough—nothing ever seemed enough lately. Likely because she'd experienced what it was like to have true power coursing through her. Dragon blood.

Unfortunately that had backfired on her eventually. She'd been filled with unstoppable power until the blood coursing in her veins had forced her into stasis, into a Hibernation like all those dragons took. It had robbed her of thousands of years' worth of her life, of the ability to grow her power.

Soon she would get it all back. The darkness inside her needed feeding and tonight was just the beginning. Poor Benjamin had barely taken the edge off.

Soon she would have enough power flooding her that she'd be able to go up against a dragon—drink it dry. Once that happened, she was never going into stasis again. No, she would take her place as the true power in the region. No more hiding in the shadows. The world needed witches now.

They needed *her*.

Once she was powerful enough, she would go after that dragon with her daughter. *Hmm.* Maybe she would even use her daughter to draw him out. The male wasn't with his clan, was isolated… Yes, maybe she would. And she would force Dallas to watch as she killed him.

That was the perfect punishment for leaving her.

CHAPTER 14

Rhys strode down the quiet, historic street, Dallas silent beside him, consistently searching each gate, mailbox or anything that looked like it might have a hint of the crest that Thurman had drawn for her. Willow flew high above the treetops, keeping them in range, but just enjoying herself in the air. When Dallas stopped and pulled out her cell phone, he froze.

"What are you doing? Did you find something?" Rhys knew King's wolves were nearby, lurking in the shadows as backup. It wouldn't do to have them out where anybody could see them, and he was glad they weren't walking with them—it meant he didn't have to make small talk with some random shifters. Especially when he only wanted to be with Dallas.

Without looking at him, she snapped a couple pictures of an empty yard in between two historic houses. The flash went off, lighting up the entire area. "I know King said that finding the crest is the priority, but this would be a great place for a community garden so I'm making a note of it since we're already here."

"Okay… Look, if you're tired, we can head back." He wasn't going to tell her she *looked* tired but her face seemed almost paler and her pace had slowed down in increments over the last half hour.

She bristled slightly. "I'm fine. It's still early enough. Besides, if people are missing, we need to find them."

He knew she was right, but that protectiveness flared to life inside him. "I know. I just don't like how hard you seem to be pushing yourself." They'd been at this for three hours straight and she hadn't complained once.

"Dallas?" a surprised female voice called out from nearby…across the street. Rhys and Dallas turned to find a petite, cute female who was most definitely human standing on the opposite sidewalk, a drink in hand. Her skin tone was a few shades darker than Dallas's, giving her a sun-kissed look. "What are you doing here?"

"Avery!" True warmth and pleasure spilled from Dallas as she hurried across the quiet residential street, bypassing a parked car before joining the woman on the sidewalk. She immediately pulled the other woman into a big hug.

They stood back from each other, both smiling as if they were long-lost friends. The scent of joy filled the air, bright and sweet.

Dallas turned to him as he joined them, her smile firmly in place. "Rhys, this is my friend Avery."

"It's nice to meet you—" He froze, withdrawing his outstretched hand as he scented multiple predators, all *dragons*. He stiffened, his gaze scanning the house the woman had come out of. And…he recognized one of the scents from long ago in his memory bank. It took a moment for the scent to register. "Mikael?" he asked into the darkness.

The human female with the curly, dark brown hair jerked slightly as she stared at him. "Your friend knows my roommate?" she asked Dallas.

He frowned down at the little female. "Roommate?"

Mikael, a feared warrior—a general of a neighboring clan—who he'd known and respected many years ago, strode out from behind a huge oak tree, a beer bottle in hand. He eyed Rhys cautiously. "I'm surprised to see you here."

"Likewise." That being an understatement.

He was aware of the females watching them curiously, so he cleared his throat and looked back at the human. "It's a pleasure to meet you."

"You too. I'm just surprised Mikael has any friends. He's always so grumpy," she said, laughing lightly.

Mikael simply snorted, his lips twitching, but he did not correct her. What the hell was the former general doing here in New Orleans? Living with a human female who was not his mate?

"So is this, like, your boyfriend?" Avery asked as she turned back to Dallas.

To his annoyance, Dallas snorted out a laugh as if that was the

ANCIENT ENEMY | 97

funniest, most ludicrous thing in the world. Then she seemed to catch herself and shook her head. "Ah, no, we're just out for a walk. We're both helping King out with something, actually. And maybe you have some insight. I saw the empty lot across the street and it looks like it would be great for a community garden."

"I swear I just said the same thing to my brothers yesterday!" Avery said, a grin spreading across her face.

As the females started talking, Rhys caught Mikael's eye and tipped his head to the side slightly. Quietly, they stepped away, a little farther down the sidewalk as the women continued talking. "It's good to see you," he said, holding out a hand.

They clutched forearms in the way of warriors and he pulled the other male close, thumping him once on the back as Mikael did the same to him.

"I see your brothers are with you," he murmured. Though he didn't actually see them. He just scented Mikael's brothers nearby, lurking in the shadows.

The big dragon grinned and nodded. "I saw your brothers in the city not too long ago. They did not remember me."

He nodded. "You never fought alongside either of them. They're both doing well at least," was all he could commit to because he hadn't seen them, much to his shame. He should have come to New Orleans when they'd been here, should have at least congratulated Lachlan in person on getting mated.

"So what are you doing here and not in Scotland with your family?" Mikael asked bluntly. "Your clan is all at home now."

"I'm hunting," was all he said.

Mikael knew of his loss, had known his sister. The male raised an eyebrow in surprise. "Still?"

"Always." Because he wouldn't rest until the monster was dead.

Mikael flicked a curious glance at Dallas, and all of Rhys's hackles rose. He didn't particularly like any male looking at her, and while he didn't think Mikael's look was sexual, it still annoyed him.

"You and the witch are...together?" his old friend murmured.

"We're friends." Though he wanted to be more, even if that was a difficult thing to admit to himself.

Mikael snorted slightly. "Ah, Avery and I are *friends* as well." There was sadness in his voice. "Do you need help with anything?" the male continued.

"No. Not right now anyway. Are you planning to stay here?" Meaning, had Mikael pledged allegiance to King? Because it was a bit odd for him and his brothers to be here. They could easily carve out their own territory. Rhys had a reason for being here, and didn't plan to stay long term.

His friend's gaze flicked to Avery, then he shrugged. That was all the answer Rhys needed. Apparently Mikael would stay here as long as Avery did.

"We're going to be heading back to our place soon, but I'll get your information from Dallas. I'm sure Avery has it."

His friend nodded again and they embraced once more before joining the females.

"It was nice to meet you," he said to Avery. She was like a bright ray of sunshine and he found himself smiling back at her. There were simply some people you couldn't be rude to. It would be like kicking a puppy.

"Oh my gosh," Avery whispered suddenly, her eyes widening.

"What?" Rhys asked, immediately alert as she pointed across the street, her mouth falling open.

Dallas's shoulders relaxed when she realized her friend was pointing at Willow.

When Mikael made a move as if to cross the street, Rhys held out an arm, blocking him. "She's with us," he growled. And he would protect Willow to the death.

"That cute little dragon is with you?" Avery asked, staring in surprise.

"She's my pet," Dallas said, smiling at her friend. "Come over tomorrow and meet her, okay? Just call me first because I'll be out doing…stuff all day."

"I will." Avery was still wide-eyed, not even looking at Dallas, but across the street at Willow who was doing little swoops throughout the air in perfect figure eights. She seriously had no problem entertaining herself and it was clear she wasn't interested in coming over here and meeting more people. Maybe Willow was maxed out on human interaction—Rhys could certainly relate.

"Willow," Rhys called out and whistled loudly.

She came to attention and met them in the middle of the street, her flying already a lot steadier. She was a fast learner.

Dallas waved at Avery again as they headed off. "Your friend seems just as brooding as you," she murmured, laughter in her voice as they continued down the street.

"Brooding?"

She shrugged. "I don't know if it's the right word, but it seems to fit you."

"I do not brood. My oldest brother is the one who does that," he said dryly.

She snickered slightly.

"So how do you know the human?"

"Well, I've known her for about five years. She's younger than me but I met her at a friend's New Year's party—another human. She knows what I am too. She's one of the few humans who do. She flips houses—or she did before The Fall. She usually lives in the house she and her brothers are renovating and then they move to the next. So they must be renovating that house they came out of. I always thought it was so fascinating to do that. So how do you know that big, sexy dragon who was hovering nearby?"

He jerked slightly. "You think Mikael is sexy?"

She snorted. "Come on, answer the question."

He bit back a growl. Barely. She shouldn't think Mikael was sexy—or be thinking of him at all. "I know him from many years ago. He is a warrior." And that was all he was going to say on the subject. He wasn't going to talk about some other male to Dallas. A male she apparently thought was good-looking. His dragon swiped at him, annoyed.

She wouldn't be looking at other males if you courted her...pleasured her. Sad, sad human. You shame us, his dragon snapped, all sharp teeth and claws now.

As they rounded the next block, Rhys made an executive decision. "It's getting late and you look tired. I'm going to shift to my dragon form and then we're going to do an aerial scan. We need to do it anyway, and we might as well try tonight."

"I'm fine. It's just been a long day." There was a stubborn set to her jaw that was beyond adorable.

But he wasn't having any of it. Not now, when she appeared ready to fall over on her feet. "Willow looks tired." He glanced back at the dragonling, who was happily doing flying tricks. *Damn it.*

"Yeah, she looks *really* tired." Dallas snorted.

"Is it because I'm a dragon and you don't want to fly on me? Is that why you're resisting doing the aerial search for the crest?" Both he and his dragon were offended by the idea.

"What?" Her voice went slightly higher pitched as she looked away from him, focusing intently on the sidewalk in front of them.

"If you don't want to ride me, I get it." But he didn't like it. Why did the word *ride* have to sound so sexual? Because when he thought of her riding him, that conjured up much different images. He could just imagine her naked in his bed, with her long, dark hair, her hips sensually rocking as she took him inside her.

"Fine," she muttered. He was surprised and it must have shown because she continued. "Just this once. I'm not committing to doing this all the time. I...am a little exhausted."

At least she was admitting it, though the way she'd said it sounded as if it had taken all of her to actually tell him the truth. "I'll strip and change in the middle of the road. Will you hold my clothing?"

Her cheeks flushed pink, but she nodded and turned away, giving him privacy.

"I don't care if you look. Nudity is no big deal to shifters." He wanted her to look, wanted to show off for her. Wanted her to want him.

"Yeah, right," she snorted.

"What? You know it's not a big deal to my kind."

"I don't understand that," she said, throwing a glance over her shoulder before quickly turning back around when she realized he'd taken his shirt off.

"You don't understand what?"

"I've met mated shifters before and they can be really territorial. So...like, you don't care if your lover or future mate gets naked in front of other shifters?"

That...was an interesting question. Because he would *not* want her to get naked in front of any other male. "That's a complicated question."

Dallas surprised him by looking over her shoulder. She held his gaze even though he was fully naked now. "Would you mind if I got naked in front of Axel?" she asked bluntly, intently watching him. As if...she cared about his response.

Maybe that was wishful thinking on his part. *Oh no.* He wasn't going to answer *that*. Because the thought of that smug lion seeing Dallas, seeing *his* female, naked? His dragon rose up like a tidal wave, ready to hunt down the cat. Instead, he turned around, letting her see his ass.

He was pleased when he heard her suck in a little breath. Then he let the magic take over, the change rolling over him in a wash of pain, pleasure and raw energy as his dragon emerged.

By the time he turned around, she had his clothing bundled up under her arm and Willow was flying above them, making happy trilling sounds. He wondered if she liked what she saw when he was in dragon form. His scales were indigo and the deepest purple, and under the sunlight they glittered like jewels. He'd been told on more than one occasion—many years ago—that he was a beautiful dragon. And his beast wanted to know if she thought so as well.

He extended his wing so it was easy for Dallas to climb up him. By the time she settled on his back, he realized that he liked the feel of her atop him, as if she belonged there. That knowledge was at odds with everything he thought he knew about himself. He'd never trusted anyone enough to let them ride him.

He waited until she settled in, then took off, angling his body as straight as he could so she would feel comfortable. He could feel her holding on tight to his scales and she seemed to have a good grip, but he still wanted her ride to be as smooth as possible. Because he wanted her to do it again.

Willow flew with him, her flying a bit stronger. But she was still learning a lot. She stayed angled to his left, mimicking his moves as he breached the treetops. Every now and then she made a little chirping sound, clearly happy. Every time she did, Dallas's laughter rang out, soothing every part of him.

In that moment he wished his life was different. That he'd met Dallas and Willow under different circumstances. Because despite himself, he could see a future with her and that scared him on every level possible. He'd never imagined a future for himself, *ever*. For so long all he'd wanted was revenge, justice. It had been his only focus and he'd never allowed the possibility of anything else.

Now, however, Dallas made him want things he had no business wanting. Forcing his mind off thoughts of a life that would never be, he focused on flying. On keeping Dallas safe.

He flew in a tight configuration over the areas they'd already searched on foot, so she could get an aerial view. After ten minutes of flying, he heard her say, "Nothing," frustration in her tone.

It was time to head back. And at least they weren't walking—now she could finally get some rest. It was close to eleven and she'd been pushing herself all damn day. He'd banked left and headed home when Willow started making scared little chirps.

Immediately he looked around, scanning for any signs of danger. That was when he felt Dallas's grip on his scales loosen.

Suddenly her hands completely fell away and he felt her slipping off him.

Willow screeched and panic punched through him as he twisted in midair. He caught her falling body in his talons and held her close. She was breathing, but unconscious.

Fear like he'd never known rattled through him, wild and hot as he angled back toward the mansion.

Flying hard, unable to slow for Willow, it took barely five minutes to get there. Though fear was riding him hard, he dove down and landed steadily, laying her in the grass gently before he shifted to his human form.

Willow landed as well, making scared little sounds as she hopped around on her feet, nudging Dallas's face gently with the end of her nose.

"I've got her," he murmured to Willow as he scooped Dallas into his arms.

She curled into him, asleep, not unconscious. Otherwise she would be a deadweight. This still wasn't great, but it was better than her being fully knocked out. And he could feel her body warmth, hear her steady heartbeat. He relaxed slightly.

He raced for the back of the house, and as he reached the yard, Bella and Harlow were already racing toward him from the shadows.

Lola jumped up from her chair, her rainbow-colored hair in double pigtails today. "What's wrong?" she demanded as he hurried toward them.

"I'm not sure. She might just be overtaxed and tired, but I was flying with her on my back and she passed out." And he'd lost a decade of his life when she'd fallen off him.

"R...Rhys?" Dallas's tired voice snapped his gaze back to hers.

She was staring up at him in confusion, her gray eyes unfocused.

He shoved out a breath of relief as he clutched her closer to him. Ignoring the others, he raced toward the back door and hurried into the kitchen. He hated leaving Willow but it had to be done. "You passed out on me while flying. I need to call a healer."

"No, that's not necessary." She struggled in his grasp so he set her on a chair in the little breakfast nook that overlooked the backyard.

Bella was with them but she remained silent, on the periphery, clearly waiting to see if they needed help.

"It is damn well necessary," he snapped out, placing the back of his hand against her forehead, checking her temperature—as if he had any idea what he was doing. He wasn't sure if witches ran hotter than humans, and damn it, he didn't know *anything* right now. And he'd never felt so helpless in his entire life.

"I swear I'm fine. I just need to eat and sleep. The finding spell took more energy out of me than I realized. I haven't done one in a very long time. They can be energy-draining and I'd already been running on fumes. In hindsight, I should have waited to start my search."

"And you didn't think to tell me?" he demanded as he hurried toward the fridge. He started tugging stuff out as Lola stepped into the kitchen.

"Harlow's getting Willow settled," Lola said.

"Thank you," Dallas murmured, true relief rolling off her, the scent sharp and sweet. She really did love her dragon.

Wordlessly Lola joined him and started fixing Dallas a sandwich, cutting up a tomato as he started toasting the bread.

"You guys, you don't have to do all that—"

"Just sit there and hush," he snapped with more force than he'd intended. Damn female was aging him prematurely with her stubbornness.

She blinked at him. "Did you really just tell me to hush?"

"You put yourself in danger." And the very thought of that had him strung tight with nowhere to target his annoyance.

She shot him an almost confused look but took the carbonated drink that Lola slid over to her and sipped on it. "Thank you," she finally said as he slid the completed ham and cheese sandwich over to her.

"That's just the beginning. You need more energy than this." And he wasn't taking no for an answer.

"Ooh, there's some leftover lasagna in the fridge I can heat up. How does that sound?" Lola asked. "Axel made it and it's delicious."

He didn't want her eating any food that damn lion had made. She should only be eating food made by *his* hand.

"That sounds really good. I feel like I could eat half of the contents of the fridge right now." Then she started eating, demolishing her sandwich in seconds.

As he watched her, he realized her cheeks looked a little hollow. Just like that, his possessive, protective nature fully took over.

Rhys nudged Lola out of the way and grabbed the lasagna from her. Some deep-seated need was driving him to take care of Dallas, and his dragon simply wouldn't allow anyone else to.

He'd never felt like this and didn't understand the compulsion, but he wasn't going to fight it. Because deep down he knew he would do anything to take care of this female.

Because Dallas was his.

CHAPTER 15

Brielle stalked through the woods in human form, her backpack strapped tight to her.

"They've left a trail as wide as the Mississippi River," Axel murmured next to her, his movements just as quiet as he stepped over a fallen tree. He was dressed similarly to her in dark pants, a long-sleeved T-shirt, shit-kickers. Though his hair was pulled up into a bun and hers was braided.

The moon guided their way tonight, bright and full, illuminating the thick woods. They'd been tasked with looking into reports of bears harassing a bunch of people at a campsite. Since The Fall it was all hands on deck, and Brielle and Axel lived in King's territory now—so they pitched in with security or border issues any time they were asked. Brielle's tiger was still getting used to a new Alpha and hadn't decided if she'd accepted King fully yet. She liked the guy, respected the hell out of him, but actually accepting another as an Alpha was a tricky thing for shifters. Especially since before now, she'd had one Alpha since she'd been a cub—Star. And now Star was gone, thousands of miles away.

She shrugged, her mouth quirking up. "They're bears. They don't have to be quiet. People just run when they see them coming."

Axel, laid-back feline that he was, looked truly annoyed. "It's shameful. They're shifters."

She bit back a laugh. Axel got annoyed at the most random things. Always had, ever since they were kids. She'd started to respond when she heard a scream—a terrified, curdling sound ripping through the night air.

Neither of them paused, just sprinted in that direction. It didn't take long to break through a clearing. In moments, she processed everything. Four tents set up in a semicircle, a fire dwindling, at least eight humans and two bears.

And blood.

A huge bear shifter was on his hind legs growling at a human male who held a pipe of sorts in his hand. A human female lay on the ground, bleeding, while two humans knelt next to her, trying to stanch what appeared to be a leg wound.

"Hey!" Brielle shouted, racing into the group.

Both bears paused and fell down onto all fours.

"Shift now," Axel demanded as he came to stand next to her. Anger vibrated off him in waves, and yeah, she felt the same way.

It was pretty clear that these bears had been more than harassing these humans. Maybe there was more to the story, but the strong picking on the weak? That always brought out her inner tiger.

The two bears snarled, growling loudly at the two of them, but not making any advances in their direction.

"All right, looks like we're doing this the hard way," Axel muttered. Then he looked at her and grinned as he stripped his shirt off. Why the hell was he grinning? "Lions, tigers and bears, oh my!" he laughed out before he finished stripping.

She shoved her shoes off as she kept an eye on the bears. "There's seriously something wrong with you, dude. Like...you were clearly dropped on your head as a baby."

Axel simply shifted to lion and raced for the nearest tree.

"I'm giving you a chance to shift to human and talk this out," Brielle said as she tugged her shirt off. She hadn't bothered with a bra because she'd had a feeling she'd be shifting tonight. "We've been sent by King to see what's going on."

The bear on the left charged at her in response. *All right, then.* She didn't get to take off her pants, just called on her tiger. The shift took over her immediately, fur and magic exploding as she dove through the air at the lumbering bear.

Quick on her feet, she jumped high in the air, aware of Axel pouncing down from the tree onto the other bear's back. The fight was over before it began.

Brielle was a Siberian tiger and this bear was about to learn that it wasn't at the top of the food chain. That it couldn't bully whoever it wanted. She jumped onto its back and hooked her claws into its rib cage, slicing up hard.

The bear screamed in pain, trying to throw her off. She jumped and turned in midair, landing on all fours. She could hear the gasps of humans around them, but ignored everything but the predator in front of her.

She'd given these assholes a chance, after all. Behind her she heard Axel snarl in rage and knew he was doing all right. He might be laid-back, but he fought dirty. He'd win this fight.

The bear pawed the ground once, as if he was a goddamn horse, then stood up on his hind legs and roared, his jaw opening wide.

She yawned as she watched him, knowing it would piss the beast off. Yep, she thought as he fell back onto all fours and charged her.

She crouched low, and the moment before he would have barreled into her she rolled to the side in a practiced move. Then she whipped around and launched herself onto his back, this time with the perfect angle to attack his neck.

She released her claws into him again, digging into his shoulders as she bit down hard across the back of his neck. She heard and felt multiple bones break as the big beast went limp underneath her.

The moment he did, the male's body shifted to human to reveal a dark-haired male who was now a bloody mess.

Breathing hard, Brielle shifted back to human form and strode for her backpack. She pulled out two sets of the spelled cuffs they'd brought for just this occasion. She tossed one to Axel, who slapped them onto a groaning bear turned human.

The male she'd fought wasn't even groaning, but his chest was rising and falling. He might survive, he might not. As soon as she had his cuffs on—ensuring he couldn't shift back to bear—she pulled out a phone and texted their backup team. They were going to need to transport these bears in for questioning and they needed to help anyone injured.

Not bothering with clothes, she hurried over to the injured female. "What happened to her?" she asked the blonde female who was busy trying to rebandage the woman's leg.

"The bear you took down swiped her. He was…playing with us. They both were. They came out of nowhere. We didn't even realize they were shifters at first," she said, tears rolling down her cheeks. "Until one shifted and told us what he was going to do to us." Her voice broke then as more tears fell freely.

Brielle gritted her teeth and resisted the urge to stride over to him and kick his teeth in. "They won't be able to hurt you anymore. Let me see her wound." She was aware of Axel talking to the others, trying to comfort them. "Also, I don't smell any other blood but is anyone else hurt?" she asked as the woman started unwrapping the bandage.

"No. Not really," a male said from behind her.

She scored her palm with her claws and started dripping blood onto the wound. She didn't do this often—rarely, in fact—but she wasn't sure how close backup was and didn't want to risk this human bleeding out. There had been enough blood and death in the world. She wasn't going to let any more happen on her watch.

"Tiger blood," the injured female said, her words slurred as she tried to focus on Brielle.

"Just lie back," she said as she smeared more blood on the slashes. Damn, that bear had got her good. It was amazing she was even talking at this point.

"Iz…my favorite snow cone flavor."

Brielle frowned as she withdrew her hand.

"Honey, you're rambling, just close your eyes," the female said as she reached into her small first aid kit and pulled out another bandage.

"Love…tiger blood," she slurred again before passing out.

Brielle blinked at the other human. The human liked tiger blood?

"She's delirious, I think. But tiger blood—the strawberry, watermelon and coconut-flavored syrup—is her favorite for snow cones. Also, it sounds really freaking offensive now that I'm saying it out loud so I apologize." She finished wrapping the bandage, her frown in place. "Can I wrap your hand?"

Tiger blood was a flavored syrup? She was so looking that up later. Brielle snorted as she stood. "I'm good, but thanks." Before she'd even turned Axel was in front of her, clothing in hand. "Thanks," she murmured, dressing in seconds.

"We've got backup on the way and we're going to get you guys the help you need," he said to the others who all looked a little shell-shocked as they huddled together.

"Thank you," the only human she'd spoken to said. "For saving us."

Brielle simply nodded, not sure what else to say at this point. She looked over at Axel, then the trussed-up bears. It would be so easy to finish them off.

"Don't," Axel said quietly.

"I'm not doing anything," she muttered.

"I know that look. Let King's pack take care of them."

She gritted her teeth and looked away from the bears. Because if she didn't get some distance, she was going to beat the shit out of them even more. Since she figured the humans had seen enough bloodshed for the day, she held off.

Barely.

CHAPTER 16

Dallas braided her damp hair, feeling somewhat better, though still exhausted. After hanging up her towel on the bronze hook, she opened the bathroom door and stepped out into the hallway. She was surprised to find Rhys there, leaning against the white and gray art deco style wallpaper along the hallway with his arms crossed against his chest. And she really hated that she noticed how his forearms flexed in that position. "What are you doing?"

"Waiting for you. I wanted to make sure you were okay."

She wasn't sure how to read him, whether he was genuinely concerned for her, or if he simply cared about her well-being because she was the key to his revenge. She was the one who could see that crest and Thurman had told them that locating it was the only way to find what he was looking for. So while she wanted to think his concern for her was real—that he'd been like a hovering mother hen in the kitchen because he cared—she wasn't so sure of his intentions. "I'm fine. Just exhausted."

"Is it normal to get so tired from doing spells?" he asked as he fell in step with her, his feet silent along the hallway as they headed back to her sleeping quarters.

"Usually no. But I used my own blood, something I almost never do. And I tapped into a part of myself I rarely use. It's…complicated. But the short answer is no."

He stayed right on her heels as they stepped into the office and she froze for a moment when she saw the new bed in the room. Rhys curled his hands around her shoulders, his chest colliding with her back at her abrupt stop. "What's wrong?" he demanded, quickly moving in front of her to block her from the nonexistent threat.

"Nothing's wrong. I'm just surprised they moved a new bed in here." They'd moved some of the furniture out and now she had a fluffy queen-sized bed that looked so damn inviting she wanted to fall into it and sleep for twelve hours. The fact that they'd done that warmed her heart.

"I asked them to," he muttered as he strode toward the French doors. She blinked at his words. He had?

As he pulled the doors fully open, she smiled to see Willow already waiting there for her like a little sentry. Her sweet girl lifted her head and chirped when she saw Dallas. Then she crept partway through the doors, laying her head on the rug before closing her eyes in exhaustion.

"She wants to be close to you tonight," he murmured.

Her heart full, Dallas walked over, bent down and scratched behind Willow's ears before stumbling toward the bed. Sleep was necessary now and she was barely holding on. She figured that Rhys could just go when he wanted because she had no small talk left in her.

To her surprise, Rhys sat down on one of the club chairs in the corner, his long legs stretched out in front of him as he leaned back, attempting to get comfortable.

Okay, sleep could wait for a second. "What are you doing?"

"I'm sleeping here," he said as if that was the most obvious thing in the world—as if her question was dumb.

"Why?"

"Because I'm concerned about you. Because you fell off my back midair because you were so tired. I'm keeping an eye on you tonight."

She snorted and the sound came out bitter as she sat on the edge of the bed.

He frowned at her. "What's that sound mean?"

"Nothing," she murmured, not wanting to get into it. Mainly because her pillow was calling her name.

"It's pretty clear that it's not nothing. Explain."

She let out a growl of frustration at his arrogant, demanding tone. He really was every inch a dragon. "Look, I get it. You're worried that I'll get injured and won't be able to help you find that crest and eventually get your revenge. But I'm fine, I swear. You don't have to stay here and watch over me like a mother hen. It's ridiculous."

He stood up and stalked toward the bed, his big body looming over hers. But then he crouched down so that they were at eye level. His dark blue eyes flared hot for a long moment, his dragon peering back at her. "I'm not in here because I'm worried about that. I'm worried about *you* as a person. You scared me tonight."

There was so much truth in his words, she felt it wrap around her. She might not have the same scent capabilities as shifters, but she could feel that he was telling the truth. "Oh." She felt a little bit like a jerk in that moment even though she was pretty sure she had every right to have made those assumptions.

"Scoot over," he gruffly ordered.

She stared up at him and didn't even think to argue as she followed his direction and scooted to the other side of the bed. Only when he slid into bed next to her did she jerk straight up. "What the hell are you doing now?" She really should have known what he was doing when he told her to scoot over, but her brain was firing on two cylinders right now. She felt as if she was in a haze, just struggling to keep her eyes open.

"Just roll over and close your eyes."

She sat there staring at him, heat prickling all over her body as he stretched out on the bed, his long legs hanging off the end as he watched her closely.

She was very aware that this bed was a perfect fit for her and him, forcing them to lie close to each other. Too close. "I should tell you to get out and that you're being ridiculous and kind of obnoxious."

"I'm a dragon, I'm always obnoxious." Then he closed his eyes and simply tugged her toward him, holding her close and making her yelp. "More sleep, less talking," he murmured.

She curled her back into his chest, sinking into the pure warmth of him. Dragons really did run hotter than witches. This whole situation was crazy. She shouldn't be letting him take over like this, she thought as she closed her eyes.

As she inhaled his rich, masculine scent, she knew she should be ordering him straight out of her room. But it was so nice to be held. In fact, she couldn't remember the last time she'd been held by anyone like this. Years. Maybe decades. And in his arms, she felt so safe and warm for the first time in... Forever.

She would yell at him tomorrow for being so arrogant, she promised herself. Then she closed her eyes and let sleep take her under.

* * *

Dallas shifted against the big, warm…chest? She opened her eyes and realized she was curled up against Rhys. Or more accurately, she had her leg thrown over his hip, her arm over his shoulder and her face buried against his chest. And holy hell, he smelled sooooo good. Oh goddess. That scent made raw heat and hunger curl through her. She wanted to get even closer to him—much, much closer.

"You're awake," he murmured, making her jerk slightly against him.

That was when she realized that he had a very possessive grasp on her hip. His fingers flexed against her, but didn't move from her body.

"You're like a furnace," she murmured, rubbing her face against him before she could think better of it. The only thing she wished was that he didn't have a shirt on. And something told her that this male didn't often sleep with clothing on. Nope, she bet that he slept completely naked the majority of the time. And that thought was very, very hot.

"I'm a dragon," he said simply.

Still in between sleep and wakefulness, she inhaled deeply, wanting to memorize his scent. *Screw it.* She was being a weirdo this morning because she couldn't help herself. "Dragons smell good," she murmured.

"Not *dragons*, just *me*." His breath was warm against the top of her head.

The absolute seriousness of his words made her laugh against him. It seemed like such a Rhys thing to say. She didn't even know him that well, but what she did know of him, yeah, that seemed right on target. Arrogant and sexy. And okay, he was also protective, given that he'd stayed with her all night.

"Next time you tell me if you're doing too much," he murmured again, his breath still warm against her head.

She wanted to burrow up against him, to just stay in this bubble for a little bit longer. But she knew that wasn't smart. Shifting slightly so that she could see him, she found herself looking into beautiful dark blue eyes that mesmerized her. "What are you talking about?"

"You did too much magic yesterday. I want to know if you're expending too much energy. I'm your shadow, I'm watching out for you. I need to be able to take care of you, protect you. That means you have to take care of yourself too."

She knew what he'd told her last night, that he cared about her as a person. Still, in the light of day, with her brain not so fuzzy, she wasn't sure if he was being protective because she was a means to an end, or because he really cared.

Realizing that she was staring at his mouth, she pushed back and sat up slightly. Or she tried to, but he didn't let go of her hip.

She flopped back against the bed. "Where's Willow?"

"Doing drills with Harlow."

"Wait...what?" She rolled toward him again, wondering what it would be like if she had the right to touch him everywhere. To stroke her fingertips underneath his shirt and tug it off completely.

"I'm not sure entirely. Harlow 'kidnapped' her this morning—her words, not mine. She bribed her with some treats and said they were going to do flying practices. Said that she would make a warrior of your Willow soon enough."

Glad her dragon was fine, Dallas wanted to fall back on the soft, fluffy bed and wrap herself around Rhys. But she knew that was a recipe for trouble.

So. Much. Trouble. The naked kind.

She could see the heat in his gaze and she was feeling weak and needy. And he still had his fingers draped possessively around her hip.

Her body was starting to heat up for one very specific reason.

This was not good. Not good at all.

If she let her emotions get chaotic and out of control, he would scent her desire. And even if he reciprocated her hunger, they were far too different. And yes, he'd been apologetic about his preconceived ideas about her kind, but she didn't think he was the type of male to ever forget that she was a witch. Or to ever fully accept her for who she was.

On that thought, she rolled over and sat up. "I need to brush my teeth."

To her surprise, his fingers clenched around her hip once before he finally let her go.

As she slid off the bed, she found that she could breathe easier again. Being so close to him short-circuited her brain in more ways than one. Distance was soooo necessary right now.

"Your phone went off a few times, so I silenced the ringer," he said as she headed for the door.

"Who was it?"

He lifted a shoulder. "Doesn't matter. You needed your sleep."

He was right, she knew that, but she still worried that maybe it had been an emergency. What if one of her neighbors had called? She grabbed her phone and strode for the door because she hadn't been lying. She really did need to brush her teeth and take care of some other morning things.

But she needed distance from him more. She just hoped that by the time she got back to her room, he was gone. She needed a few minutes of space from him, especially since she'd spent the whole night in his arms.

It was some of the best sleep she'd ever had, and that disturbed her. She should *not* feel safe in his arms, shouldn't feel so warm and comforted.

And she would do well to remember that he was a dragon who up until very recently had viewed her kind as the enemy. He was hunting down the witch who had borne her, after all.

Once he found out *that* truth, she knew he would want nothing to do with her. So she needed to keep those walls up between them.

And build some new ones for good measure.

CHAPTER 17

By the time Dallas had showered and made it to the back patio, breakfast was spread out, and to her surprise, Avery and her dragon friend Mikael were there. Rhys was also there, looking good enough to eat and watching her with that predator gaze as she stepped out toward everyone. It seemed he was always watching her.

Some of Dallas's tension eased when Avery smiled and stood, shoving her chair back and meeting her on the edge of the lanai. In jeans, sneakers and a pullover sweater, she looked like she always did—adorable. "Lola asked me over, so I hope it's okay that we came so early," she said as she pulled her into a hug.

"Hey, I'm just staying here. You can do whatever you want," Dallas said, laughing. "But I'm so glad to see you."

Avery's eyes narrowed slightly. "I can't believe you have a pet dragon and didn't tell me."

"To be fair, I've only had her for a little while and the world *has* been kind of crazy."

"No kidding. We've been so slammed with construction lately, trying to get people housed. It's like this never-ending race to work faster."

"I can imagine. So you have roommates now?" She glanced over to the big dragon, who was pretending that he was *not* watching Avery, but it was pretty clear that Mikael was keeping Avery in his line of vision.

"Yeah. King wanted me to house some ancients who'd woken up right before The Fall, and now I'm living with a bunch of dudes. It's good for my brothers at least—now they have actual decent male role models to look up to instead of their annoying older sister. Even if they are all sort of more or less adolescents." She shook her head, her dark curls bouncing.

Dallas knew that Avery's father took the cake on being the douche king of the world, so she understood what her friend meant by decent role models. Really, an avocado was a better role model than their father—though the boys weren't teenagers anymore, they were in their early twenties, something she sometimes forgot. They just seemed young to her. The two young men took after their Cuban mother in the looks department, dark hair, darker skin and very handsome. Avery was adorable and had a natural bronzed glow year-round, but for the most part she took after her father—something Dallas knew the human hated.

"It's so cool that you're friends with Avery too," Lola called out, motioning for them to come sit at the table with the others. "And you need to eat, from what I hear."

Dallas shot Rhys a dry look as she and Avery headed back to the huge table, but he shrugged and pulled out a chair for her. Which was oddly sweet.

"Thanks," she murmured as she sat next to Avery. Rhys sat across from her in a spot next to his friend Mikael and immediately poured her coffee from the carafe. When he added the amount of sugar she liked, she realized he really did pay attention.

"So do you think I could ride Willow?" Avery asked as Dallas started piling fruit onto her plate.

Dallas glanced over at Willow who was busy entertaining herself with a volleyball someone must have given her. It was a miracle the thing wasn't smushed yet. "You really want to?"

"You wish to ride a dragon?" Mikael asked suddenly, straightening in his seat, all his focus on Avery.

Avery's eyes widened. "Uh, yeah! Who wouldn't want to?"

He frowned at her. "You never said anything. I will take you flying."

"Well you guys never asked if I wanted to go flying, and now the cutest dragon in the world is one of my friends' pets." She grinned as she looked at Dallas. "So, what do you say?"

"I think she'll be fine with you. She's really good with me and Rhys—and all the ladies here."

"Hey, she likes me too!" Axel called out from the other end of the table.

She glanced down the table at Axel and shook her head at the lion. "And she likes Axel too. I think it's because he sneaks her treats he thinks I don't know about."

"Well, Axel is very lovable," Avery said before spearing a strawberry with her fork. "He's a big, squishy lion."

Dallas noticed that Mikael's expression went dark at the mention of Axel. Dallas caught Rhys's gaze and realized that he was simply watching her, all intense and sexy and brooding. Snagged in that stare, in those eyes, she found that she couldn't tear her gaze away. Damn it, she needed to get her concentration off him but it was pretty impossible, especially after he'd held her in his arms all night. She distinctly remembered what it felt like to have all those muscles pressed up against her, to have his arms wrapped around her, comforting her.

Blinking, she managed to look away from him and simply focus on the fruit on her plate.

"So where are your brothers?" Lola called out from the other end of the table.

Mikael jerked slightly, looking away from Avery. "Are you talking to me?"

"Yes. Where are the hotties who hang out with you? You know, the ones who don't talk much but look like they'd be a lot of fun in bed."

"Quit teasing him," Avery called out, then shot Mikael a grin. "She's just messing with you."

Lola snickered and took a sip of a mimosa. "I so am not."

"She's definitely not," Bella said, rolling her eyes. "Keep your brothers away from her, she'll eat them alive!"

Mikael looked a bit like that proverbial deer caught in headlights. But when his gaze landed back on Avery, he seemed to settle himself.

Warmth filled Dallas's chest as she listened to their interaction. She really did like her solitude on her farm and all of her friends out there, but in the country she saw everyone in small doses. Here she was inundated with people and she found out that she really liked the company. And she could admit that she liked being included and accepted for who she was with this group.

She'd always tried to tell herself that she was fine and didn't care what people thought of her, and for the most part that was true. But it was a hell of a drug to be accepted. She glanced over at Rhys again and he was still watching her, a definite hungry look in his expression.

He wasn't even trying to hide it, which was a bit disconcerting. This male was seriously messing with her head. If she was into casual sex maybe she could have something fun, a fling with him. But she wasn't wired like that—she needed more trust with someone before she contemplated anything intimate. Getting naked and letting all her guard down was a big deal. It required so much trust.

At that thought, she looked down at her plate and focused on her food. Her stomach was a tight ball of anxiety but she knew she needed to eat. Especially since they would be out again today searching for the crest. She was feeling hopeful, however, that they could cover a lot of ground since they were starting early. She just wished she had some witch friends she could call on to help. She actually *did* have a few who she trusted, but someone had once told her that the best way to keep a secret was not to tell *anyone*.

Right now she knew this needed to remain a secret among only those who were currently aware of it. Because someone could make an offhand comment to someone else, not meaning to, and alert the wrong people that King was looking for them.

"I have to head out soon," she said to Avery when there was a lull in the conversation. "So if you want to ride Willow now, you can."

Avery had pushed her chair back before Dallas had even finished her words, practically jumping up and down like a kid on Christmas Day.

"All right, you're definitely ready." Dallas laughed as she pushed her chair out and joined her. Then she looked over at Rhys. "We won't be long. As soon as we're done, will you be ready to go?"

He simply nodded, and she wished he wasn't so damn sexy, so damn delicious looking. Because she could eat that male right up, whether he hated witches or not.

* * *

Rhys stood next to Mikael, who was leaning against an oak tree, his arms crossed over his chest as he watched Willow swooping up and down throughout the yard with Avery on his back.

"She's a good little flyer," Rhys murmured. "She's not going to drop your female."

"Avery is not mine."

"Okay, then." He could say it all he wanted, but Mikael watched her in the same way that Rhys watched Dallas.

"She's not yours, then?" Axel dropped down from the damn tree—sneaky feline.

Even though he'd surprised Rhys, Rhys remained immobile—and made a note not to underestimate this lion. He might act genial and fun-loving, but Axel was clearly skilled at sneaking around.

Mikael shoved off the tree. "Who the fuck wants to know?"

The lion just grinned, far too much mischief in his eyes as he shoved his hands into his jeans pockets. "Pretty sure it's clear that I'm asking. And I can't help but wonder if maybe she would prefer riding a lion instead of a dragon." Then he laughed to himself and strolled away—as if he wasn't baiting a giant, deadly predator who could set him on fire.

When Rhys realized that Mikael was literally blowing out smoke, he grabbed his forearm. "Get your shit together. He's just screwing with you."

"I've never had a lion pelt before. I think it would make a nice throw rug." Mikael's tone was dry—with just a hint of truth ringing in his words. "I would toss it in front of my fireplace."

"Something tells me Axel gets that a lot. So are you going to tell me why you're here?" Rhys asked the other dragon.

"It's as good a place as any." He lifted his shoulders. Then he shoved out a sigh. "We woke up near here and my clan is gone. We are the last of our family."

"I didn't realize."

Mikael's jaw was tight as he watched Avery squealing in delight. "For now, this is my home."

Rhys had a feeling that his home was wherever Avery's was, but he didn't comment. "I told you why I'm here. I'm close to finding my sister's killer," he murmured, low enough for only his old friend to hear. "She was so...sunny. Happy. It kills me that her life was cut so short."

"If you need assistance, let me know. I remember her." The faintest smile played across his expression.

"She is impossible to forget."

"So how close are you?" he asked.

Rhys couldn't give any details about what they'd discovered, but he nodded. "*Very*. Closer than I've ever been before."

"Then we will all help, my brothers and I." Mikael rolled his shoulders once, seeming anxious, before settling against the tree again. "It will be nice to have someone to track down."

Many years ago, Mikael had been the enforcer for his clan. He'd worked with trackers to hunt down rogue dragons or other supernaturals who got out of line and broke their rules.

Rhys was glad to have an ally, someone he trusted. Because he wasn't doing this alone; he needed someone else to have Dallas's back as well. He was hunting down an evil, and if that evil figured out Dallas had helped him, she would become a target. He was determined that never happen.

And while he was willing to die for his cause, he would never do anything to cause harm to Dallas. Not even for his own revenge. That knowledge shook him at a molecular level but it was true.

He would sacrifice his own life for vengeance, but he would not sacrifice her life.

CHAPTER 18

"Just one second," Dallas murmured as she finished sending a long text. Rhys couldn't help but stare at her, drink in every inch of her as her fingers flew across her screen. Her phone pinged as it broke the text into multiple messages. She'd pulled her long hair back into a ponytail and had on a formfitting sweater that showed off her perfect breasts. Comfortable like him, she also had on jeans and well-worn sneakers.

"Everything okay?" Rhys asked. They were heading out to search again. At least today they were starting in an area close to the mansion. He'd asked her about driving or riding a bike today but she'd wanted to walk. She said she preferred to in case the symbol was somewhere more at eye level, which apparently it often was. She said it was the type of thing usually half hidden and she didn't want to miss it.

"Yeah." She tucked her phone away into her crossbody bag. "I just wanted to let King know about some of the spots I found for community gardens, including the one across the street from Avery and your friend. I forgot to tell him about everything I'd found and didn't want to forget."

He fell in step with her as they headed down the walkway to the open gates. He inhaled subtly, her sweet scent wrapping around him, making his dragon purr right under the surface.

"So tell me about your friend Mikael," she said as they stepped onto the sidewalk.

What. The. Fuck. He realized he was growling when she stared at him in shock.

"What? Is he not a good guy?" She whispered the last part as she glanced over her shoulder, as if she expected Mikael to overhear them. "Because it's pretty clear that he's interested in my friend, so I just wanted to check that he was decent and not a giant dick."

His beast retreated immediately. For some reason he'd thought she was asking for herself—she *had* called the male sexy. Which was annoying. "Yes, he is a trusted friend. And he was a brilliant warrior." And it made Rhys sad that Mikael had lost his family. He'd wanted to ask him more about his clan, but it hadn't been the time for it. He would wait until they had more privacy.

"Good." Dallas looked down at the little map she'd brought. "I'm pretty sure Avery likes him too. But she's kind of oblivious to things and I don't think she realizes he's into her."

He snorted, drawing a look from her. Her friend wasn't the only oblivious one.

"What?" she asked.

"Nothing," he murmured, "though I'm fairly sure that Axel is going to get his head knocked off for flirting with her so mercilessly."

She snickered. "I don't think you're wrong about that. He is a *terrible* flirt. With males and females," she added.

Yeah, he'd picked up on that as well. The guy seemed like an equal opportunity flirter, and it was all harmless as far as Rhys could tell. He didn't want to talk about that damn lion, however. Didn't even want to think about him. His only concern was Dallas. "So we're going to start where we left off yesterday?"

"Yep. We can start here," she said as she pointed to her map. "And then move inward this way. There's really not a way to tell which is the best position to start. For all we know, the location is on the outskirts of the circle. It's just a crapshoot."

"There's no way to narrow it down any?"

She paused and shook her head. "Not really. I mean, if I knew which coven was behind this or had a personal relationship with one of the humans or vampires taken, I could try a few other tricks. But then I'd get into some gray areas."

He wanted to push her a little but she was already giving so much of herself and it wasn't really his business anyway. The old Rhys would have pushed her, demanded information. But...he was trying to be better. For her. He'd spent so many years racing after his vengeance and he was ashamed of who he'd become. Ashamed he'd let hate consume him.

"If you get tired or hungry, we stop. Okay?"

"You're very bossy," she murmured as she glanced at the upcoming house, scanning it for the invisible crest.

"I'm *right.*"

She didn't respond one way or the other, just made a sort of humming sound.

At least she'd brought a bunch of snacks in her bag, mainly nutrient bars for protein. And he'd brought a satchel with containers of water. He wasn't going to be unprepared today.

"So what's your Hibernation like?" she asked, the random question surprising him. "You don't have to answer," she added, adjusting her bag as a breeze rolled over them. "I was just curious. The whole concept of Hibernation is kind of foreign to me."

He nodded at a couple out walking their dog and sidestepped them on the sidewalk before he fell in step with her again. "Mainly I'm unconscious the whole time but I occasionally dream. It's like, well, a really long sleep. For the most part, it's supposed to be a time for our brains to truly rest and reset. My kind ages differently than humans, or even you, as you know. And because of that, the way we store our memories is different. It can be difficult to compartmentalize so many memories, good or bad. Because if the bad outweigh the good ones..." He lifted a shoulder. A dragon could go truly mad. He almost had.

Her expression thoughtful, she nodded. "That makes sense. I can't imagine carrying around so much pain for thousands of..." Wincing, she looked up at him. "Sorry. I know you lost your sister. I wasn't trying to bring that up." She winced again. "And I've done it twice."

Because there wasn't an ounce of maliciousness in her tone or expression, he reached out on instinct and squeezed her hand. "I know. It's okay. I haven't actually talked about her in a long time."

"You can talk about her to me if you want." She scanned the next house.

He knew she didn't find what she was looking for because her shoulders slumped just a little bit. Rhys wished there was more he could do to help her, that he could actually contribute.

As they continued, he realized he was still holding on to her hand.

He told himself to let go of it, that it was the smart thing to do, but he couldn't force himself to let go. And she wasn't pushing him away. So he linked his fingers through hers and his dragon practically purred underneath the surface.

Finally, you do something right, his dragon sniffed imperiously.

He rolled his eyes at himself. His beast could be such a jackass sometimes. Even if he was right.

He started to talk about his sister. "She was kind, definitely the best of all of us. She was younger than me, but she still liked to mother me. She sort of bossed all of us around." A smile tugged at his lips. "We didn't mind though. To us, she could do no wrong. Your friend Avery kind of reminds me of her. She's got that same sunny disposition."

"She's one of the kindest people I know."

"Eilidh was like that. She was so trusting, just believed there was good in all people. There was this cranky old human who lived on the outskirts of a nearby village—one my clan protected. He was mean to everyone, raging and bitter even to children. I assumed he was simply an angry human. But she told me it was because he had lost his wife and baby when she went into labor. Eilidh said that dragons were lucky because when they lost their mate, they died too. She said no wonder he was so angry and bitter all the time. Eventually he came out of his depression and ended up marrying again and having a whole brood of children. If it hadn't been for my sister's kindness, I don't know that he would have made it through that winter."

She squeezed his hand tight, her gray eyes filled with warmth. "I'm so sorry you lost her."

He nodded once, his throat tight.

"You said...when dragons lose their mate, they die too?" There was surprise in her voice, which made sense.

His kind didn't broadcast their weakness. Or maybe it was their strength. He wasn't sure. It was simply the way dragons were. And his sister had been right—if he was ever so lucky to be mated, he wouldn't want to continue without his other half. "Correct."

"You feel like expanding on that?" She looked over at another yard.

"No. But...it is exactly how it sounds. If a dragon is mated, whether to another dragon or not, if their mate dies, they die too. And if a non-dragon mates a dragon, that becomes their burden to bear as well. They will die if their dragon does."

"Wow."

He lifted a shoulder, surprised at himself, but apparently he couldn't keep secrets from this intoxicating female. "I was supposed to be with her that day, the day she was taken," he suddenly blurted, even though he'd had no intention of telling Dallas this at all. "I promised her we would go swimming even though the waters were ice-cold. We'd planned to go in dragon form. But I was late because..." He cleared his throat.

"Because?"

For some reason he didn't want to tell her this. "I got distracted by a female." And he'd hated himself ever since.

She raised an eyebrow at him. "That's not a crime."

"I know." But the guilt was still there, deep inside him, and it wouldn't go away. If he hadn't been thinking with his dick, things could have been different. "Eventually we figured out what had happened. Through some of her friends we discovered who she'd gone to meet when I didn't show up that day. And eventually we found her...bones." It hurt to even say the words.

Dallas squeezed his fingers again, but remained silent and steady. A soothing presence, just letting him talk.

"It's not your fault, you know," she murmured when he didn't continue. "Only one person is at fault here. Which I think you know. But that guilt you're carrying? It's not yours to hold on to."

He knew that, could say it until he was blue in the face. But it didn't change the fact that he hadn't shown up that day. That he'd broken a promise. That he'd let his sister down. That if he hadn't been so stupid, his sister would still be alive.

"She could've taken her another time, if it hadn't been that day," Dallas continued quietly. "Sometimes there's nothing we can do to help people, to save them. I'm not saying our fates are written in stone, because I don't think they are. Sometimes bad shit happens. And it sucks."

He squeezed her hand, but froze when she suddenly stilled in front of two gates overgrown with green tangles of ivy.

Past the gate he saw a two-story home with simple, clean-looking construction. White shutters open against the windows, wide balconies on both upstairs and downstairs, and the house was a simple pale blue. There weren't any hanging plants on the balconies, no chairs, nothing. The neighborhood was quiet, with a few dogs barking nearby and some kids laughing. He didn't hear anything out of the ordinary, didn't see anything… But the back of his neck prickled in awareness. "What do you see?"

"I see the crest." Her words were quiet enough for his ears only. "Do you see any video cameras?"

He scanned the two big gates and the surrounding wall but didn't see anything that stuck out to him. Just pretty ivy growing over the edge of it and a huge house beckoning them from inside. There was something else there, however, scraping at his skin. He rubbed the middle of his chest and looked around.

"There's something here, a darkness," she whispered as she strode up to the gate. Using the magic he'd seen her control before, a rainbow of colors sparked from her fingers, then the lock opened and the gate swished forward without a sound.

"I'm texting King." He pulled out his phone, already scrolling to the Alpha's name. King's wolves hadn't come with them today and now he was cursing that they hadn't.

"Okay, but I'm going in."

He reached for her forearm, but she was too fast, striding forward ahead of him.

Cursing, he hurried after her. "We don't need to do anything stupid."

"I'm not afraid," she said, looking around the empty yard. The house was large and well-maintained, but the yard was…plain, only a few potted plants. The lawn itself was trimmed neatly. Something was off, however, but he couldn't figure out what it was. He simply sensed it, right on the edge of his vision. It was there, but it wasn't.

"Stay back," she murmured. Then she stepped forward and held out her hands, pressing forward with her fingertips as if she was touching a wall.

And that was when he saw a ripple in the air, as if she'd touched a waterfall. Colors sparked everywhere, and he saw the huge dome of…raw magic surrounding the house.

Hissing, she jumped back, her fingertips bleeding.

His dragon roared, beating against him. "Hell no." He scooped her up into his arms and raced right back out the gate. He might want to charge in there, but he'd seen enclosures like this before. They would be hell to penetrate. Heart racing, he held her close, the need to keep her safe a live, visceral thing pulsing through him.

"Rhys, let me down," she demanded, squirming in his arms.

He only let her go once they were on the sidewalk again. And it was taking everything in him not to shift to his dragon and fly her far, far away. In fact…maybe he would do just that.

"I'm fine, see?" She held up her fingertips, which were now completely healed. "The power of the barrier took me off guard. That's all. I know what I'm dealing with now. I can handle this, promise."

"Are the humans and vampires here?" He kept his voice pitched low so that only she could hear. There was no one else on this quiet street that he could see, but that didn't mean they weren't being watched.

"I don't know. But this place has the crest, not to mention the barrier spell to keep nosy people out. We can wait for King or we can try to rescue any survivors now. I don't want to wait." She watched him, her jaw set tight.

Damn it. He gritted his teeth and glanced at his cell phone. King still hadn't responded. So Rhys called.

No answer. Rhys shoved his phone back in his pocket. It wasn't in his nature to walk away from a fight but he also had to worry about Dallas. "On a scale of one to ten, how powerful are you compared to other witches?" he asked bluntly. He didn't know how the hierarchies of witches really worked, and while she put off subtle waves of power, he had no idea how to measure it.

She blinked in surprise. "Ah, I don't know, I've never really thought about it. I've never fought another witch. Not truly anyway. I'm secure in my powers, however."

His dragon roared at him again, not satisfied with the answer. But he bit back his initial response. "At the first sign of danger we can't handle, I'm shifting to my dragon form and flying us out of here. Do you understand? Because I will grip you in my claws and fly straight out, even if you don't want me to."

"I understand," she said, then patted him on the chest as if he was overreacting. "Come on." Turning away from him, she headed for the still-open gates.

He jumped in front of her, even though he couldn't do anything about the dome—not easily anyway—as they approached the shimmering wall of magic. He inhaled deeply, ready to blast the thing with fire. It would take a while to burn through it, but he was up to the challenge.

Dallas held up a hand. "No. If it's booby-trapped, I don't know how it will react to dragon fire. And yes, I can tell that's what you're about to do. Just let me try something first. If my way doesn't work, you can set it on fire."

Without waiting for his response, she took a deep breath and closed her eyes. Then she started murmuring something quietly and reached out for the wall. When she did, she gripped the shimmering material and pulled it apart as if she was ripping apart a piece of fabric. The seams split open so easily, a wash of rainbow colors sparking as she created an opening big enough for them to step through.

He blinked at how quickly she'd ripped it open. That was...impressive.

He followed after her and, beyond the invisible wall, could see what had been hidden before. The grass wasn't green on the other side, but a dead brown, and the pale blue house was instead a cracking, dull purple.

He could feel the dark magic rolling against his skin but since he was a magical creature himself, it sloughed off like water off a dragon's back. His dragon shoved to the surface, uncomfortable at the oily feeling scraping, slithering across his skin.

Don't like this, his dragon rumbled. *Not natural.* Growling, he scanned the yard.

Dallas paled slightly but she shook her head when he started to talk. "I'm fine. I can feel...I can feel their souls calling." She took off at a dead run across the lawn.

Hell. Rhys jerked into action, panic punching through him, but he caught up to her in a few long strides. "Don't run away from me," he ordered.

But it was like she didn't hear him as she hurried up the rotted steps to the front door. The knocker was barely hanging on to its hinges, flakes of puke yellow paint crumbling off the door.

He held out an arm, stepping in front of her. "I go in first." He was a dragon, fireproof. And not completely magic-proof, but he could withstand a whole lot. He still wasn't sure how powerful she was and he wasn't letting her put herself in danger.

He kicked the door open and heard her sigh behind him.

"I could've just picked the lock," she muttered as they stepped into what turned out to be a completely empty house. No furniture in the foyer or two attached rooms. Nothing—just wood floors that had seen better days.

"Can you smell that?" he murmured. Because he could.

Death. And a lot of it.

Next to him she wrinkled her nose and nodded. So this wasn't just his supernatural senses picking up on it, it was strong enough for her to smell as well.

Not waiting for her to lead the way this time, he hurried past the set of winding stairs toward a long hallway and stopped in front of a doorway. He looked at her and she nodded.

He tried the knob and it swung open easily. As soon as the door opened, the stench of rotting flesh greeted him. The faint decay wafted upward, the coppery remnants of dried blood filling the air. And pain. Because that had a scent too. And the sharp bite of painful memories clung to the walls, as if the screams of victims had imprinted themselves there.

She covered her nose with her hand and made a gagging sound, but stepped forward with him, completely unafraid. Goddess, she really was a warrior. A soft, sweet one ready to dive right into battle.

He wanted to keep her back, didn't want her to see what he feared was down this short set of stairs. Because there was no life left in the room beyond, he was certain of it. He couldn't hear any heartbeats at all. No one drawing breath. Nothing. Just blood and death waited for them.

As they stepped onto the first stair, he flipped on the first light switch he saw. The stairwell flooded with light immediately, highlighting splatters of blood on the short set of stairs and the concrete floor below.

He vaguely thought that this room had maybe been a garage or someone had wanted to convert one into a room, but it was all cold concrete. As they descended the steps, the stench grew almost unbearable.

His eyes immediately focused on the arrangement of bodies on the cold floor and he started to grab Dallas and haul her back upstairs but she moved lightning quick around him.

"This is really dark magic," she murmured, horror in her expression.

He looked at the neatly placed circle of naked men and women. Vampires and humans. Blood pooled in the middle of the circle, staining the concrete. And their bodies... Symbols had been carved into their backs, arms, legs. Everywhere. Some people had died with their eyes open in horror—some had lost their eyes.

She stepped closer and pointed to the middle of the circle. "They've been drained of their blood. They did the spells here because that drain would catch the fallout. Whoever is behind this is doing ritual spells. They could be killing these humans and vampires to open a Hell gate or...to increase their life span," she said, looking up at him with pain-drenched eyes. "But humans won't give them what they want, not like supernaturals will. Human blood will only be a short-term thing, a patch, for what they want."

He looked back at the corpses, his rage punching through him and his dragon. He'd seen enough. "We don't need to be here anymore." And the truth was he didn't *want* to be here. He'd killed enough during battles. But those had been justified killings during war—skilled combatants, dragon warriors, not civilians and never innocents who couldn't defend themselves. This was...this was savagery for the sake of it. It was evil. There was no other word.

Dallas didn't argue as he guided her back toward the stairs.

He didn't remove his hand from her elbow, needing to touch her, to keep himself grounded and remind himself that she was alive. That she hadn't been touched by this darkness. Because he felt it clawing at the air, wanting her.

CHAPTER 19

Dallas barely made it out the front door and down the steps before she threw up her breakfast everywhere. Her mind was full of the images and smells inside that house of horror.

She was suddenly aware of Rhys next to her, holding her hair away from her face and rubbing her back as she emptied the contents of her stomach. The bright red from the strawberries she'd eaten covered the dead lawn in front of her, the splash of color macabre. As she finished, breathing hard, still bent over, he handed her a napkin. She had no idea where he'd even gotten it from—maybe from his bag—but she took it gratefully and wiped her mouth.

"Here," he said as she stood, shaking.

She took the already opened bottle of water with trembling fingers and held it to her mouth. When she spilled it down her chin, he steadied it for her and held it to her lips.

As the cool liquid rolled down her parched throat, she focused on him. In that moment she saw real concern in his gaze.

"I want to get away from this house," he said as she held the water at her side. "I don't have any bars on my phone. I think it might be interfering with cell phone service."

"The dome is definitely affecting your phone. I only opened it. I didn't destroy it." Her legs wobbled slightly as they strode toward where she'd ripped a seam in the wall of magic. By now, whoever owned this place would know that their magic spell had been tampered with.

Dallas doubted whoever had murdered all those people would come back now. The people inside were all dead and now their little hiding spot had been discovered.

Before they'd made it across the yard, King and five of his wolves strode through the ripped magic wall. He was the only one in human form. He took in her and Rhys with one visual sweep, looked around at everything else, then withdrew his sword.

She didn't have time to react before he turned to stab his sword into the wall and ripped upward.

A shrieking sound, like thousands of bats screaming, filled the air. She winced as the wall suddenly dissipated in a sharp blast of sparks and colors. *Holy hell.* So that sword was apparently more than just a regular sword.

She tried to get the cap on the water bottle to twist it closed, but couldn't manage it so Rhys took it from her. By the time he'd tucked it back into his bag, King was in front of them, his expression dark.

She shook her head before he could ask the question. "They're all dead. All the humans and vampires inside are gone," she murmured, as if he would have any trouble finding them. Wolves' sense of smell was powerful. He and his packmates could probably smell the stench of death from out here.

"Don't go anywhere," he ordered before he hurried off, his packmates racing after him.

"They've been dead a while. We couldn't have saved them," Rhys said to her as he started gently swiping his thumbs over her cheeks. Comforting her.

That was when she realized she was crying.

"There were so many of them," she whispered. She closed her eyes, trying to banish the images, but they wouldn't go away. Something told her they would never go away. All those bodies, their skin carved up...the blood. The expressions of pain and horror. She shuddered.

"I don't care what King says, I want to get you back to the mansion."

"Yeah, wouldn't want to damage your tool," she muttered even though she wasn't even angry at him. She was just angry at the loss of life. Still, she wondered if he truly saw her as a tool, a way to hunt down his sister's killer.

"What the hell are you talking about?"

"Nothing. I'm just edgy and angry." Angry at all the senseless death, senseless murders.

"You think I see you as a tool?" he pushed, not letting it drop.

She met his gaze. "Well don't you? Thurman said that once we found the crest, we would find what you're looking for."

"I don't give a shit about that," he snarled, seeming to surprise himself with the words before he frowned at her again. "I just care about you. You're pushing yourself too hard and I don't know enough about your power level to know if it's too much. If you're going too far," he snapped. "I don't like feeling out of control. And you make me feel just that!" Breathing hard, he stared down at her for a long moment. "And for the record I really want to kiss you. But I won't because King's people are coming back outside right now."

She stared at him in shock, especially as his last words registered through her foggy brain. He wanted to kiss her? She was really glad he hadn't, because she'd just thrown up and that was gross. Not to mention...they were still too close to that crime scene. She shuddered and wrapped her arms around herself. Before she'd even done that, he slid off his jacket and wrapped it around her shoulders before his arm followed. He pulled her close, tugging her right up against him as King approached.

She was thankful for Rhys's presence, for his warmth and the solid feel of his muscled body as chills skated through her. Being so close to him helped ward off some of the cold, but it had seeped into her bones.

"You ripped open the magic wall?" King was watching her with a new respect now.

She nodded.

He blinked. "By *yourself?*"

She nodded again.

He opened his mouth as if to say something, then frowned. "Do you know who did that?" He jerked his thumb over his shoulder.

"No. I didn't stay down long enough to check to see if there were any kind of signature markings or carvings. I'll go back though."

"No," Rhys snapped out.

King gave him an arch look but didn't say anything one way or the other before he focused back on Dallas. "We've caught their scent. There are at least six of them. I'm going to leave some sentries here to keep guard, but I'm going to hunt the killers down. Is there any way whoever created that wall will figure out you're the one who ripped it open?" His expression was dead serious.

"I didn't even know that was possible," Rhys breathed out in horror.

"No. They won't be able to figure it out. But only because I thought to put up a blocking spell before I tore it open," Dallas said.

King breathed out a sigh of relief. The fact that he'd asked told Dallas that he knew a little bit more about witches and witchcraft than most people. Which shouldn't be surprising, considering he was Alpha of New Orleans.

"Good. I want you to go home and get some rest. Or drink an entire bottle of vodka. Whatever will help you unwind, because you've been a huge help today. And I know how much energy it took to open that wall. I can't believe you're still standing. Go get some sleep." He looked at Rhys. "I don't need to tell you not to leave her side." It was clear he was ordering Rhys, regardless.

"No, you don't. She is mine to protect."

King's eyebrows raised only slightly, then he nodded and let out a loud whistle. Two of his trackers raced up to him, one male, one female. Then they all raced off, leaving the other two wolves standing guard at the house.

"I don't think I can walk home," Dallas whispered, the confession hurting. She hated being weak or vulnerable.

But Rhys didn't hesitate. He scooped her up into his arms and held her close. "If I fly us back, can you hold on to my scales long enough to make it to the mansion? I guesstimate it'll take me seven minutes max."

"I can do that," she said, but he still didn't let her go even as he stepped onto the sidewalk.

"I don't like any of this," he muttered more to himself than her as he headed down the street, waiting until a car passed before he set her on her feet. "I'm going to shift forms in the street. Are you sure you're okay to ride on me? Because I can carry you in my talons."

"I'm okay, promise." If it would only take seven minutes, she could hold on long enough to make it back to the house.

Well, she was almost certain she could. But if she fell, she knew he would catch her, regardless.

* * *

Dallas felt as if she was on autopilot as Rhys landed in the mansion's front yard minutes later. She could barely pet Willow, who was chirping excitedly as she greeted them. Those excited chirps quickly turned to distressed sounds, and to her horror, Dallas started crying.

A wave of emotions cascaded over her and she knew it was because of the blocking spell she'd created before she'd ripped open that wall. Not to mention ripping the magic wall itself was something that normally took at least six witches at once to do. But she'd been so worried about what was behind it, had been terrified that people would be killed if she didn't get inside the house fast enough. Turned out she'd been too late after all. And she was having a really hard time processing that. Those screams she'd heard had been their souls desperate to be free.

Rhys shifted to his human form immediately, completely uncaring about his nudity as he hooked an arm under her and scooped her up once again. He carried her as if she weighed nothing. She felt as if she could just close her eyes and float away into nothingness. The remnants of the magic dome skated over her fingers, arms and legs, making her want to take a shower. A really long one.

"We'll be out soon," Rhys said to Willow, who Dallas swore must've understood because her sweet girl made an affirmative sound and then flew to the back of the house as he hurried through the front door still holding her. "You're going to take a quick shower because I know you want one," he said as they approached the small guest bathroom nearest her room. He set her on her feet and continued. "Leave the door unlocked. I'm going to grab you some clothes from your room."

She simply nodded because he was taking over completely and right now she liked it. It was nice to have someone in charge, to make decisions. She actually couldn't believe she'd ripped that wall open by herself. She was just glad she'd had the foresight to block her identity.

Because whoever had created that wall was powerful. She hadn't gotten a read on the magic, however. There had been no signature. But that in itself was telling. When there wasn't a signature left behind, it meant the witch was powerful and smart enough not to leave one.

She wondered if whoever had created it had planned to come back for the bodies. Maybe, maybe not. If they'd planned to keep using that place to murder and drain their victims of blood, then it was highly possible they'd had eyes on it. So someone might know Dallas had done it anyway. And at that thought, another wave of exhaustion swept through her.

She rubbed her temple as she turned the shower on to hot. By the time she brushed her teeth, steam started to billow out in soft white waves. She began stripping off her clothes. Her fingers seemed to move at a snail's pace, as if she was pushing through a thick fog. Suddenly the door swung open and Rhys was standing there, pants on, and a bundle of her clothing in his hands.

He stared in shock at her as she held her sweater loosely in her hands by her side. Her skimpy bra was all lace, barely covering her breasts.

He abruptly turned his back. "Ah, apologies. I thought you'd be in the shower by now. Do you feel strong enough to get inside by yourself?"

"I don't know," she said, not even caring that she was partially undressed in front of him. She felt like she should care but...couldn't muster up anything right now.

He turned back around then and averted his gaze as he held out a hand. "Just hold on to me as you finish undressing." He seemed to choke on the last word, his voice growing raspier.

"Did you mean what you said about wanting to kiss me?" She shoved at her jeans, somehow managing to get the stupid things off.

He made a strangled sound. "I really don't want to talk about that right now."

"Well I do." Apparently she'd lost her mind. Now definitely wasn't the best time but she felt almost compelled to ask him about it. And clearly all the synapses in her brain were misfiring. She felt disconnected from everything, her entire body trembling from the shock of all the energy she'd used in that sudden burst. Witches weren't supposed to use their spells like that, but she'd had no choice.

He leaned around her, carefully avoiding any type of contact as he pushed the shower curtain open. "Get in," he ordered softly.

His chest was rising and falling rapidly as he continued to look away from her. Dallas figured that if she pushed, she could get a reaction—

maybe get him to kiss her. But yeah, that no-energy thing was real. She managed to step into the small enclosure, grateful for the warmth as the jets pounded down around her.

"Don't worry about washing your hair or anything," he murmured. "You just need to get warm because of your shock. Then you're going to get some rest." His deep voice sent delicious waves of awareness pulsing through her.

"You don't have to wait for me."

"Yes I do. And to answer your question, I meant what I said. I want to kiss you senseless more often than not." And he sounded absolutely frustrated about that.

She wasn't sure what to say as she grabbed her loofah and poured bath soap on it. She quickly scrubbed her body, and despite what he'd said she decided to wash her hair anyway. She knew soap and shampoo couldn't wash off what she'd seen but she felt the overpowering need to get clean. As if her body was tainted by the evil and death in that house.

"No response to that?" His deep voice cut through the sound of the pounding water and her thoughts.

"I'm…." *Hell.* She didn't know what to say. Couldn't find the words.

"I'm sorry if I made you feel uncomfortable."

"You didn't. My brain is just mush right now. But for the record, I've thought about kissing you as well." A lot. But it didn't matter right now. She was going to slip into unconsciousness soon and she needed to be in bed before that happened.

He made another one of those strangled sounds, then was silent. He was so quiet, she thought he might've left so she slid the shower curtain open and peered out only to find him still standing there, leaning against the dainty little sink, his gaze colliding with hers.

She quickly pushed the shower curtain back into place, making the hooks jingle on the rod. She knew she was close to her collapsing point so she finished rinsing her hair out and turned off the water. Before she could reach out to grab a towel, Rhys's big hand slid behind the shower curtain, her little microfiber hair towel she used for her hair in his hand.

"Thank you." She grabbed it, squeezed the water out of her hair, then wrapped it up in the towel. A moment later, he handed her a big fluffy towel for her body.

He really was thoughtful. He'd shown her in so many little ways that she could trust him. That he cared. It was…disconcerting.

Once she was dry and had the towel wrapped securely around her, she pushed the shower curtain open.

He had his back to her. "Are you okay to get dressed?"

She was tempted to tell him no, that she needed his help. But that felt wrong. "Ah, I'm good. You can just wait in the hallway."

He hesitated, then nodded and stepped out, his movements jerky. "I'm not going anywhere," he called out as the door shut behind him.

She tugged on the little sleep shorts and tank top he'd gotten her. He hadn't gotten her any panties and she didn't know if she should be glad that he hadn't rummaged around through her intimate things. More likely, he'd just forgotten. At that thought she wondered if maybe he'd forgotten them because he didn't wear boxers or briefs or…yeah, she couldn't actually see him wearing anything like that. He likely just went commando. Her cheeks flushed as she forced herself to not think of what he wore or didn't wear underneath his pants.

Though she didn't want to bother with it, she combed the tangles out of her hair before braiding it into a long, damp rope. When she opened the door, Rhys was there, his gaze sweeping over her in semi-clinical fashion, but she saw the heat flare as his eyes landed on her mouth and then her breasts. Her nipples tightened underneath his scrutiny, but he turned away abruptly. She told herself it didn't matter. She wasn't up to anything physical tonight anyway. She was likely to pass out on him mid…anything.

"I've already ordered food to be taken to your room." Not waiting for a response, he stalked off in that direction.

She hurried after him on wobbly legs, but before she'd taken four steps he turned and scooped her up again.

"This is becoming a habit," she murmured, curling into all his warmth. The male was so comforting and warm.

"A habit I don't mind," he rumbled in the deep, sexy voice she felt all the way to her core. In that moment she had absolutely no defense against him. All of her self-preservation was stripped away as he held her close, taking care of her.

Heat flooded between her legs as she curled into him. And he must have scented her need because he sucked in a sharp breath and made a sexy, low rumbling sound in his chest.

Once they were in her room, he didn't stop until he set her on the edge of the bed oh so carefully. There was already a tray of food waiting for her. Hot soup, crackers, and three energy bars. Which she definitely needed.

"I wasn't sure how much food you could eat right now, but you've got to get something in your stomach before you sleep. You'll sleep better," he added, as if he thought she might argue.

"Thank you for doing all this." Exhaustion swept through her now, tugging her under, telling her to close her eyes.

"You don't need to thank me for this. And you also don't need to worry about Willow. I spoke with Aurora and she's going to be keeping Willow company for the next few hours. She said they were going to do some flying lessons. Your girl is completely fine."

She smiled as she leaned back against the headboard and settled the tray more fully in her lap. "You thought of everything."

"I don't know about that. And before you try to argue, I'm staying with you. Even if King hadn't ordered me, I'm not leaving your side. I didn't know it was possible for anyone to track you when you disturbed that magic wall."

She nodded as she picked up the spoon. "It is possible. But luckily I'm smarter than the average witch."

He was silent as she started eating, then he started pacing only to stop when his phone buzzed in his pocket. "I'll be right back." Then he left, allowing her to breathe for a moment as she dug into her vegetable soup.

After she finished the soup and all the crackers, she didn't feel like eating three energy bars, but knew she needed to. She'd used up so many calories. And he was right, this would help her sleep and recover faster. So she choked them down, eating them in little bites before she slid under the covers. She was so cold and had been secretly hoping he would join her again.

As if she'd conjured him, the door opened, but she didn't turn over, exhaustion sapping her strength. She actually recognized his footsteps as he approached the bed. She heard him pick up the tray and he must've set it outside the door before it closed again.

"Are you still awake?" he whispered as he slipped in behind her.

She made a humming sound as he wrapped his arm around her and pulled her back against his chest.

It was kind of bold, him getting into bed like this with her. But she liked it. She wanted to tell him that he didn't need to bother, that she didn't need anyone to take care of her, that she would sleep just fine by herself. But that would be a big fat lie. She liked having his arm around her. She liked having someone take care of her like this.

No one had ever taken care of her, not truly. Certainly not her mother. To her mother, Dallas had just been a tool, power to wield. Until she'd gotten old enough and seen through all the lies. So many lies.

"I know you said not to thank you," she said around a yawn. "But thank you again anyway." She curled her hand over his bigger one and patted it.

In response he simply wrapped his arm tighter around her and held her close. The steady beat of his heart and his even breathing lulled her into a deep, soothing darkness.

CHAPTER 20

Dallas jerked in Rhys's arms, her eyes flying open. She'd only been asleep for three hours and he knew she needed more. It was clear in the wild, almost unfocused glaze of her beautiful gray eyes.

"Is Willow okay?" she rasped out.

His heart clenched. She was always thinking of other people, other beings. He'd never imagined a female like her in his life. "She's fine. Currently being spoiled. It's only been a few hours, Dallas." The blackout curtains were firmly in place but bits of the late morning light still peeked through.

Dallas sighed and seemed to settle more against the sheets. "Good." She nuzzled her face against his chest, wrapping her arm around him and throwing one leg over him as if it was the most natural thing in the world.

Just like that, his cock hardened. He'd already been in a semi-state of arousal on and off for the last few hours. Every time she shoved her ass up against him, or turned over and wrapped her body around his, he got hard. Then he'd have to think of shitty things so his erection would go down. It was a vicious cycle.

Now with her curled up against him, her full breasts pressing against his chest, it was definitely too much for his waning self-control.

He closed his eyes and took a deep breath, fighting to steady the wild beat of his heart, and tried to think of anything but Dallas's lush body pressed up against his.

"I wouldn't mind that kiss right now," she sleepily mumbled against his chest.

Oh, hell. He rolled his hips against her, leaving no doubt how aroused he was.

She leaned her head back to look up at him. She was half awake, but he saw the fire simmering in her bright eyes that had gone almost silver and he could clearly scent her desire. It was sweet and overpowering, leaving him no doubt that she wanted him as badly as he wanted her.

Without second-guessing himself, he crushed his mouth to hers, tasting, teasing, taking. Goddess, he wanted to consume her, to bring her so much pleasure that she passed out from it. His female needed rest—and an orgasm.

Moving quickly, he caged her body underneath his, glad they had an actual bed in here now as opposed to that flimsy cot.

Moaning, she stretched out underneath him, arching her unfortunately covered breasts against his chest. But he felt the beaded points of her nipples rubbing against him as he plundered her mouth. Her taste was perfection. *She* was perfection.

He slid his hands up the tiny shirt he'd picked out for her earlier, cupping her breasts, shuddering at the feel of them in his hands, at the fact that she wanted him to touch her at all.

She groaned into his mouth and the scent of her desire spiked in the air as he slowly teased her nipples.

He needed to see her naked, or at least more of her. And he needed skin-to-skin contact, was desperate to feel her against him. When he leaned up to tug her top off, he realized he was slightly glowing.

The mating manifestation. Dallas was…his mate.

He jerked at the reality of what was happening to him, even as his dragon sniffed that of course she was. He'd just been too foolish to see the signs. He…would digest this later.

He tugged on her shirt, wanting to see all of her.

She stared at him, a soft, sleepy smile playing across her face. "I think you're a little bit magic too," she whispered, running her fingers over his biceps and down his forearms. "You're glowing."

That he was, and clearly she didn't know what his glow meant. He would tell her later.

Once she was bared to him, he stared down at her breasts, feeling as if he had the most precious thing in front of him. She was better than any dragon hoard, better than…anything he deserved. "And you are perfection," he managed to growl out as he reached for the top of her sleep shorts and tugged them down.

He dipped his head to one breast even as he got rid of her shorts— and it was taking all his self-control not to simply incinerate her clothing and just be done with it. She should be naked all the time around him. As he tugged her nipple into his mouth, she let out the sweetest moan and arched into him.

Hell yeah. Hearing that sound from her lips made him shudder.

As her back lifted off the bed, he slipped a hand underneath her, palming her back, feeling more grounded as he held her. The beat of her heart was wild and out of control as he teased her breasts, moving from one to the other, so that her skin was slick with his kisses.

She clutched onto his back, her legs spread wide for him as she moaned out his name.

Her scent was driving him crazy, making his glow even brighter. He'd heard about the mating manifestation before. Hell, he was just surprised it had taken this long to manifest. A week ago he would have scoffed at anyone who told him that he was destined to mate a witch. A week ago he was a fucking fool who needed a good punch in the face.

Mine. That was the only thing he and his dragon knew with certainty. Dallas was his.

He reached between her legs and gently teased a finger between her folds and found her soaked. All for him.

Finally, you please her, his dragon purred.

He was rock-hard between his legs but he didn't dare take off his pants. He needed to taste her, needed her to come. His sweet Dallas deserved all the orgasms.

And he needed her to find the release she so desperately craved so she could get some more rest. She'd done so much, and he'd learned in the few hours she'd been asleep that the amount of power it had taken for her to rip that wall open was superhuman. It should have taken a whole coven to rip it open but she'd done it all alone and in *seconds*.

His female was truly remarkable.

She speared her fingers through his hair as he started kissing a path lower along her body. Her skin was soft, smooth, and he nipped everywhere, giving her little love bites. She gasped out in pleasure every time he did and his cock pushed even harder against his pants.

When he knelt between her legs, she tried to close her thighs.

He looked up the length of her body and realized her cheeks were flushed red and not just from desire. Was she nervous? Or was this something else?

"Is this okay?"

She nodded, her breathing erratic but her gaze hesitant.

"Say it," he murmured. "Yes or no." He needed the words, wanted to make sure she was all in for this. Because he never wanted her to regret them. Regret him.

Her thighs slowly fell open. "Yes."

It was clear she was nervous and he didn't think it was because she'd never had this done to her before, but more likely because of the way their relationship had started off. She was at her most vulnerable with his face between her thighs. He had to do this right, had to make this perfect for her. Because he didn't think he could let her go. He didn't want to.

Ever.

He bent his head between her legs, inhaling the sweetest scent of her as he slowly licked up her slick folds.

In that moment she clenched her legs around his head, her desire filling the air and making him light-headed as it overpowered everything else.

As he started flicking his tongue against her clit, she cried out. "Rhys."

Hearing his name on her lips was almost too much. His cock jerked against his pants again. He felt like an untried adolescent, ready to spill his seed in his pants, instead of the ancient he was.

He dipped two fingers inside her and her inner walls clenched around him as he continued teasing her clit. He could tell she was close. She was riding the edge so hard it wouldn't take much to push her over it.

He continued teasing her, increasing the pressure on her sensitive bundle of nerves, and when her fingers dug into his scalp, pleasure mixing with pain, he knew she was about to come. So he slid another finger inside her.

She arched up against his fingers and mouth as she climaxed, crying out his name as she trembled with the pleasure. When she fell against the sheets, boneless and satisfied, he crawled up her body, caging her in with his forearms. He could look at her all damn day and not get tired of it.

She gazed up at him, a slightly dazed expression on her beautiful face. "Thank you," she murmured, looking sleepier by the second.

But then she reached between their bodies and rubbed his cock over his pants.

He took her hand away. "You need sleep," he murmured.

"I need you to come too," she whispered back, wildfire entering her gray eyes as she tried to dip her hand underneath his pants.

"Fine. But you lie here and do nothing," he ordered. She'd given way too much of herself and he wasn't letting her do anything else. Not even for his pleasure.

"So bossy," she murmured as he freed his thick length from his pants.

He started stroking himself, pinning her with his gaze as he did, imagining it was her hand stroking him. It wasn't going to take long and that should probably embarrass him, but he had the most perfect female underneath him. And he had the taste of her orgasm on his tongue. Yeah, it wouldn't take him long at all.

He covered her mouth with his as he stroked. She joined him, wrapping her fingers around his. *Oh, goddess.*

His balls pulled up tighter at the feel of her fingers skating against his hard length, and that was what set him off. Her touch.

He started coming in long, hard waves.

All his muscles pulled taut as he found release on his stomach and hers. When he was done, he felt a bit savage and primal as he rubbed himself into her skin. He had the most primitive need to mark her, to claim her so that all other supernaturals would know she was his and *only* his.

She gave him a sweet kiss, then curled on her side as she made that soft humming sound he was coming to realize she often did. As she started to drift off into sleep, he slid in behind her and tucked her up against his chest before he pulled the covers over them.

He wasn't one to let his guard down, but he knew the house was well protected, and hell, he needed sleep too. Once he was sure she'd finally drifted into oblivion, he allowed himself to close his eyes and fall asleep with the woman who meant far too much to him.

The female who he now knew, without a doubt, was his intended mate.

CHAPTER 21

Dallas slowly came to consciousness, very aware of the heavy arm draped over her middle. She was also very aware of the hard erection pressing against her back. She couldn't believe what they'd done earlier in the day, but had no regrets. She just hoped he didn't either. Waking up like this, with him, was surprisingly pleasant. She'd always had her space, slept alone for the most part. And she liked it. But...this was really nice too. Really, *really* nice. The kind of thing she knew she couldn't get used to.

Rhys nuzzled her neck gently. "I know you're awake," he murmured, the deep rumble of his voice reverberating through her.

"Just barely." She stretched out slightly, shifting against the sheets. Her brain wanted to take over and immediately figure out what those sexytimes meant for the two of them, but yeah, that wasn't happening now.

"How do you feel?"

"Better," she said after she took stock of herself. She actually felt kind of incredible, even if she was hungry. "I could probably eat something in a little bit."

"Good. Someone just restocked the fridge and I even think that lazy lion cooked, so you'll have plenty to choose from."

She laughed lightly because Axel wasn't lazy. He seemed to enjoy cooking for the whole house. But she now understood that Rhys was simply jealous of Axel. It was ridiculous, but shifters could be wildly territorial when it came to lovers.

"So are we going to talk about what happened earlier?" Settling against him, she laid her hand over his—which was draped possessively over her bare stomach. She liked it there, liked being in his arms where she felt secure and safe. And she didn't care if the safety was an illusion. For now, she'd take it.

"We can talk about it in the shower," he murmured against the back of her head, his warm breath sending tingles of pleasure racing through her.

"As in together?"

"Yes." That one word came out all deep and sexy and made her clench her thighs together.

She definitely liked the sound of that. "What time is it?" She didn't think she'd slept a whole day away.

"I'm not entirely sure. The sun is about to set pretty soon."

So she *had* slept all day. "How's Willow?"

"Napping, last I checked. Trust me, she's fine. This whole crew here loves her and she hasn't been alone for one moment. I think I heard Lola say something about painting Willow's claws.

She laughed even as warmth settled through her. Knowing that others were looking after Willow made her feel so much better and less guilty. She knew she had nothing to be guilty for. Still, she never wanted Willow to think that she'd abandoned her or forgotten about her.

Feeling bold, she shifted her ass against Rhys's hard length.

He groaned, his grip tightening. "Let's go now," he rasped out, suddenly pushing up.

She rolled over and looked up at him as he grabbed a pair of lounge pants, likely putting them on since they had to walk out into the hallway. Right about now she really wished she was in a regular bedroom with an en suite so they had more privacy.

In the light of day, so to speak, she felt incredibly vulnerable and exposed after what they'd done, after what they'd shared. But she still didn't regret it.

She'd been half awake before, but she'd known exactly what she'd been doing. And she had enjoyed it a whole lot. Waaaay too much. "Will you grab my robe?" She nodded at the silky black robe draped over the chair by the desk.

Wordlessly he picked it up, then held it up to her to put on. Which meant she had to drop her sheet and get naked in front of him again. He'd already seen her, tasted between her legs, made her climax—she shouldn't be feeling shy at all. But a sudden wave of it rushed over her as she dropped the covering and stood, slipping into the robe without meeting his gaze.

"You have no reason to be shy. You have the most beautiful body I've ever seen." Matter-of-fact words from her big, sexy dragon.

Though he wasn't hers at all. At least not long term. This thing between them, whatever it was, was likely just physical and short term. She knew she didn't factor into his plans—he was all about his revenge. And that was a whole mess of complications she didn't want to think about now. Or ever, really. She was just going to enjoy this time with him and take it for what it was.

She cleared her throat, unused to compliments. "I don't know if you're going to fit in the shower with me," she murmured as she grabbed an extra set of clothing and underwear.

"Oh, I'll fit." There was something about his tone that implied he was referring to far more than the shower.

Another rush of heat slid through her and she avoided his gaze as she hurried to the door. Even though she didn't need another shower, the thought of one sounded divine. So did food. And really, so did another orgasm but she wasn't brave enough to ask for one.

Though they *were* about to shower together, so maybe she would get one anyway. And she wanted to make sure he got one too—all from her. He'd been all bossy earlier, jerking himself off mostly by himself, but it had been sexy. Oh soooooo sexy. Especially when he'd come all over her stomach and rubbed himself all over her. Goddess, her inner walls tightened as she remembered the intense look on his face when he'd come on her.

Once they were alone in the bathroom together, he surprised her by gently freeing her braid and combing his fingers through her now dry hair. She leaned back, enjoying the feel of his fingers grazing her scalp, of the simple intimacy of this.

"I'll start the shower," he murmured, slipping past her and doing just that.

The guest bathroom wasn't huge but it turned out it was definitely big enough for the two of them.

Feeling nervous, she played with the tie of her robe as he shoved his pants off, clearly fine with his nudity.

"I'll leave if you don't want me here," he said quietly when she still hadn't undressed.

She met his intense gaze and shook her head. "I want you here. I'm just feeling nervous, I guess." Things had changed so quickly between them and she was feeling untethered. As if the reality of her world had suddenly shifted and she wasn't sure what to do.

"We don't have to do anything but shower. We *never* have to do anything you're uncomfortable with."

"I'm not used to casual sex," she blurted out. "So I'm just feeling out of sorts." She wanted to blame it on all the magic she'd expelled earlier but that would be a lie. And the thought of lying to him felt wrong on many levels. She was already withholding something from him. She didn't want to add to that with lies.

"I'm out of sorts too," he murmured, his dark blue eyes holding hers.

For some reason it was hard to believe because this arrogant male was always so confident. Before she could think of a response, he pulled the shower curtain back and stepped inside. Steam billowed out behind him, and when he pulled the shower curtain half closed she was able to breathe out a sigh of relief.

He's already seen you naked, she reminded herself. *And he obviously liked what he saw.* Rolling her eyes at herself, she stripped off her robe. She wasn't a coward so it was time she stopped acting like one.

She stepped into the shower with him and he immediately moved to the side, allowing her to get under the water. Just like that, most of her tension fled. This dragon was so damn thoughtful and possessive and it was almost enough to undo her.

"Tell me more about your family, about when you moved to New Orleans," he said as she stepped under the water.

She frowned up at him. "Why?" she demanded.

His lips quirked up. "Ah, because I'm making conversation. Because I want to know more about you."

Oh, that made sense. She inwardly winced at her paranoia, that he'd somehow figured out who her mother was. She needed to tell him the truth but...later.

Closing her eyes, she let the water completely soak her, then stepped out of the stream so he could get under it. But instead, he grabbed a bottle of shampoo and started washing her hair. For some reason the action was incredibly intimate and sweet, and she didn't care that she'd just washed it that morning. The peppermint scent filled the shower as his expert fingers magically massaged her head. Goddess, he was talented with those fingers. Another rush of heat spiraled through her and she knew he would have to scent her desire. Not that she wanted to hide it or anything.

He let out a low groan behind her and she felt his heavy erection brush against her back so yeah, he was in the same place she was. But he'd asked her a question and she'd never answered.

"My family history isn't really great. I never knew who my father was. Just someone my mother used because she wanted to get pregnant. He was powerful, that much I know. She alluded to it more than once," Dallas added, surprised she was telling him this.

But he'd told her about his dead sister, and considering that her mother had been the one to kill his sister, she could be honest. Plus, she cared for him—more than she wanted to think about.

"I think she held back the knowledge of who my father was as a way to control me. Though I didn't realize that until much later. When I was young, my mother was decent enough, even if she wasn't a very caring parent. For the most part, our coven at the time raised me. Witch covens are like shifter packs in that respect—everyone helps out when needed. And I like that, in theory. But it just gave her an excuse not to have much to do with me until I was old enough for her to actually care about my growing power."

Now that Dallas had started it was like she couldn't stop. The words just poured out of her.

"By the time I turned sixteen, I realized that she didn't love me. I wish I could say that her love was just conditional but...there was simply *no* love there. She doesn't know how to love anyone but herself. And she was the queen of gaslighting. The only thing she cared about was how powerful our coven grew—how powerful *she* was. There's a darkness in her..."

She swallowed hard, but forced herself to continue. Behind her, he was silent, still massaging her head.

"The week I turned eighteen I left town. I didn't tell a soul I was leaving, because I knew she would try to stop me. I backpacked around the country for a while." Decades. "I worked odd jobs, got a couple degrees. Eventually I made my way to New Orleans and I've been here the last twenty years. Something about this place called to me on a fundamental level. This is my home and I love it."

He'd finished massaging her head and was now just holding her close.

"So that's my sad story," she said on a nervous laugh. "So you have to tell me more about your family." She stepped forward and started rinsing the shampoo out of her hair.

"Or I can go down on you again." His voice was all raspy, sexy.

His words punched through her and she sucked in a breath as the shower jets cascaded around them. "Rhys…"

"Is that a yes or no?" His eyes glowed slightly now as he watched her.

"Yes, no, I mean…I still want to know about you." She was getting whiplash from his change in topic, but she liked it. Liked him.

"And I'll tell you later. But I need to taste you now. I can feel the sadness rolling off you. I don't like it."

Oh goddess, and he wanted to take it away by giving her pleasure? This male was going to destroy all her walls.

Before she could respond, he had her pinned against the wall and was devouring her mouth with his. He plundered her mouth the same way he had earlier, possessing her completely in a way she'd never experienced. Never even allowed herself to fantasize about.

She arched her body into his, clutched onto his shoulders as he cupped her face with one big, callused palm.

She felt like a cat in heat, wanting to rub all up over him.

He groaned into her mouth as he slid his hands down her body, cupping her breasts as if she was made of spun glass.

She loved the way he was with her, but she needed a little more.

Reaching between their bodies, she palmed his thick erection and slowly started stroking him. He'd been in control earlier and she wanted to make him come. Just from her, with no help.

She had no idea what would happen between them after this. They'd made each other orgasm once and now apparently they were about to do it again. But that didn't mean anything. Soon he'd be going back to Scotland—once he got his revenge and killed her mother. And if he ever found out who Catta truly was to her, he would hate her for the rest of his life.

She shoved those thoughts out of her mind when he cupped her mound. She didn't want to think about her crappy family or the secret she was keeping from him. She just wanted to enjoy this moment. Especially after she'd nearly expended all of her energy earlier.

She rolled her hips against his hand, her inner walls tightening around his finger as he slid it inside her.

"I can't get enough of you," he murmured against her mouth before he crouched in front of her.

She stared down at his broad shoulders and dark hair. He should look ridiculous in this small shower but he just looked sexy as hell.

"Put your leg over my shoulder," he ordered softly, pinning her with those dark blue eyes.

He'd been so gentle and careful with her over the last couple days. And she really wanted to believe that he cared about her, not because she could do something for him, but because of who she was. He made her feel special, treasured. That alone terrified her because she'd been rejected so many times before. It had become second nature to reject people first. She was always waiting for the other shoe to drop, for her former partners to reveal that they were just using her for whatever reason. It had gotten to the point that she'd stopped dating, stopped sleeping with anyone.

She didn't want to walk away from Rhys though.

He leaned forward as she did exactly as he ordered and put her leg over his shoulder. There was no purchase against the slick tiles of the shower but he gripped one of her hips securely and held her in place.

When he flicked his tongue against her clit, she forgot everything else. He teased her over and over until she was climaxing against his face. She didn't care how loud she was, didn't care about anything other than the spirals of pleasure punching out to all of her nerve endings as he completely consumed her. By the time he'd wrung multiple orgasms out of her, she collapsed against the wall but he caught her, pulling her into his arms.

Her nipples brushed against his bare chest and she savored the skin-to-skin contact. Craved it.

His erection was still thick between them, heavy and pulsing. "I'm going to take care of this," she murmured and wrapped her fingers around it even as he kissed her deeply. It was kind of weird to taste herself on his mouth but she found she liked it.

He shuddered under her touch, his big body trembling as she stroked him over and over until he completely lost control just as she had. It hadn't taken much to push him over the edge. Getting him off like this was a huge turn-on, and she realized that if they had sex right now, she would likely come again, the instant he slid inside her. But she wasn't ready for that intimacy. Not yet.

He came with a growl against her mouth, coming all over her hand and stomach. Just like before he rubbed it all over her skin, and in that moment she knew he was definitely marking her. It must be a shifter thing—and she liked it way too much.

She liked being claimed by this male, liked feeling as if she belonged. As if maybe...they could have something real together. It was a fantasy but one she was allowing herself to have.

"You're going out tonight with me," he murmured against her mouth, giving her gentle little kisses before snagging the shampoo bottle for himself.

She stared up at him. "What?"

"You, me, some of the others. We're all going to the Quarter later tonight. I spoke to King before you woke up and they're still searching for the witches. Per him, there's literally nothing you can do right now. Nothing I can do either, because I'm not leaving your side. And I know you're overdue for having some fun. So after this, you're going to eat, then I'm taking you out dancing."

She stared up at him, a swirl of emotions mixing inside her. She wanted to say yes, but doing this almost felt like going on a date. It felt real. More real than what they'd just shared. "So if we go out tonight...we're...together? For the night, I mean? Not like..." She cleared her throat.

He watched her, his dragon peering back at her for a brief moment. "We're most definitely together. And if that sneaky lion flirts with you, I'm punching him in the face. So fair warning," he murmured before he leaned down and brushed his lips over hers.

Okay, then. She fell into his kiss, marveling at how natural this felt.

When he stepped back under the jets, she grabbed her conditioner as he washed out his shampoo. The thought of going out with him on a pseudo-date sounded almost fun.

Fun?

She'd almost forgotten what that was, she realized. She had no regrets about her lifestyle and loved where she lived. She missed the peace and security of her land and she looked forward to eventually returning home. Her land was a part of her in a way non-witches wouldn't understand. But the truth was, she said no a lot to people. Especially her friends in the city when they asked her to come visit and stay a night or two. Because it was easier to reject people first. A habit she'd allowed herself to fall into.

But for tonight at least, she was going to turn off her brain and have fun with the big, sexy dragon in the shower with her. Because he was right—there was nothing they could do if King's pack was still hunting those witches.

King was Alpha, and if he wanted her and Rhys on the sidelines, it was the way it was. And that was fine with her.

Besides, she got to spend the evening with Rhys. She knew it wasn't going to last between them, but she could enjoy the here and now and pretend that they had some sort of chance at a real relationship.

CHAPTER 22

"I feel weird being out and having fun right now," Dallas murmured as she linked her fingers through Rhys's. She also felt pretty weird holding hands with this big dragon when there was so much up in the air between them. She hadn't been kidding when she said she didn't do casual. Apparently she was breaking all of her rules tonight. And for the foreseeable future with him.

Until he learned the truth. Because he'd end things with her then, no doubt about it.

"I understand," he said as they followed behind Lola, Bella, Brielle and Harlow. Axel was in his actual lion form, swishing his tail back and forth as they trotted down the street. It seemed so...on brand for the lion.

Music poured out from multiple places on St. Peter Street as they headed deeper into the heart of the French Quarter. Unlike the many times she'd been here before The Fall, now there were plenty of supernatural creatures in their animal form just walking around. Minding their business, having a good time.

"I take it you haven't had a lot of fun in the last year since waking up?" she asked as she sidestepped a jaguar running down the street.

"No. Not until I met you." He kissed the top of her head and warmth spread everywhere as they continued onward.

"We don't need to wait in line," Bella tossed over her shoulder. "I called ahead and—"

"Dallas!"

She turned at the sound of a male voice coming up on her left from the street. Her eyes widened in surprise when she saw her friend Javier striding down the road.

His dark hair was cropped close to his skull, very likely a throwback to his Marine Corps days. The half-demon hybrid moved with a liquid grace that belied his other nature. His amber eyes glowed slightly as he stepped up on to the sidewalk to greet her.

"Oh my God!" She threw her arms around his neck and pulled him into a tight hug.

Laughing, he hugged her back.

"What are you even doing here?" she asked as she stepped back. "I thought you were living in Biloxi under Finn's rule."

Rhys wrapped his arm around her shoulders and pulled her close, the possessive gesture not lost on her. She wanted to laugh because Javier was definitely just a friend.

"How about you introduce me to the big dragon first before he bites my head off? Then I'll tell you everything." Javier's smile was genuine as he held out a hand to Rhys. "My name's Javier, or you can call me Javi. I am *just* a friend with Dallas and have only ever been a friend. For the record."

She elbowed Rhys gently and he held out a hand, returning a semi-polite "Hello."

"This is my friend Rhys," she told Javier. "He's in town for a little bit and we're helping King out with some gardening stuff."

"Gardening?" He snickered as they hurried to catch up with the others.

"You know what I mean." Then she looked up at Rhys. "Javier used to run a farm back in Alabama. Agriculture and livestock. We actually met on an agricultural forum ages ago. Later we discovered that we were both supernaturals and formed a real friendship."

Rhys frowned slightly.

"Oh, a forum is a computer thing. Like a group where people chat online. Sort of like a group text."

He nodded slightly and Javier gave him an interested look. "Did you just wake up or something?"

Rhys's back straightened. "What do you know about dragons?"

"Well, my brother is a dragon hybrid, so I know enough."

Rhys seemed to ease at that. "I woke up about a year ago. I'm still adjusting to this world and learning many things."

"You woke up at the wrong time. Or maybe the right time. I don't know," Javier said, shaking his head as they reached the corner of the next street. "Where are you guys going, anyway? Because I'm surprised you're out at all."

"Oh, we're actually going to your sister's club." Cynara, half vampire, half demon badass warrior.

He laughed lightly. "What a coincidence. That's exactly where I'm going."

"How long are you in town?" she asked.

"Few weeks. Maybe a month. King asked Finn if I could help out with tracking down some things. Since this is my night off, I figured I'd better go see my big sister, or risk getting my ass kicked later."

As they rounded the corner, she saw the line to the club was incredibly long and she was glad they weren't going to have to wait in it.

"You have a familiar scent," Rhys said bluntly as he looked at Javier. "Bo is your brother also?"

Javier's eyes widened slightly. "Yes. And you have really good scent abilities. Are you a tracker too?"

Rhys shrugged. "I'm a warrior."

"And I can tell you're talkative too," he said, laughing.

Rhys's mouth kicked up slightly.

"Come on you guys!" Lola called out ahead of them. "And bring your sexy friend!"

Javier's eyes widened slightly as he looked at Lola. "You gonna introduce me to her?" he asked Dallas quietly, eyeing the petite snow leopard with the rainbow-colored hair.

"Of course. I'm pretty sure she'll eat you alive though."

"I am so okay with that."

Rhys actually grunted in what sounded a lot like laughter so she leaned into him as they headed for the VIP door, which was being held open by Cynara—who tackle-hugged Javier.

In that moment Dallas was glad she'd listened to Rhys. Getting out tonight felt good. Weird, but hanging out with people who genuinely liked her, people she hoped that she could be friends with—yeah, she was going to enjoy tonight for all it was worth.

And just maybe it would end with her and Rhys getting sweaty and naked. At that thought, a burst of heat bloomed inside her and Rhys let out a little growl as they stepped into the fairly loud club.

Leaning down, he growled low in her ear. "Keep that up and I'm tossing you over my shoulder and heading back to the mansion."

Why did that sound like the best idea ever?

She held on to this feeling because she knew it was fleeting. Something told her a fight was coming, that there was something on the horizon she'd need to deal with. And she had to be ready.

Reality would crash back on her head sooner than later.

* * *

Rhys glanced around the club as they entered, scanning for exits and potential threats. Technically, this place was full of threats—there were a lot of supernaturals here, including some in their animal forms.

As they ascended a set of stairs, a few familiar scents teased his senses, one in particular making him pause, then smile. He scanned again, looking for an old friend.

"What is it?" Dallas murmured next to him, her hand firmly in his.

He loved the feel of her fingers intertwined with his, loved that she was here with him tonight. That part of him that told him he needed to be out hunting was finally at ease for the moment. "I scent an old friend. And there he is," he said as they reached the top of the stairs into what was apparently a VIP section.

A big male held back a velvet rope to allow them to enter the private area that overlooked one of the dance floors below. A rope seemed like an ineffective way to keep people out but he dismissed the strangeness.

"Rhys!" Arthur, a huge dragon much older than him shoved up from his seat, clearly having had a few drinks, before he stalked over and pulled him into a bone-crunching hug.

"It's good to see you, brother." They weren't blood related but came from the same region. Arthur had taught him many things as a child. He was surprised the male was here at all. Well, he was surprised until he spotted a tall, deadly female dragon with ice gray eyes and jet-black hair striding across the floor.

"I would ask what you're doing here, but it's clear you're here for this lovely lass," Arthur boomed out as he turned to greet Dallas with a hug.

Rhys held out an arm, blocking the male from touching Dallas. He genuinely liked Arthur but the male wasn't touching her. His dragon was too close to the surface as it was.

"Ah." Arthur held out a polite hand and took Dallas's much smaller one in his. It didn't matter that he was in modern-day New Orleans, he had on a kilt and his giant red beard should probably be trimmed. Or hacked off. He looked exactly like the barbarian he was. "It's a pleasure to meet you."

"You too." Dallas stared at Arthur, clearly curious about the dragon in a kilt.

"What have we here? Another stripling has woken up." Prima greeted him with a smile that reached her eyes. "I just saw your brothers not too long ago and that fascinating new mate of his. She's quite talented."

"You know I'm thousands of years old." Which meant nothing to this female who was one of the only dragon twins in existence—and one of the few dragons to have been hatched.

"Of course you are." She patted him once on the upper arm before smiling politely at Dallas. Power rolled off Prima in potent waves that even humans would be able to sense. "I'm Prima."

"Dallas. Nice to meet you."

In response, Prima sniffed her and then smiled. "You are the female with the pet dragon. I've heard about you."

Rhys shot a look at Arthur, who simply shook his head.

"I am," Dallas said, slightly laughing. "Can you smell her on me?"

"Yes. It's a sweet, wonderful scent. Long, long ago," she said, cutting a sideways glance at Rhys, "before this child was born, there was a group of wild dragons who allowed themselves to be tamed by humans. Those humans were aptly titled dragon riders. Your dragon has the same scent of them. I've missed them."

"Oh...wow. Do you have any idea how big she'll grow?" It was something that Dallas had been wondering.

A casual shrug. "No bigger than a dragon shifter. Oh and your pet will likely be a child for a couple decades. They age very slowly, like us, so it will take time for her to grow into her wings. So be patient with her as she will be maturing for the next…maybe ten or twenty years. It just depends."

As if patience was going to be an issue. But Dallas was so grateful for this knowledge. "Thank you so much. I have *so* many questions."

"I will happily answer them later. Right now we're heading out to hunt down some rogue bears who are bothering some wolves out in the bayou. King just called and asked if we could head out for a quick hunt. It's just Arthur and me going but I don't think King would care if you two came along. Care to join us?" she asked, looking between the two of them.

"No," Rhys said before Dallas could respond. "My female has had a long few days. We're relaxing tonight." Not that he thought she wanted to go hunting, regardless.

Arthur clapped him once on the shoulder, hard. "Good for you! How long are you in town? We need to share an ale at least before you leave."

"I'm here for a while. We will definitely share a beverage."

"And I'll contact you about your dragon. I'd like to meet her," Prima said to Dallas, a warm smile on her face.

"That sounds great, thank you."

Rhys pulled Dallas into his arms the moment they were alone again. Relatively alone, since the VIP room was crowded. Lola waved them over to their table, pointing at a bunch of shots lined up.

"So they seem pretty intense," Dallas said as they strode around the edges of the dance floor toward the group. "How long have they been mated?"

"They're not mated." He'd forgotten that Dallas couldn't scent a mating link the way he could.

Her eyes widened slightly as they reached the table. "They sure act like it."

"Eventually Arthur will wear her down."

"Who, scary Prima?" Javier asked as he slid two shot glasses in front of them.

Dallas held the small glass up and clinked hers with his. "I'm glad I'm not the only one who thinks she's scary. Her eyes…"

Rhys understood what she meant. When you looked in Prima's eyes, you saw the beast almost all the time. There were thousands of years' worth of experiences and savagery looking back at you.

"Uh, terrifying is more like it," Bella added.

Rhys smothered a smile as he picked up his own and toasted Dallas. Something told him that Prima would love to be called scary or terrifying. She would wear that title as a badge of honor. And as he looked at Dallas, who was relaxed as she tossed back her shot, he knew in that moment he wanted more normal nights with her.

Days, nights and everything in between.

CHAPTER 23

King resisted the urge to kick the door off its hinges as he strode out the front of the Bonavich vampire coven's French Quarter home with Ari and Delphine, two of his lieutenants, on his heels. He was barely containing his rage as he strode down a long, brick walkway toward the sidewalk.

As he reached the end, his eyes widened to see Aurora waiting there, her legs crossed at her ankles as she leaned against a parked car. There were humans and supernaturals alike milling down the street, some heading home, others searching for the nightlife.

"What are you doing here?" he asked, more than surprised to see her. *Don't ask stupid questions*, his wolf snarled. *Just be happy she's here.*

She shrugged and flicked a quick glance at Delphine behind him.

He gritted his teeth and looked at Delphine. "Really?"

She shrugged and clapped him on the shoulder once before heading off with Ari, who simply gave a half shrug. The big male rarely talked. He just got shit done, something King appreciated.

"Delphine texted me. Said you guys hit another dead end, and I was in the area. Figured you could use someone to vent to." Aurora fell in step with him and linked her arm with his, guiding him down the sidewalk.

His wolf immediately settled at the feel of her touching him. "Delphine needs to—"

"She was just doing her damn job. You're her Alpha and you're stressed right now. So she texted me. How is that a bad thing?"

He shoved out a breath, but didn't respond. It wasn't a bad thing, not exactly. But the fact that his packmate knew that being around Aurora would calm him down was important. He wasn't used to depending on someone, not on this level.

Of course he depended on his pack, but at the end of the day he was the one who made the hard decisions. They all looked to him to keep order, to make the right decisions. Right now he was hunting down witches who were killing and draining humans and vampires. And even though he'd tracked them with his best trackers, he still couldn't find them. He might need to call Dallas again and see if she had another way to locate them.

"So what happened?" she continued.

He just grunted again.

She let out a sound of exasperation. "You're killing me, Smalls."

He shot her a confused look. "What?"

Her eyes widened slightly as she looked at him. "You know, from *The Sandlot?*"

He lifted a shoulder.

"Oh my God, you've never seen that movie?"

"My life has not allowed for a lot of movies." For the most part he didn't get the attraction to cinema. He was too busy running a pack. And now he was trying to keep the city from burning so they could actually rebuild with the hope of coming out stronger on the other side.

"Have you ever seen *The Goonies?*" she continued, staring at him as they headed down the sidewalk.

"I don't even know what that is."

She blinked at him. "What about *Deadpool?* That's newer."

He just lifted a shoulder.

Now she stared at him in mock horror. "Well you're in luck since we can't stream anything anymore. Because I have those DVDs with me. We're going to have a movie night in the near future... Once these psychopaths are found and brought to justice."

Yeah, and that better be sooner than later. He realized he had no clue where they were even going, but being with her was taking the edge off. So was this ridiculous conversation. *Deadpool* sounded vaguely familiar at least. "You brought DVDs with you from St. Augustine?"

She shrugged as they reached a crosswalk. "My sister packed up my entire room and she knew to bring the important things."

Aurora had been kidnapped over a year ago, held prisoner for the magic blood in her veins. He hadn't known her then, hadn't known Aurora long at all, though somehow it felt as if they'd been friends for a lifetime. Her sister, Star, had launched a rescue mission, and once she'd saved her, they'd ended up in New Orleans a couple months ago after a long-planned escape. "Then I will watch these ridiculous movies with you."

She let out a little huff. "Why do you think they're ridiculous?"

"How is something called *The Goonies* not ridiculous?"

"Friend, you are going to be proven so wrong." She shook her head as they turned onto a side street filled with bars and restaurants currently bustling with activity.

He was glad to see it, glad the city was alive tonight. It was a delicate balance, but people had to be able to go out, to see friends and feel as if the entire world hadn't been destroyed. It was a psychological thing and it wasn't just the humans but shifters as well. Shifters needed pack, needed contact. Needed to know life wasn't just about survival, blood and death.

A few patrons sitting outside the first bistro they passed nodded and waved at him, but more lit up and waved at Aurora. She hadn't even been in New Orleans long, but she was this bright, shining beacon people gravitated to. He understood because he was one of those people. After that video feed of her killing those rogue dragons with her wild phoenix fire, people were more than curious about her.

"Come on, let's grab a drink," she said as she dragged him into a hole-in-the-wall bar and restaurant called The Fried Alligator.

The bar was full but as soon as he stepped inside, half a dozen people slid off their barstools to make room for him.

He nodded his thanks and sat down with Aurora, who took over and ordered for him.

He shot her a sideways glance. "Tequila? Really?"

"Just do what I say," she said as she glanced at the menu and ordered food for them as well.

No one told him what to do. Ever. Even when he'd been a pup, he'd exasperated his mother with his Alpha tendencies. But somehow he didn't mind it with Aurora. She wasn't challenging him, she was just being his friend. And he valued her friendship. "You're incredibly bossy tonight," he muttered, no heat in his tone.

"Well you've been making decisions nonstop and busting your ass for who knows how many days in a row. So I'm making things easy for you. So eat and drink what I say and relax for ten freaking minutes."

The bartender, a man named Antony Carter who he'd known most of his life, simply snickered and took the menus from Aurora. "Sounds like you've got a smart female here," he said as he tucked the menus away.

King wasn't sure how she'd been right about the tequila, but as he tossed the shot back he realized, yep, this was what he'd needed. It went down smooth. So did the second shot.

"Can I help with the tracking?" Aurora asked as he pushed the two shot glasses away.

Right now his best trackers were still searching for the witches. "No, but thank you. I recently called in a favor from a friend." Javier, brother to Cynara, who ran a huge club downtown, had just arrived. In the morning he'd be taking over for King's other trackers if they didn't have any luck. King planned to head back out there soon as well, because he wanted to stop by a small witch coven and see if they knew something. He'd already stopped by a week ago, but this trip was going to be a surprise.

"Good. I have an idea of what will take your mind off things. We can do it in your training area."

He shot her a surprised look. "Do what?"

"Oh, you'll see. Bring that big sword of yours."

His mouth kicked up. "Is sword a euphemism?"

She blinked, her mouth falling open, then laughed, the sound deep and throaty, wrapping around him like the sweetest embrace. "Nope. Trust me, you'll like what I have planned. So will your pack."

"They could be *your* pack," he murmured quietly enough for her ears only.

She stilled and looked at him in surprise. "I'm not a wolf."

"So? There are plenty of other beings in my pack other than wolves. Pack is about love and loyalty. That bond is more than blood."

She went motionless for a long moment and he wondered if he'd made a mistake asking her. There was so much about her he didn't know, so much about her *kind* he didn't know.

Finally she spoke, her words measured. "You obviously know that my kind are rare. It stands to reason that others could come after me in the future. Just like before. I am out to the world now. I can't hide what I am and I don't want to, regardless."

His wolf flared to the surface so he lowered his gaze, not wanting her to see the rage in his eyes. If someone came after her again, tried to take her for her blood or any other reason, he would destroy them. Rip them apart limb by limb. And he would enjoy it. No one touched what was his. No one touched her.

He cleared his throat, feeling more in control now. "And?"

"And, I'm just saying that I might be a threat to your pack."

Now he laughed as Antony set two small plates in front of them—fried alligator for him and fried jalapenos for her. "If someone comes after you, we'll take them out. Just think about the offer," he added, not wanting to pressure her. Because he didn't want her to say no.

"I will. Thank you," she said as Antony slid two more plates in front of them. Greek salad for her and a medium-rare burger for him—and she'd told Antony to hold the onion on his, just the way he liked it.

Something shifted inside him then, something he didn't want to acknowledge, but couldn't deny. His wolf had claimed Aurora—and so had he.

* * *

"I'm not going to battle you," King murmured for Aurora's ears only. Now that they were back to his compound, she'd told him what she planned two minutes ago.

And it was nuts.

She snorted as they strode through the wide-open gates to his compound. His people owned a city block in the Quarter and most of the structures were connected. But they also owned houses on a few other blocks throughout the city, including a condo complex in the Irish Channel and a mansion in the Lower Garden District. He liked having his pack dispersed throughout the city. More eyes and ears everywhere was a good thing.

Right now they were at the Lower Garden District compound, and since it was a nice night most of his packmates were out in the yard. *Just great.*

"Not battling. It's practice. I'm simply going to throw lightning bolts at you and you're going to block them with your sword. You're a freaking tornado. You need to let the steam off and this is the way to do it. Otherwise you're going to lose it with one of those dumbass vampires and create an incident."

He shot her a sideways glance. "Did you just call them dumbasses?"

"Everybody is a dumbass once in a while. Myself included."

"Am *I* ever a dumbass?"

"I have never witnessed it firsthand, but I'm sure you have been. I'll just ask Delphine or one of your packmates for examples."

He snorted slightly as they strode up the long, curving driveway lined with thick oak trees dripping with Spanish moss—some older than him.

"You need to change or anything?" she asked, eyeing him.

He wondered what she thought when she looked at him then he shoved that thought back just as quickly. They were just friends. He wanted more but she'd never given any indication that she would offer him anything other than friendship. The truth was, her friendship was worth more than…anything.

"I don't know if this is a good idea," he said instead.

"Are you scared?" Then she made an actual clucking sound. Like a chicken.

His eyes widened as he turned to stare at her. "Are you clucking at the Alpha of New Orleans?"

She clucked again and then giggled kind of manically.

He'd never seen this ridiculously playful side of her before, not fully. And he liked it. Despite the tension that seemed to live in his shoulders, he couldn't help the smile that spread across his face.

"Is King turning down a challenge?" Marco, one of his youngest wolves, walked out of the shadows in human form, a mischievous glint in his eyes. He was a warrior, not a beta, but he wasn't challenging King.

"I'm pretty sure he did." Aurora's grin was infectious.

Sighing, King stripped off his jacket and tossed it to Marco. "Let's do this."

"So what's the challenge?" Marco asked.

"It's not actually a challenge," Aurora said as they started across the lawn where various shifters were patrolling or just relaxing. "He's just going to deflect my lightning bolts with his magic sword to blow off some steam."

Marco let out a low whistle. "Oh, hell yeah. The whole pack will want to watch this. I'm gonna take bets on how many he can hit."

"You gotta do better than that," Aurora said. "It should be more along the lines of how many he can hit per minute. Otherwise that's just sad because you *know* he's going to hit all of them."

"I'm right here!" King said, even as he fought another grin. When he was around her, he felt decades younger. He didn't have the weight of his people, his city, on his shoulders. He was just King.

By the time they strode to the middle of the yard, at least twenty wolves had gathered on the lawn, some drinking beer, some eating, others in full tactical gear.

He withdrew his sword from his back sheath. "Let's get this over with," he muttered.

"That's a terrible attitude," Aurora said as she slipped off her sneakers.

He frowned, wondering what she was doing.

But then she started glowing, and her wings shot out of her back. He heard a faint ripping sound and realized she'd ripped her sweater. Clearly she didn't care, going by the grin on her face.

He stared in awe, unable to stop himself as pale blue fire licked over her entire body and she lifted into the air on wings of the same pale fire. She really was the most stunning thing he'd ever seen in his hundred-plus years on this earth.

The only reason he didn't care that he was staring so boldly at her was because he guaranteed every other pack member was staring at her as well. It was impossible not to. She was goddamn perfection.

He unstuck his tongue from the roof of his mouth and found his voice. "So when do we—"

She flapped once, hard, and a bolt of blue lightning shot straight at his face. He dodged to the side, lifted his sword and slammed into it.

The power of her lightning ricocheted into him, straight to his core. But it didn't hurt. If anything, it rejuvenated him, made him feel as if he could take on an army all by himself. He'd had his sword for close to a hundred years and thought he knew everything about it. But in that moment, he realized his sword was soaking up her power as well. *Holy shit.* He hadn't known that was possible.

She shot at him again. He dodged, this time swinging at it as if his sword was a baseball bat.

Her lightning bolt sparked in the air, creating a beautiful shower of blue and silver before his sword sucked up all the energy.

"You're pretty good," she called out and shot three bolts at him at once.

It said a lot about what she thought of him that she thought he could take on her lightning. Because he didn't think she was holding back. He was glad—he never wanted this female to hold back from him. He wanted all of her, every authentic bit.

He twisted and turned, slicing each bolt of lightning she threw at him.

It was a deadly dance between the two of them and he wondered what would happen if he missed and her fire slammed into his chest instead. It was something he didn't plan to find out. He was an Alpha wolf but he wasn't immortal, and he'd seen her bolts of lightning take down an Alpha dragon. Of course *he* had taken down multiple Alpha dragons himself.

Around them, everyone else faded away as he danced with her, slicing and jabbing at bolt after bolt. His sword ate up the power, singing with pure pleasure with each strike.

Finally, she threw her head back and laughed, her wings flapping beautifully in the night air. Her long chestnut hair blew back in soft waves. She looked like a warrior goddess as her feet touched the grass once again.

Sweat rolled down his back and neck as he grinned at her. He felt like a teenage pup as he stared at her, but he didn't care.

When he looked at his pack, most of them were staring at the two of them with wide eyes. He frowned. "What?"

"I think you broke some personal records," Delphine called out. "I've never seen you move so fast! That was incredibly impressive."

He took a couple mock bows and everybody started laughing, a few clapping and others wolf-whistling.

Aurora approached him, her wings still bright as she pulled them tight against her back. He loved when she let them free, when she allowed herself to be everything she was meant to be. "How do you feel?"

"Incredible," he said honestly.

Her grin grew even wider. "Good. Then my job here is done. I'm probably going to head home and grab a shower. I just wanted to make sure...you were okay." She murmured the last part subvocally so only he could hear.

He appreciated it. He was Alpha, had to appear indestructible. It was strange to have someone worry about him the way she did, but he liked it. She would make an incredible Alpha's mate. Hell, would *be* an incredible Alpha.

He held out a hand and clasped her forearm like he would one of his warriors. He thought of her as so much more than that, but he respected her on this level as well. And he wanted her to know it.

She clasped his forearm as well and nodded once at him. "Anytime you need to practice, let me know."

He nodded because he couldn't find his voice at the moment. As he looked into her eyes, he found himself wanting that future he dreamed of with her.

A future with her as his mate.

CHAPTER 24

*R*hys *raced across the grassy incline, his heart in his throat.*
    Blood.
    He scented blood. A lot of it. Too much. And he recognized that scent, though he wanted to deny it as he reached the top of the hill.

He scanned the valley below. Green, lush grass as far as the eye could see. His sister was there...somewhere. He sensed it, but couldn't see her. Couldn't see Eilidh.

He was supposed to have met up with her earlier but had blown her off. For what? He raged at himself, his selfishness, as he called on his dragon, letting his clothing shred as his beast took over.

He launched into the air, the tatters of his clothing falling behind him as a burst of thunder rolled across the darkening sky. The thick scent of impending rain hung in the air, sharp and crisp. No! He needed to follow the scent trail before the rain washed everything away.

On a surge of power he swooped downward, his wings making the grass ripple underneath him like the ocean.

Faster, faster he flew until he passed the valley and over a copse of trees. The scent of blood was heavier here.

Behind him he heard rain starting to pound into the earth. He flew harder, as if he could outrun it, scenting his sister somewhere far below him.

He swooped downward and followed toward the side of the mountain, rage already boiling hot inside him. The blood was too strong. The scents all wrong. His brain refused to accept what he was smelling.

But he knew. Death. Thick and cloying.

As he approached the side of the mountain his dragon eyes caught on a small cave opening near the bottom of it. He arrowed downward, scanning for any signs of life.

Rain started splattering against his wings, pelting him harder and harder until the rain turned to hail, slamming into his back, wings and tail as he landed.

The hail rocks rolled off him until he shifted to his human form.

Ignoring the huge rocks that slammed into his back and arms, he raced toward the cave opening.

As he breached it, he stumbled, staring in horror.

"No," he whispered. No, no, no.

Bones. Dragon bones. And blood, splatters of it. Everywhere. Eilidh's blood, he was certain of it. And even if he hadn't been, this was his sister. These were her bones. Someone with powerful magic had done this—it was the only way possible that Eilidh was now mere bones.

The walls of the cavern shook and he realized he was screaming, roaring with the rage and grief of her death. Her murder. He couldn't stop roaring even as rocks started falling down on his head. Couldn't stop the red-hot agony bursting inside him as the need to kill nearly overwhelmed him.

Whoever had done this would pay with their life. With everything inside him he vowed that he would make them suffer excruciating agony in this life or the next. Eilidh would have her justice.

Rhys's eyes snapped open with a start but he knew where he was. Knew he had been dreaming. Or remembering, more accurately. A nightmare he couldn't outrun no matter how hard he tried.

Because it was real. And it had been his fault.

His heart was an erratic, wild beat in his chest as he pulled Dallas a little closer to him. She had her back nestled against his chest as he curled around her. He wanted to stay right where he was, but something was tugging at him.

Pulling him away from the warm bed with the warm female who'd gotten under his armor.

Rhys slipped out of bed and pushed down the feeling of guilt as he got ready to leave. He wasn't doing anything wrong, he simply didn't want to wake Dallas. But he didn't like the thought of leaving her, regardless.

He pulled the covers over her so she'd stay warm and gave her one long look, drinking in every inch of her peaceful face, the way her dark hair fell against the pillow and sheet. He'd be back soon, he promised himself. He just needed to do this now.

Willow stirred in the doorway, lifting her head. He held a finger to his mouth and he swore that dragon was a little genius because she simply nodded as if she *completely* understood him. He was already naked so he strode outside and called on his camouflage, but not before telling Willow to stay put. When he did, she sat up straight like a sentry and guarded the open door.

Once he was camouflaged, he shifted to his dragon form and took to the skies. He'd put off hunting Catta only because he thought that crest would lead them to her. And maybe it would eventually. But something about that house of blood and death was calling to him. He flew easily, the skies quiet at four in the morning. He spotted a couple dragons far in the distance, recognized their colors and stuck to his own path.

He circled the house with dead grass and the stench of death roiling up from it, then landed. The brown grass crunched underneath his paws before he shifted to his human form. He kept his camouflage wrapped around him because he scented one wolf nearby, likely watching the place at King's orders. He wasn't doing anything wrong but he didn't feel like asking for permission.

Instead of going inside, he slowly circled the house, searching for... *Something.* Something was bothering him. It was at the back of his mind but he couldn't put his finger on it.

He circled once, twice, three times, and on the third loop he caught a vaguely familiar scent through the stench. And that was when he realized what was bothering him. One of the scents underlying everything almost reminded him of Dallas. But not that sweet, pure quality of hers. It was more like a familial type of thing. The way he'd been able to sense that Javier was related to Bo and Cynara.

But that didn't make sense, did it?

He inhaled again and this time couldn't catch the scents, as if they'd been lost on the breeze. Or maybe he'd imagined it altogether. But he didn't think so. He also didn't know what to do with this knowledge.

Frustrated, he walked around the rest of the property again, even though he knew there weren't clues just lying about. Once he was done, he eased open the front door, which was still unlocked.

The moment he did he saw a shadow drop from one of the oak trees near the front of the property.

Damn it. He'd hoped he'd be able to get inside unnoticed.

"Show yourself," the female voice called out.

He strode down the stairs, and it took a moment until his eyes caught on the slim, lean figure who'd moved to hide near another tree. A wolf. Delphine, he thought her name was. Her long braids were pulled back into a tie, she wore black pants, a long-sleeved black T-shirt, and her pale amber eyes glinted brightly against her brown skin.

Sighing, he let his camouflage fall.

When she spotted him, she frowned and strode forward, crossing the distance between them. "What are you doing here?"

"I'm honestly not sure," he said, knowing she would smell the truth.

She frowned at him. "I was informed that you and Dallas found this place. Why are you back?"

"I couldn't sleep tonight and...I don't know. I thought maybe we missed something. I heard that King and his trackers haven't found the witches and it's bothering me." That dream had woken something inside him. He could feel it on the edge of his consciousness, if only he could figure out what it was.

Her jaw tightened and she nodded. Not like he needed the confirmation—King had already told him—but very clearly Delphine was frustrated too.

"Did you bring any clothes to change into?" she finally asked.

He shook his head. "I wasn't planning on being here long. I just thought maybe if I could catch the scent, I'd be able to track it."

"If our trackers couldn't find them, then you won't either." Her tone was matter-of-fact.

He snorted because wolves were just as arrogant as dragons, it seemed. "Maybe, maybe not. But I'm not interested in some sort of pissing contest. I just want to find out who's responsible." Again, she would scent the truth rolling off him.

And his words seemed to satisfy her because she nodded in approval. "Go ahead and go inside. We've already removed the bodies. Just don't touch anything."

He lifted an eyebrow. "You're sure?"

"I'm one of King's lieutenants. Of course I'm sure. Unless there's a reason I shouldn't let you in there?"

He grinned and shook his head. "No. If I find anything, I'll tell you."

"We've combed over the place, just FYI."

"I figured. I don't expect to find anything." But he still wanted back in there nonetheless. "Did you guys find out who the humans and vampires were? Notify their families?" That was a hell of a thing, not knowing what had happened to a loved one. He wouldn't wish that on anyone.

"We're working on it. It's a process."

"We'll catch who's behind this," he said.

"We?"

He lifted a shoulder and turned back toward the house. "I'm including myself in that."

She muttered something to herself about dragons but he ignored her as he hurried up the steps and pulled his camouflage on once again. He didn't doubt that the wolves had searched the place, but he still liked being covered in case there were random cameras inside. Inside the foyer, he paused and looked around. It was the same as before—empty.

Still, people always made mistakes. He started on the bottom floor and quickly realized that the majority of this house hadn't been used for anything recently. Just the bathrooms, but even the kitchen didn't appear to have been utilized. Everything gleamed as if it had been cleaned within an inch of its life. No, all the scents came from the direction of that *room*. Whoever had used this house had used it for one purpose only.

He headed down the small set of stairs once again, and even though the bodies were gone, he could still see them in his mind as he stepped onto the cold concrete floor.

Though he knew it wasn't possible, he swore he felt fingers dancing up his feet and calves, the evil remnants left in this place scraping against his skin. Wanting his blood. Wanting him.

The scents down here were far more complex, the blood and death not as strong as it had been before, and he was able to sift through other scents more easily. Once again he caught that familiar scent and this time it didn't disappear. He inhaled deeply and tried to figure out what was bothering him. It almost smelled like Catta, but not. He couldn't figure out if his mind was playing tricks on him or if perhaps he *wanted* to smell something that wasn't there.

After ten minutes, he decided to call it a wash and leave. There was nothing new to be gained at this point.

Once he was outside, he let his camouflage fall so that Delphine could see him, and shifted to his dragon. The sun still hadn't risen and wouldn't for another hour, he guessed. The flight back to the house didn't take long, but when he landed in the yard he found Dallas sitting out there, a cup of coffee in one hand and Willow lying lazily at her feet as she petted the dragonling's head.

Dallas gave him a neutral look as he shifted back to human and strode toward her. "Is everything okay?"

He wasn't going to lie to her. "I went back to the house. I couldn't sleep and... I don't know why exactly. I almost felt like I was being called there."

"Did you find anything?" Her expression thawed as she spoke. Maybe she'd thought he'd left for another reason. There wasn't much that could have torn him from her bed, something he thought she understood.

"No. I don't think so. Just a lot of different scents." He was tempted to tell her that one of them reminded him of her, but didn't want to insult her, and wasn't sure what it meant anyway. So he sat next to her and she quirked an eyebrow. "What?" he asked.

"You're just going to sit out here in the buff?"

He laughed lightly and shrugged. He hadn't even thought about it. "I can go put some clothes on. Or we can just go back to bed and you can take all yours off?"

Her eyes heated at his words, gray going almost silver, and she set down her cup of coffee. "I like the second option better. But I'm not ready for...full-on sex." She bit her bottom lip.

Willow let out a fussy sound as if she knew they were going to leave her.

"I don't care," he murmured. He just wanted intimate contact with her. Whatever she was offering, he wanted. He turned to a fussing Willow. "We won't be long, I promise."

"It's weird that I'm pretty sure she understands us—and I'm also kind of disappointed that it won't take long," she murmured.

He let out a startled laugh at her words. Something told him he would never tire of this female. The longer he was around her, the more he realized he couldn't imagine his life without her. He didn't *want* to imagine his life without her.

Maybe this was the choice Thurman had been talking about. Well if it was, he chose Dallas.

CHAPTER 25

"I feel like you're holding something back from me," Dallas murmured as she drove down the quiet residential street with brightly colored one-story homes. Each house had a big wreath hanging on the front door, all in purples, green and gold, as if the whole neighborhood had coordinated it.

Today they'd opted to drive instead of walk because there were a few garden and food plots King wanted them to look at that were on the far side of the city. And they needed to take the ferry to get to one area. Rhys had offered to fly them, but the ferry was fine with her. Though it felt weird to be in a vehicle and she could tell that Rhys didn't care for it at all. Probably because he could fly anywhere he so chose.

"What do you mean?" he asked.

"This morning, when you told me about going to the house. I just feel like you're holding something back from me." She lifted a shoulder, wondering if she was being paranoid. It was her instinct, after all, to reject people first. She didn't want to fall into old habits and do that to him with no cause. When she'd woken up alone this morning, all those past feelings of being rejected had swelled up, threatening to suffocate her.

"It's nothing." He turned away from her and glanced out the window.

On instinct she reached out and skated her fingers down his forearm. She loved touching him, loved the skin-to-skin contact. It made her feel even more connected to him. "Clearly it's not nothing. Come on."

"When I was at the house…" he said as he turned back to her. Then he grasped her hand and brought it to his mouth once, brushing his lips over her knuckles.

Spirals of awareness rolled through her at that brief, intimate touch.

She really could get used to this, to him. And that was a terrifying thought. He'd be leaving soon, something she would do well to remember. It was taking all she had not to cut and run, to end things because she knew how they'd end anyway. Because that tiny little flicker of hope inside her refused to die. She didn't want to run from Rhys. "And?" she prodded since he seemed to have lost his train of thought.

"There were a bunch of scents there. Random scents, the ones that King tracked down. Or tried to. I know King and his trackers are out there, and not to sound all arrogant but I have great olfactory senses. There was a darkness there, and this is going to sound messed up—and I swear I'm not trying to insult you—but it almost smelled like you a little bit. But...*not* you. I don't know how to put it into better terms."

At his words, ice chilled her veins, slicing and sharp, making it hard to draw in a breath.

Her mother.

Heart pounding, she slowed and paused, waiting to turn the car around as they pulled up to a stoplight. There was hardly any traffic now, or ever, lately. Even though the light was red, since no one was coming she flipped a U-turn.

"What are you doing?"

"I'm heading back to that place." She didn't need to say where. "If you scented someone like me it might be someone from my former coven." That was the truth because it would be her mother. She'd already witnessed that he could smell familial connections among shifters, so it made sense that he could between her and her mother as well.

Nausea swirled inside her. If he was right, then her mother was in New Orleans. That knowledge was revolting. But if Catta was here, she had to be stopped sooner than later. Dallas couldn't stick her head in the sand and do nothing.

"Why are we going back there?"

"I didn't know that my former coven members were involved in whatever this is. But if they are...I may be able to track them."

It was clear he wanted to ask how, but he simply nodded and pulled out his phone. "I'm texting King."

She was glad he didn't push her on how she could do this—she didn't want to lie to him and wasn't sure she could at this point. He'd scent it anyway, but just the thought of lying to him made all the muscles in her stomach ball up tight, made her anxiety spike.

She was quiet as he texted. Tension ratcheted up inside her, her shoulders tightening as she thought about what she had to do. "Look, I'm going to do a type of finding spell. I just need to know that you're going to have my back."

She could feel the same tense energy rolling off him in potent waves as he set his phone down. "How could you doubt that I would?"

Because you don't know my secret.

Her fingers tightened around the wheel as she made a right-hand turn. "I don't doubt you, I just…I'll be a little weak after the spell. I'm going to need you to take care of me. Literally. I'm going to have to trust you to have my back if someone attacks me, because I won't be able to defend myself."

"This sounds dangerous. You're not doing it," he snapped out. "Nope. It's not happening." He was shaking his head, his jaw tight.

"Even if I can help you find Catta?" she asked bluntly.

He jerked in his seat. "I don't understand. You can find her?"

"Maybe." It would come at a great personal cost, making her weak and vulnerable—susceptible to any supernatural beings who wanted to hurt her. Hell, even humans if they wanted to.

She wouldn't be able to tap into her powers for a while if she did this spell. And it would only work if Catta was in the area, if she was within a certain radius. She hadn't thought her mother was here but if Rhys was right and he'd scented her back at that awful house, then… It was highly possible that she was.

"Not even if it finds her," he finally said.

She wasn't sure who was surprised more, her or him. She glanced at him. "Don't lie to me."

"I am *not* lying." His words were whiplash sharp. "I'll find her without you hurting yourself. I'll find her on my own. I've been searching long enough and I'm not going to risk you hurting yourself over this."

She couldn't even put into words what that meant to her. Throat tight, she parked a few spots down from the house and got out of the car before he could protest.

"What the hell are you doing?" Rhys asked as he jumped in front of her on the sidewalk, completely blocking her.

She went to step around him but he moved again, holding his arms out so she still couldn't pass. "Rhys!"

"I can do this all day. In fact, I can throw you over my shoulder and fly you back to the house. I'm not letting you do whatever this is. You will *not* hurt yourself!"

She placed a hand on his chest, touched by his concern but anxious to do this and get it over with. "It's not going to kill me or anything. I'm just going to be *really* tired. Weak. And...I'm going to want to go home immediately after. *My* home. To sleep and be at peace, surrounded by my own things. I'll rebound faster if I'm on my own land. The spell won't hurt me though."

"You swear it won't kill you?" His jaw clenched tight as he stared down at her, a mix of riotous emotions in his eyes. Eyes that had gone pure dragon. Oh, his beast was not happy.

"I swear. If any of my former coven members are involved in this and they're nearby I can track them. It'll just take a lot of power." And she'd recently expended a lot when she'd ripped the magic dome down here, so she was tapping into her reserves again far too soon. It would be worth it, however, if it found Catta.

"King is meeting us here," he finally said. "We'll talk to him."

"That means you have to actually move out of my way," she murmured, dropping her hand.

He grabbed it and basically stalked down the sidewalk, holding her hand tight in his, as if he was afraid she'd bolt.

King was already waiting for them with a handful of wolves at the property when they stepped through the open gates.

She nodded once at the Alpha. "Have you had any luck finding the witches?"

King shook his head, his frustration clear.

"I might be able to find them. Or one of them. But if I do, it's going to drain all of my energy and I'm not sticking around the city afterward. I'm going home. That part is not up for negotiation. I know you want me here going over different garden plots. And I'll come back and do it in the future. But if I do this right now I'm going to need to go home almost immediately." All of her healing teas, her house, and her land especially would help rejuvenate her. She'd injected so much love and energy into her own land over the last two decades that it would be a natural balm to all of her.

"You're not a hostage here. If you want to go home, it's fine. I appreciate all you're doing and I still need more information from you, but finding who's involved in these killings is a hell of a lot more important."

She liked that he was putting the lives of humans and vampires above anything else. If she'd had a doubt about what kind of Alpha he was, she wouldn't anymore. But she'd never doubted King to begin with. His natural aura radiated a rare kind of caring and kindness she didn't often see in others. Something inside him needed to take care of others. It was woven into his DNA.

"Okay, then." She took a deep breath and stepped back from them. When she pulled out a little pocketknife from her back pocket, Rhys frowned at her. "What—"

She sliced her palm open and he jerked forward, maybe to stop her, but she shook her head. She wasn't going to get into the specifics right now, she was simply going to do this. She clenched her fist once and blood started dripping from her palm. So she bent down and shoved her hand straight into the dead grass and tainted soil.

She sucked in a sharp breath as she felt her mother's power. *Goddess,* it had been Catta after all.

No, no, no.

She hated that she hadn't picked up on Catta before. There had been no damn signature on all those dead bodies. But somehow that evil woman who had borne her was in the city. Killing people.

That stopped now.

Aware of Rhys hovering next to her and King a few feet in front of her, she stared out into the distance but she wasn't actually seeing anything in front of her. Instead she was using all her energy to focus on her mother's location and any coven members who might be with Catta.

A big room, maybe a basement, appeared in her vision, the details becoming crystal clear as did her mother's beautiful face. Big green eyes that looked beguiling, innocent. Flame red hair the color of fire. She was an artist's dream—and a walking, living nightmare.

She had a sharp athame in her hand, was smiling prettily down at the vampire who was baring fangs at her. Catta laughed lightly, the twinkling sound magical as she stroked the female's face.

Dallas hated that about her, hated how beautiful she was.

Forcing herself to focus on the room, she mentally reversed course and looked around, trying to find the exit to the room. Because she was seeing Catta in real time. Looking at that beautiful, murderous face and cursing her existence wouldn't do anything for anyone.

Dallas needed to get a damn location. So she started looking at the surroundings. They were in an empty room. Like maybe a garage converted to a game room. No windows, no closets, just an exit door. So she went through it, floating really, her spirit finding its way out until she was in another yard looking up at a smaller house this time.

One story instead of two. A fairly nondescript house. Gray brick, black shutters, a turquoise-colored door and wind chimes that looked an awful lot like bones hanging from the front porch. She drank in every detail, including...

Her gaze snagged on the actual numbers of the house. She could feel the spell fading and spectrally raced across the yard, needing to see the name of the street.

"Dallas." Rhys's voice came as if from a long distance. She could feel him touching her shoulders, holding her tight.

No. She ignored him, blocked out his presence, needing to stay right where she was. She scanned the street as she hurried down it, taking in everything she could, trying to remember every detail. *There!* She had it.

She closed her eyes and when she opened them again, found Rhys staring down at her, his dragon in his eyes as he pulled her to her feet and held her close. "You're never doing that again," he snarled, his big body trembling.

"Your eyes... They were glowing silver." King was staring at her, but she had to blink a few times before his face came into focus.

Her eyes didn't matter. Nothing did but finding Catta and the others. Saving those people. "I need a piece of paper and a pencil," she managed weakly. "Now."

He barked out an order and moments later, sitting on the dead grass, her hand already healed from the knife slice, she started drawing what she'd seen.

Though it was difficult to grip the pencil and her hand trembled, she managed to draw everything. She included the street sign, the numbers on the house, even the little flamingo-shaped potted plants and wind chime hanging on the front porch. "I think this is where they are," she rasped out, her words stilted. "The witches are there. They're holding humans and vampires. They're alive. Some of them, anyway. I didn't see all their faces. It was all a blur, but this is happening right now."

She felt as if she'd been through a blender, as if she could sleep for two weeks straight. Invisible sandbags weighed down her eyelids but she forced herself to her feet, and thankfully Rhys helped her stand. He immediately wrapped his arm around her waist and held her against him, steadying her.

King looked at the paper, nodded once. "This is incredible. I know where this is. What can we do to help you?"

"Stop them," she rasped out.

He nodded and stepped away from them but she held up a hand. "And take Rhys with you." She knew she'd asked him to have her back, but she could go see Thurman and get enough healing tea to make it to her land by herself. And Rhys needed to be the one to kill Catta. "He deserves to—"

"I'm not leaving you. I promised—"

"I can have someone drive me back to the house. I can wait while you take care of this." He had been hunting his sister's killer for so long. "Catta is there!" Maybe he wasn't getting that.

"I don't give a shit about any of this. That's not true, I do care." He shot a sharp look at King. "Their leader, her name is Catta, and I want to see her head on a spike. She killed my sister and hundreds, maybe thousands of others. She needs to die."

It was clear that King had questions, especially since he'd had no idea that Rhys had been in the city hunting someone. But the Alpha simply nodded. "Every single person involved in this will die today." He turned to Dallas. "You're sure they're there now?"

"I believe so. When I do spells like that, everything I see is in real time. I recommend getting there as quickly as possible. I was careful about cloaking my presence but...they might have sensed me. Go." She was weak. Too weak, and fading fast.

King nodded again, barked out more orders to his people, and then they took off at breakneck speed.

"We'll swing by the mansion to grab your things and Willow, then I'm going to fly you back to your house," Rhys told her. "But we leave now. I don't want you flying on her. She's still too wobbly."

She simply nodded.

"You're being very acquiescent," he said as he scooped her into his arms.

"I'm too tired to do anything else."

"I have things to say but I'll say them later. I think you lied about putting yourself in danger and I don't like that. I don't like that one bit," he snapped out.

She closed her eyes as he hurried them back to the car. "I guess it's a good thing you don't make decisions for me."

He made an angry sort of growling snarl but didn't respond otherwise as he helped her into the passenger seat and strapped her in.

"Take me to the Magic Man," she murmured without opening her eyes, leaning her head back against the headrest. "Before we get Willow."

"No problem." She felt the vehicle turn in a different direction. "Why now?"

"My energy is fading faster than I expected. He'll have a healing tea that should help me recharge long enough until we get back to my place. It'll give me a couple hours respite."

"You can just sit in the car and I can grab it from him if you want."

"That's fine with me. He'll know exactly what I need." Her words trailed into a whisper as sleep threatened to pull her under.

But she forced herself to stay awake. She didn't want to be unconscious and unprotected until she got back home.

Her land would protect her. And she had to believe that Rhys would too. She was counting on it.

CHAPTER 26

Rage and energy hummed through King as they approached the house Dallas had directed them to. It was just two blocks away from the original place he and his trackers had hunted them to before.

They'd lost the trail, obviously due to some kind of dispersing spell if he had to guess. There was a whole lot he didn't know about witches, but one thing he did know: Dallas was an incredibly good and powerful one. She didn't let on that she was powerful, however, which he found interesting. Though she hadn't tried to hide her powers or anything.

But the fact that she'd been able to handle a finding spell of this magnitude by herself *and* ripped the magic dome down by herself in seconds told him she was a power to be reckoned with. Especially if she ended up mating with that dragon—she would have a much longer life span and even longer to grow into her powers. He also had a hell of a lot to discuss with Rhys too, but that was for another day.

King knew he should've pushed for more information about why Lachlan's brother was in New Orleans but he trusted the other Alpha and his mate Star not to steer him wrong. He still did.

As he and his team of trackers neared the end of the block, he held up a hand then circled with his finger. He hated doing an infiltration in the middle of the day but they were all wolves and this couldn't wait. They should be able to sneak in better than any black ops team with their skills, and they would be going inside in human form. At least to breach the doors and windows. Then he would see what happened.

He scented that elusive dark magic on the air and steeled himself. His sword practically hummed behind him, ready for battle. It was vibrating with all sorts of wild energy after sparring with Aurora. He still needed to ask her about her magic, about what those lightning bolts had done to him and his sword. Because he still felt like he could take on an army by himself. Good thing too, since they were about to go up against a bunch of powerful beings.

There were a couple humans jogging past as he and his wolves strode down the street. He stopped in front of a pair of college-age girls and held up a hand.

The fear that rolled off them didn't exactly surprise him. He had that effect on humans now that he was out as a shifter and in charge of the city. Hell, he'd had that effect before.

"You guys live on this street?" he asked.

The one on the left nodded. "I do. That's my family's house." She pointed to the right.

"Get inside and stay inside. Call any human neighbors you have and tell them to do the same. Now."

The girl nodded and they both hurried toward the house.

But he stopped them when something occurred to him. "That gray house with the black shutters." He gave the address. "Do you know who owns it?"

The girl frowned. "No one lives there."

Well, that wasn't true, but that meant the home was definitely spelled to make it appear as if no one was living there. At least no one would be calling the owners of that home. "Go. Work quickly."

The two of them raced off, their sneakers pounding against the pavement as he hurried back to the sidewalk. The feel of the magic grew stronger and darker the closer he got to the edge of the bushes surrounding the house. His wolf shook it off, but he still didn't like being this close to darkness.

He withdrew his sword, knowing he was going to have to tear through another wall of magic and give away the element of surprise. There was no way around it, however.

"In seven seconds, I'm ripping through the wall," he said through their earpieces. "As soon as it's down, infiltrate. Anyone involved in this dies. Lethal force is approved." Hell, it was encouraged at this point. "Try to keep one alive for questioning, but not at the risk to your own life." If they did manage to keep one of them alive, they wouldn't be for long. He was the judge and jury right now and these murderers had broken every species' laws.

There were murmurs of agreement as he stepped out from behind the privacy hedges. Sword out, he strode straight down the driveway toward the house.

The sword vibrated then screamed as he made contact with the invisible wall. Waves of energy spiderwebbed out, revealing the magic veil. He shoved his sword deeper.

The dome shimmered and rattled, red sparks of magic shooting everywhere.

He gritted his teeth as he shoved inward hard and ripped up. The second he did, his sword split the dome.

For one long moment, time seemed suspended as everything froze. Then the spiderweb shot out in all directions, a loud crack rending the air. The dome burst, magic shattering everywhere like glass.

On instinct he braced himself for impact but the glass disappeared into nothing instead of shattering all over him.

And that was when he saw what truly lay behind the dome. It was the same as the other house. Life had been sucked out of everything—the grass, the trees, even the brick was no longer the bright gray it had been, but dull and flaking.

Without pause, he raced straight for the nearest side door. At this point, the element of surprise would be mostly gone. As he reached the door, he slammed his boot against it.

It flew open, ricocheting off the wall as he stalked into what turned out to be a kitchen.

He heard breaking glass and doors being kicked open elsewhere as he faced off with a woman who was at the stove, teapot in hand. Her eyes widened when she saw him, her irises flashing black. She let out a scream and lifted her hands as if to throw a spell at him but he dove forward, lightning fast, sword at the ready, and cut her head off.

He didn't stick around as her head flew through the air, blood arcing everywhere. He was already moving toward the attached hallway, his wolf senses picking up on moans of pain. He reached a doorway in a long hallway at the same time Delphine did. Her wolf was in her eyes, her canines and claws already descended. Ari was right behind her.

Whoever was in charge had to know they were here by now. He kicked the door in and saw four short stairs descending into what had likely been a game room at one time given the paint on the far wall.

Instead of jumping down the stairs and around the wall blocking them, he tapped his sword against the wall once, sending tendrils of magic spiraling down the staircase. He wasn't sure where he got his magical powers from but they'd always been a part of him, just like his wolf was. His mom had always told him he was special, but had never given him any more than that.

Screams started and he knew his magic was working—searching out the darkness and destroying it.

He started forward, jumping down the stairs in one leap.

A half circle of six witches stood at the ready, one of them screaming under the onslaught of the magical assault from his sword. But the others were standing strong, feet shoulder-width apart and hands out as if ready to do battle.

Behind them naked vampires and humans alike lay in a circle of blood, moaning in agony. It was clear they were pinned to the ground by some sort of magical force. He digested everything within seconds as he strode forward. "Release them," he growled, his wolf in his throat and definitely in his gaze.

The woman in the middle, a stunning redhead, threw her head back and laughed. Then she lifted her hands and threw a ball of red-hot fire at King. He didn't think, just reacted on instinct and training. He lifted his sword and swung at the magic. Instead of absorbing it, his sword repelled it straight back at her chest.

The ball of fire slammed into her, tossing her back a few feet as a giant hole created by her own fire ate away at her from the inside out.

Her eyes opened in horror as a raw scream tore from her throat.

It died immediately as the spell consumed her body within mere moments.

The sharp stench of fear rolled off the other witches as he raced at them, his wolves doing the same.

He stabbed the nearest one, and the magic from his sword shoved inside her, bursting in all directions as it destroyed her.

Meanwhile his wolves simply attacked, going straight for the witches' throats.

It wasn't a battle, it was a massacre, with his side prevailing. By the time they were done, all the witches lay in pools of blood, and the one he'd killed first didn't exist at all anymore. Her body had turned to ash.

He knew the moment the spell had been broken on the humans and vampires because one of the vampires sat up, breathing hard as she looked at the carnage.

"Thank you," she rasped out.

King knelt in front of her, holding out his hands to help her stand.

His wolves shifted back to human form and started helping everyone else.

"How many witches are there?" he demanded of the female vamp.

"Maybe one or two more. They're not all here," she said, looking around at the bodies. "One of them went upstairs to get tea. She likes to drink it while she torments us."

"She's dead."

The vampire's eyes flashed bright amber before returning to brown. "Good."

"We're here to help you. You're part of Ingrid's coven, right? Dahlia?" He recognized her from the file Ingrid had given him, but wanted to confirm.

She nodded. Then she tightened her jaw, and he could see that she held back her emotions. "Yes. They were draining us for immortality. Us and humans. They were going to move on to wolves next. Or they thought they were. They talked about attacking dragons." She laughed bitterly. "Foolish witches. They thought if they gained enough power from our blood, they'd be able to go after wolves."

"You don't have to talk about this now," he said, even though he needed the information.

"Yes I do." Dahlia wrapped her arms around herself and he cursed at his own stupidity.

He tugged off his shirt and handed it to her. Vampires didn't often care about nudity, the same as shifters, but she'd had her freedom taken from her, had been tortured, and would likely be feeling vulnerable. He hated that he didn't have clothing for all of them.

"Thanks," she murmured as she eased it on over her already healing body. The cuts all looked shallow, definitely superficial. The witches must have been taking their time draining this bunch.

His wolves were caring for the rest of the others in the room, but this female was cognizant and didn't mind sharing information. Information he needed to make sure this was the end of this shit.

He motioned to his wolves to get the others upstairs as he continued talking to her. "What was their end game?"

"To take over New Orleans."

"They said that?"

"Not directly to me or anything. But they didn't try to hide what they were doing. I heard them talking amongst each other. They wanted to bring in other covens, to grow stronger. Well, a couple of them did, but some of the others disagreed. Said that some of the covens wouldn't practice dark magic. They were right—I know some witches who would cut off their own arm before getting into this shit."

Like Dallas. "How did they kidnap you?" He needed to know how these people had been targeted. Looking around the nearly empty basement, his gaze stopped on a few folding chairs leaning against a wall. He grabbed one and motioned for her to sit down.

She did, practically collapsing on the chair, and he pushed back his guilt. He needed these answers while everything was fresh in her mind. Because if there was still another threat out there, there might be more people to save.

"Who is the leader?" he pressed.

"Honestly I'm not sure. The redhead that you killed—that sword thing was badass by the way—she did most of the talking directly to us. And she was the one who lured a lot of us away. She had a certain kind of magic where she could create an illusion, I guess. Make you see what you wanted to see."

"Like a shape-shifter?"

"Kind of. The magic didn't last that long. Probably because it took a lot of energy, I'm guessing. I don't know enough about witches. But the majority of us, she took by looking like either our romantic partners or luring some of us in with the intention of hooking up with our ideal mate." There was self-loathing in the female's voice as she ran a trembling hand over her pixie haircut. "It's how she got me. I've got a thing for leggy blondes."

"She's dead now. She can't hurt you. And I want to have you looked over by a healer. So let's get out of here. I'll have more questions, but this has been a huge help for now."

"Thank you," the female rasped out, emotion finally starting to crack through. "Seriously. We wouldn't have lasted through the night. They were taunting us, slowly draining our blood. It didn't matter how much we fought it, we were never getting out of that spell."

King simply nodded and helped her out of the seat, motioning that they should head up the stairs. "For the record, a witch helped me find you." He knew that witches had taken them and he didn't want all of them to hate Dallas's kind because of a bad few. He himself had been guilty of lumping witches into the same category and he knew that shit needed to stop. Especially since witches were helping rebuild the whole world. "It's just something you should know. She gave a lot of herself to find you guys."

"I'm not a bigot," the female murmured, a pained half-smile on her face as she strode toward the stairs. "But thank you for telling me."

Her strides were fairly steady as she made her way up the stairs and he was grateful that his people had already called in healers and backup by the time he got out to the front yard. Ingrid was arriving at that time too, and the relief on her face when she saw her people was very real. "Dahlia, Benjamin!" she called out. Then she called out to others, beckoning all her vampires to her.

He just hoped this was the end of it. That there weren't more threats out there, other members of this evil coven still alive. He would hunt all of them down but he wanted this finished. He had enough rebuilding to deal with, and hunting down a bunch of rogue witches would only slow that down.

People needed to start feeling a sense of normalcy again. It would be a new normal, but his city deserved it.

And he was determined to make it happen.

CHAPTER 27

"You can stay with us while you heal," Lola said as she sat next to Dallas at the table outside, wearing a slightly pouty expression. "We barely got to hang out and last night was so fun—and your friend Javi was so hot!"

Dallas half-smiled, despite the exhaustion humming through her. Lola seemed to think every guy was hot. Rhys had left her sitting outside with Willow so he could go pack all of her stuff—and ordered her not to move from her spot. "Trust me, it'll be better for me if I can go home." She took a sip from the soothing peppermint tea infused with a whole lot of healing juice.

"Well whatever you need, we can just go get it for you. We liked having you here," Lola continued, and the others nodded.

Bella reached out and laid the back of her hand on Dallas's forehead and frowned. "I think you're running a fever."

"Yeah, I think you should stay," Harlow said, arms crossed over her chest.

All their caring and concern was about to undo her. She was so weak right now and this was pushing her over the edge. "Seriously, guys, I'm going to start crying."

Brielle looked horrified at that thought. "Please don't cry."

Harlow snorted. "Yeah, my twin can't handle tears. It's the quickest way to make her run from you."

Her twin elbowed her with a sharp jab to the side.

The only reason Dallas was even still upright at all was because of the healing tea Thurman had given to Rhys. He'd also given her a couple spelled cookies—*macadamia nut, thank you very much*—that had not only tasted delicious but had given her an extra burst of energy as well. It was like she'd taken a bunch of super vitamins but she knew the crash was coming soon. And she needed to be on her own land when that happened. "You guys, I swear, I'll come back with Willow soon. Maybe a week or so."

"Look, we like Willow," Lola said. "Okay, we *love* her. But that's not why we want you to stay. We like you. And we don't like everybody."

The others nodded in agreement. Even Axel. Instead of the normal easygoing smile from him, he looked worried for her. She hadn't looked in the mirror yet, but Dallas could imagine how pale she was right now. And her eyes were probably dull as well. It was what happened when she expended so much damn energy so quickly. And that finding spell had been insane, penetrating through layers and layers of dark magic to hit home.

Lola glanced down at her phone when it dinged and her eyes widened slightly. "Holy shit, Aurora just texted me. King and his wolves hunted down those witches."

Dallas stirred in her seat, her gaze straying toward Rhys. He was walking out of the house now, bags in hand. She was so glad he'd made the choice to come with her instead of hunting down Catta. Even though she wanted him to get the closure he needed, she needed him right now. And he'd chosen to stay with her. That knowledge was almost too much to bear. Goddess, she was about to start crying just thinking about it.

"What happened?" She turned back to Lola.

Lola read from the screen. "There were half a dozen witches in a basement. They were draining the blood of vampires and humans. A couple humans didn't make it, but almost everyone else is alive. Except the witches. Every single one of them died."

Relief coursed through Dallas at the news. She'd thought that she might sense it when Catta died, but she could barely feel her own magic right now. It was deep inside her, just a tiny spark flickering as her energy rejuvenated itself.

"That's great news," she said, reaching out a hand for Rhys, who now stood by the side of her chair.

He took her hand in his, linking their fingers together. "Ladies. Axel. I need to get Dallas home."

"It's clear we can't change your mind, but if you need anything let us know," Lola said.

"Rhys packed some cookies I made," Bella said. "So don't let him 'forget' to give them to you."

"Chocolate chip," Rhys added. "And I promise I only ate one."

A smile tugging at her lips, Dallas forced herself to her feet. "Tell Aurora goodbye for us. But I'll be back soon, I promise. I just need to be at home in order to heal better."

Everyone hugged her, and then everyone hugged Willow as well. Her sweet dragon soaked up all the love, dancing around everyone, but it was pretty clear that she was ready to go home as well.

By the time Rhys had shifted, Willow was already in the air, ready to head out to adventure unknown. Any time Rhys flew, it seemed that Willow was ready to go with him.

Now that her mother was dead, Dallas knew that her time with Rhys had almost come to an end. He'd told her that he would go home once he had his revenge. Or he'd hinted at that anyway. At least she knew he would stay with her until after she healed since he'd promised.

Damn, she was just too tired to think about anything, let alone the future. She held on tight to his neck as he launched into the air, soaking up every last second she could with her big dragon. Because soon he would leave. And that was going to hurt both her and Willow.

At that thought, she leaned forward and hugged him even tighter. She was unable to stop the tears that fell, splashing onto his scales as he soared over treetops.

CHAPTER 28

Brielle crowded around the screen with Lola, Bella, Harlow and Axel as they waited for Star to pick up the video call. When her smiling face came on-screen, something inside Brielle relaxed. Her tiger knew that Star wasn't her Alpha anymore, but until a few weeks ago Star had been their Alpha for a long damn time—since they were precocious kids getting into a hell of a lot of trouble.

"There was a real dragon living here!" Harlow shouted.

"Your mate's brother is so going to mate with a sweet witch!" This was from Lola.

"Aurora is doing so well!" Bella shouted, unable to contain her excitement.

"You just missed out on the best chicken parm ever." From Axel, of course. That male was always thinking about food.

Brielle didn't say anything as the others all talked at once, shouting over each other.

Star blinked, her bright purple eyes vivid before she looked at Brielle. "You guys have a dragon?"

Brielle's lips pursed together but before she could respond, Harlow blurted, "No, but she was staying with us for a week and we're all going to visit her soon. She's so stinking cute I kinda want to kidnap her but I like her owner too much to do that."

Star blinked again as she stared at Harlow. "Who are you and what have you done to my stoic Harlow?"

Brielle grunted in agreement. She wasn't sure what had happened to her twin, but lately she'd been a raging chatterbox. It was pretty nice, if she was being honest.

"Wait, did you say…Lachlan's brother is getting mated?"

Lachlan popped into the image then, all serious dragon. "Rhys is mated?" he asked in that lilting Scottish brogue.

"No," Brielle said before anyone could answer. "But he's well on his way to claiming her. It's just a matter of time. He just took her home because she expended way too much energy from a spell. Apparently she's a pretty powerful witch."

Lachlan stared at all of them as if they'd lost their minds. Then he kissed Star on the head and murmured something too low to hear before he disappeared from sight. There was the sound of a door shutting then.

"It's just us now," she said laughing. "My mate can't believe Rhys is mating with a witch. Now…she's the one who owns the dragonling?"

Harlow answered then and for the next twenty minutes they all talked over each other, everyone just excited to talk to Star. Brielle's tiger was very much at peace, seeing how happy her lifelong friend, her former Alpha, was. It was clear that Star was happier than she'd ever been.

Once everyone was winding down, she cleared her throat. "You guys mind giving me some time with Star?"

"Of course not." Bella blew kisses at the laptop and everyone else waved before heading out.

"So what's up?" Star asked, straightening slightly. Behind her a big window was open, revealing that it was dark out, and Brielle was pretty certain she heard sheep in the distance.

"Just wanted to talk to you." She flipped the chair at the desk around and straddled it. "You look good."

"That's what nonstop sex'll do to a woman."

Brielle snorted. "It's more than that. How is everyone there? How's everyone treating you?"

"Amazing. I was nervous coming here. It doesn't matter that I'm not a dragon. They've all accepted me. I mean, there might be a few outliers but I haven't dealt with anything internal yet. External is another matter," she said, sighing.

"Supernaturals or humans?"

"Both. There are a lot of people suffering. So many people were traveling when The Fall happened and now they're displaced, in a new country. We've been able to get some people home, but others have no home to go to. It's...hard seeing so much suffering and adjusting to this new reality. I almost feel bad being so damn happy with Lachlan." Star's eyes flashed a deep violet then, a mirror of her feelings.

"I know. It's the same here. We were out on a mission last week for King and found a group of human teenagers stuck out in the middle of nowhere. On the outskirts of the bayou. They'd been here visiting an aunt when everything went to shit. They just wanted to get back to their parents. But..." Brielle swallowed hard, pushing back the wave of emotion pushing up.

"Yeah." Star's jaw tightened once. Then she cleared her throat. "So how's my baby sister?"

"Amazing." She didn't even have to think twice about that.

"Yeah?"

"She's...blossomed. She and King have a weird sort of friendship. You know she's become a liaison of sorts for him, but I don't know. She's coming into her own. She's always been incredible but it's like I'm watching a butterfly emerge. She's powerful, something we've always known. But she's growing into that power faster than I thought would happen."

"You're not just saying that for my sake?"

Brielle knew her tiger flashed in her eyes. "I would never lie to my Alpha. To my friend."

Star's lips kicked up ever so slightly. "I'm not your Alpha anymore."

"Hmm."

"King is your Alpha now."

"I live in his territory. And I follow his rules. You...were my Alpha a long time. My tiger is still adjusting."

"Do you want to come to Scotland?"

Yes. "No. I won't leave Aurora. Not yet."

"Hmm. Maybe not ever. Just give it time."

She would. "So how are the girls settling in?"

Star let out a real laugh then. "Oh my, Kartini has already broken a few hearts."

"So what else is new?"

"Exactly. Taya and Athena seem to be settling in." There was something in Star's tone though and she'd left out Marley.

"So...what about Marley?"

"I don't know. She's been quiet, reserved. Not like herself at all. I think I might ask if she wants to head back to New Orleans if I can't get her to talk to me. I don't know if Scotland is the right place for her and I don't want her to stay out of a sense of loyalty."

Brielle was surprised that Marley hadn't opened up to Star, and made a mental note to call her later that night.

"So what's going on with Harlow? Seriously?"

Brielle just laughed and shook her head. "I have no idea what's going on with my twin but I like it."

"I do too. I miss you."

She sighed. "I miss you too. It's weird not seeing you every day."

"I know."

"Being mated looks good on you."

Star grinned. "I know that too. How's my lion doing?"

"Likely to get his head cut off any day now by some male he's pissed off."

"I'm glad that some things haven't changed."

Yeah, Brielle was too.

CHAPTER 29

Dallas opened her eyes, feeling as if she'd come out of a deep fog.

She was *home*—in her own bed. For a long moment she lay there, soaking up her surroundings. Her window was open, the sheer white linen drapes blowing lightly with a breeze.

She could hear a multitude of quiet voices outside—ones she recognized. Including Rhys. He was still here—not that she'd worried he'd leave.

Willow wasn't at her window but Dallas could see her prancing around near the goats. Herding them to nowhere as usual.

She snorted softly and slipped out of bed, feeling as exhausted as if she'd run a couple marathons. She wasn't sure how long she'd slept but it was daylight, maybe afternoon. So she must've slept for twenty-four hours. At least.

She stumbled to the bathroom, brushed her teeth and took care of other business and then decided to take a quick shower. She needed it. The cold water blasted her, helping her wake up as fast as coffee would. When she was done, she ran a blow-dryer through her hair, put on some eyeliner then tugged on a loose white skirt, a soft bralette, and a blue-and-white, paisley-patterned flowy top. As an afterthought she slipped in her favorite hoop earrings that had been a gift from Hazel. In her normal clothing, she felt…good. Settled. It went a long way in helping her feel more grounded after everything.

Dressed and ready to face the day, she went in search of Rhys and found him talking with Naomi and Hazel as they sat around her patio table.

Relief bled into Hazel and Naomi's gazes the moment they saw her.

Both her friends jumped up and rushed at her.

Hazel pulled her into a tight hug, with Naomi quickly joining in. Laughing at their intensity, she squeezed back.

"I told you I wasn't keeping her hostage," Rhys muttered.

Dallas let out a startled laugh and leaned back. "Is that what you guys thought?"

Willow had joined them now and was happily dancing around, her wings held tight at her back the way Rhys had taught her so she didn't bang into everything.

Hazel's cheeks flushed pink as she shrugged and scratched behind Willow's ear. "The only reason I didn't storm your house is because Willow seems to like him. She's got pretty good taste."

Dallas dropped a dozen kisses on Willow's face before Rhys scooped her up and tucked her up against him as he sat back down.

She didn't miss the looks of surprise from either Hazel or Naomi but she was so not commenting on her and Rhys and whatever they were. Because she wasn't even sure what they were at this point. She enjoyed him holding her, however.

"We saw Willow flying and realized you were home, so we brought over some food. Actually, we've only been here about half an hour. Are you hungry?" Hazel asked as she started unpacking a cooler, clearly already knowing the answer.

"I'm starving. How long did I sleep, anyway?"

"A day and a half." Worry flickered into Rhys's gaze, his dragon peering out at her for a moment. "Is that normal?"

She was surprised at how long she'd rested, but she felt so rejuvenated. Underneath her, she could feel the magic from her land lifting up to greet her in an invisible caress, happy she was home. "It's a little longer than normal, but obviously I must have known I was safe to sleep so long." She'd done big spells before and then passed out, hiding and hoping that she wasn't attacked in her sleep. But her body must've subconsciously known she was safe with Rhys.

"So it seems a lot has changed since you've been gone," Naomi said, curiosity clear in her big eyes as she started pouring sweet tea for Dallas.

Even though she lived in the South she hated sweet tea. But she needed the sugar right now and she wasn't going to be a dick to her friend so she took it with a smile. "Yes, it has," she said, laughing lightly as Rhys tightened his possessive grip around her. She settled back against him, liking that he wasn't shy about claiming her. Deep down, she knew this wasn't a long-term thing. Even if she wanted it. He would leave once she told him the truth of her parentage. She was trying to mentally prepare for it, but wasn't doing a great job.

"Well, we're going to head out of here." Hazel shot Naomi a warning look when it was pretty clear that Naomi wanted to argue and stay. Naomi was definitely one of the bigger gossips around the farmers. Maybe gossip was the wrong word—she just liked to share information and keep everyone informed of what was happening. "We've been taking care of everything since you've been gone and have nothing exciting to report. But we are going to want to hear all about your time in the city," Hazel added as she gave Dallas another quick hug. "Especially since you apparently did some magic that required you to sleep for a couple days."

Rhys relinquished his hold for a brief moment so she could hug her friends again.

"I swear I'll tell you everything that I can." She needed to talk to Rhys, see if he had any updates from King. She just hoped that all those witches involved had been taken care of. She also needed to tell Rhys that Catta was her mother. Though she wasn't sure *how* to tell him. She was afraid that if she did, it would make him see her differently. That she'd see loathing in his eyes and he'd reject her. "Thank you guys, for watching over my farm, for all this food."

Naomi made a little scoffing sound. "Please, you would do it for any of us."

She nodded because it was true. "Thank you all the same."

"Take a day and rest, but tomorrow I guarantee everyone's going to be over here wanting to see you and Willow," Hazel said as she and Naomi headed out.

Willow made a little chirping sound and flew after them as they walked to their car.

"Thirty-six hours, for real?" She leaned her head on Rhys's shoulder for a moment, soaking up his warmth.

"Yes. I was worried about you," he said as he reached for one of the sandwiches Hazel had made and placed it in her hand.

Simple turkey and Swiss. And it sounded like heaven. Food in general sounded amazing right now.

"I'm definitely rested. So what did King say?" she asked before taking a bite. Because Rhys would have talked to him by now, probably more than once.

"He questioned all the survivors, and there might be a straggler witch or two out there but no one could confirm that anyone was missing from the group King and his people killed. He sent over a description of all of the dead witches."

She stopped chewing and turned to look at him. "And?"

"One of them is—was—Catta."

Her stomach tightened at his words. "You're sure?"

His jaw tightened. "Not a hundred percent. But from the description he gave, it sounded exactly like her. Flame red hair, green eyes, a beautiful monster. And she appeared to be the leader."

The muscles in her stomach remained bunched. That sounded just like Catta, but she had no problem changing her appearance, something Dallas knew.

"I know this sounds morbid, but can we see the body? Or see if the scent is what you've been hunting all these years?"

"He incinerated her with her own magic." Rhys quickly launched into King's description of the battle.

The little food she'd eaten tumbled around in her stomach. She knew exactly what kind of spell Catta had thrown at King. It was one of the earliest ones she'd taught Dallas. It was a dark, dark spell and the fact the King had been able to launch it back at her was incredible. "That sounds like her."

"Eat," he simply said.

She ate two sandwiches, a bunch of fruit, cheese, and two protein bars. And she still felt like she could eat even more but she leaned back against him, feeling settled as her energy returned. The magic from her land infused her, settling into her bones.

"So are you going to tell me how you tracked them?" Rhys murmured into the quiet.

Sitting in his lap, she looked out on her garden, her land, all the acres in front of them. A few white clouds dotted the sky, and her trees rustled under the light breeze, but it was quiet, peaceful. "I don't want to tell you."

"Why?"

She closed her eyes, knowing she needed to be honest. Somewhat at least. "I'm related to Catta. Part of the same bloodline." Somehow she couldn't force herself to tell him that Catta had borne her.

Rhys shifted slightly underneath her but he didn't curse or act shocked.

She opened her eyes and looked at him in surprise. "You knew?"

"I guessed it was something like that. I don't know a ton about spells or witches, but that scent that triggered the familial recognition was my first hint. And then the spell you did. I knew it had to be more than just a common link from an old coven, but an actual familial relationship."

"You don't hate me?" She still couldn't tell him that Catta was her mother. The words wouldn't come. Maybe later. But she didn't want anything to spoil the here and now with him. Because if he knew the truth, she was afraid he would despise her. And Dallas couldn't bear it. God, she knew that made her an asshole, but she was so damn touch-starved. She just...wanted to hold on to him for a little bit longer. She'd dealt with a lifetime of hiding what she was, of being hated for who she was. She just wanted to keep what they had a bit longer in case he did reject her. Her scars ran deep, no matter how much she wanted to trust that he wouldn't hate her once he knew the truth.

"Of course I don't hate you." He sighed and brushed his lips over hers. "I understand why you didn't tell me. I was a giant dick about witches before I met you."

"I'm sorry you didn't get to take your revenge personally." It was a weird thing to apologize for but she knew it had been important to him.

He shook his head. "I only wanted justice for my sister. And she's gone. I thought I would feel different... And I guess I do. Catta needed to die. *Clearly.* I'm just glad that you're alive." He looked like he wanted to say more but stopped himself.

"What?"

"Nothing. Thurman told me I would need to make a choice. And I'd like to think I made the right one."

"You mean going with King, or staying with me?" Because it still stunned her that he'd decided to stay with her, to bring her home while King killed Catta and her coven.

He nodded once and leaned forward, brushing his lips over hers again, deepening it this time.

She knew he was going to leave soon. How could he not? So she wanted to soak up every second with him. She wanted to cross that line with him, wanted to feel him inside her. They'd only skated the surface of intimacy and she wanted so much more.

Turning in his arms, she straddled him, clutching onto his shoulders tightly.

"We don't have to do anything," he murmured against her mouth, trying to hold her away from him.

"I'm fine," she said, smiling. He stared into her eyes, the concern there slaying her. "I *promise*."

"Do you think Willow will be okay if we do…anything out here?"

Need punched through her at his question, at the hunger she saw mirrored in his own eyes. She glanced over her shoulder and saw her dragon doing little dips over the pond in the distance, splashing up water with her wings and amusing herself. She didn't think Willow would care one bit what they did. Turning back to him, she reached for the hem of his shirt and tugged upward, needing to touch him. Needing skin to skin.

He grappled with her light top and bralette, doing the same, tugging it up and tossing it somewhere.

She stroked her hands up his chest, savoring the feel of all that raw power underneath her fingertips as she kissed him—and was kissed right back. She swore she'd missed him even in sleep. She felt consumed with the need to have him inside her, claim her.

It wouldn't be a real claiming but she would take this time with him and hold on to the memories of it when he left and she went back to her regular life.

He was glowing again, she realized. She sucked in a breath as she took in his soft blue glow. She stared at him even as heat rushed between her thighs. It didn't feel like magic, not like hers anyway, but there was a charged quality to the glow he was giving off.

His eyes were dark indigo, hungry with need. "It's a dragon thing," he said, as if she'd asked a question. She'd seen the glow before, but it was no less awe-inspiring.

He clutched her hips tightly, his long fingers clenching against her.

"It happens during sex?" she asked.

"It can," he said carefully. "It's never happened to me before. Not until you."

She felt like there might be something he was leaving out, but she didn't even care at this point. She was just glad that this beautiful glow was all for her and kissed him again, harder this time as he reached between them and slid her skirt off.

Soon they were both naked, their clothes piled on the grass as she was straddling his lap. His cock arched up between their bodies, thick and beautiful. As she looked down at the beauty of him, heat rushed between her legs. There had never been a more perfect male than him.

He cupped her mound, groaned in appreciation as he slid two fingers inside her with ease. "You're so wet," he growled out against her mouth.

Desperate for all of him, she lifted up on her knees as he guided his thick cock to her slick folds, teasing for just a moment.

When she sank down on him, it was like coming home, like this was exactly where she belonged. Where *he* belonged. Right with her.

"Fuck," he groaned out as she rolled her hips and tightened around him.

She sucked in a breath as she took all of him, enjoying the feel of him inside her. She tried to get out of her head, to stop thinking about the future, about losing him, but she desperately wanted one with him.

He nipped at her bottom lip and her inner walls clenched around his thick length in response.

No more thinking, now she was just living in the moment. She started riding him and all thoughts of the future ceased. The only thing that mattered was the two of them and pure pleasure.

His glow grew brighter around them, the soft blue a bright beacon casting its light all around her yard. It was the most beautiful thing she'd ever seen, as if they were surrounded by pure magic manifesting from the two of them.

She really did care for him—more than just care. She knew she loved this big dragon, but was too afraid to tell him. Way too afraid that she wouldn't be enough, that he would be another person to reject her. Especially when he found out who her mother was.

She rode him faster and faster even as he grabbed her hips and thrust upward to meet her stroke for stroke. He seemed as manic as she was to find release together.

His big hands stroked all over her—her back, her breasts, anywhere he could reach. It was like he just wanted to touch her.

She hadn't realized exactly how touch-starved she was until now, until she soaked up every single graze from his callused fingers.

He kissed a path down her neck, growling against the sensitive spot behind her ear. His growl reverberated through her, sending delicious shivers to all her pleasure points. Then he reached between their bodies and teased her clit, immediately setting her off. He'd learned her body so quickly, seemed so in tune with her.

She surged into orgasm, waves and waves of pleasure punching through her. As her climax rose, he increased the pressure, growling against her neck as he did. The extra sensation sent waves of heat and pleasure rushing through her as her climax built harder and harder until she finally couldn't stand it anymore.

"No more," she said, practically shoving his hand away. She didn't realize there was such a thing as too much pleasure, but her body was trembling with it.

"It's never enough," he growled against her neck even as he grabbed her ass tight. And that was when he let go, crying out her name as he thrust up hard inside her, finding his own release in long, hard strokes.

They both came down from their high together, the sun beating down on her back as she looped her arms around him and laid her head on his shoulder. "I could stay like this forever," she murmured, slightly drowsy.

"Let's get you inside in case more of your neighbors stop by," he finally murmured, making her laugh lightly. "I don't want anyone else seeing you naked."

"I think you're going to have to carry me," she said, because she was completely boneless. She figured she could probably go back to sleep again.

Laughing, he stood and lifted her into his arms.

And there was no place she would rather be in that moment. Unfortunately she knew things would change once she told him the truth. The full truth.

Which she would. As soon as she worked up the courage.

CHAPTER 30

Dallas stroked her hand up and down Rhys's chest, savoring the quiet with him. The sun would set in an hour but time had lost all meaning at this point. She just knew that she loved being with him—loved *him*. She wanted to ask him if he would stay with her for a while. Maybe forever. But that was crazy, right?

"So how do you feel about your old coven members...being killed?" Rhys suddenly asked into the quiet.

She jolted slightly but the answer was easy. "They were practicing dark magic. Really dark." And she needed to tell him that her mother was Catta. If they were ever going to have a chance at something real—and she hoped that they could—he had to know every part of her. Or at least the important ones.

"Still, gotta be hard." He idly stroked a hand down her back.

"Not really. I ran away from them in the middle of the night." She pushed up to look at him. "Literally as soon as I was legally old enough, and honestly I shouldn't have even waited that long. But I had a plan and that meant I had to save some money. Plus I stole some spells from one of the coven's books. And when the timing was right, I made my escape. I put as much distance as possible between them and me. I didn't stop running until I was clear across to the other coast that first week. I don't feel any sadness if that's what you mean."

He gently stroked her cheek. "King texted me again. He wanted to see if you would come to the city later, identify them in person? He said something about witches being able to spell their appearances and he wants to make sure everyone from your old coven is there."

"I don't actually want to see them, but it might give me a sense of closure. That part of my life is long closed anyway, but still…" If she saw her old coven members, maybe she truly would get closure about that part of her life and Catta. She wanted to believe her mother was dead, hoped she *was* dead. But as she lay there, some part of her magic was starting to tingle in awareness— *Oh, goddess!*

Dallas jerked up in bed, shoved away from him as raw panic punched through her. She needed to get to Willow, get her dragonling to safety. "She's close!"

Rhys stared at her as she grabbed his discarded shirt and tugged it over her body. She wasn't going into this battle naked. Just as quickly she grabbed her jeans and yanked them on with shaking hands.

"Who's here?" He jumped to his feet, all his muscles pulled taut, as if he was ready to battle.

"Catta."

He stared at her. "How do you know that?"

She stared back at him, her heart racing because they had no time to spare. She couldn't hold this back any longer. "I planned to tell you before. But then I thought she died… And I got scared," she whispered. She closed her eyes and turned away from him. "She's my mother. She's a monster, but she is my mother." With no time to spare, she raced toward the doors leading to her backyard. She couldn't stand to look at his hatred, couldn't stand to see the rejection in his face. "I wanted to tell you but now there's no time to talk about it. She's come to kill me. She knows what I did. I can feel her magic on the air." Yanking the French doors open, she raced outside, Rhys right next to her, waves of emotion vibrating off him.

She spotted Willow racing toward them and some of her panic eased. Then she looked to the skies, scanning for Catta on the horizon. Because yeah, Catta? She could fly. Technically Dallas could too, but not in the way Catta could, and it took far more energy. The kind of energy she couldn't afford to waste.

"She'll have backup." Rhys's words were clipped as he strode forward, completely naked.

"She's powerful." She wasn't sure why she said it; of course he knew that. "She shouldn't be able to break through your fire, but don't let any of her spells touch you," she ordered as she mentally prepared for the challenge. Goddess, she couldn't stand it if she lost him. Though she was pretty sure she'd already lost him, regardless. But she wanted him to live, to kill Catta and then go home to his family. He deserved all those things and more after what he'd been through.

Willow joined them, had very clearly picked up on the tension because she was letting out tiny little chirping sounds as she shifted nervously next to them.

Dallas laid her hands on Willow's head and chanted a small but powerful protection spell. It wouldn't last forever but it should help against any attack.

"There!" Rhys shouted and she followed his gaze. On the horizon were five witches, flying toward them, Catta in the middle. Her flame red hair was a beacon. It was a bizarre sight, seeing them ascend with no wings, just her mother's raw magic suspending them in air.

They were dressed in all-black, full-body suits that were likely fire-resistant. Yeah, well, they wouldn't resist Rhys's fire for long.

"Shift!" she ordered him, her fingers tingling with all the wild magic she kept inside her.

He grabbed her shoulders and kissed her hard before he pulled away, waves of anger rolling off him as magic burst into the air, his dragon unleashing in a kaleidoscope of colors.

She would *not* think about that kiss, would not think about the fact that it was probably her last kiss with him. Once they killed Catta and these other monsters—and she had to believe they would—he would leave. That much Dallas knew.

Her mother was so powerful, had always told her what a disappointment Dallas was. That if she would only tap into dark magic, she could be just like Catta. She would have everything she desired. Youth, beauty, riches forever. As if Dallas wanted all those things to begin with.

Even as tension and adrenaline hummed through her like angry bees, Dallas crouched down and ran her fingers over the soft grass. She whispered out words of love and encouragement, reaching deep for the stockpile of magic she'd stored underground over the last two decades. Every crop she planted, every tree or plant she added to her land, she injected part of herself, her magic. And she was going to need every ounce of it now.

She could see her mother's flaming red hair against the horizon. Still as stunning and evil as ever.

Rhys let out a roar of rage as he arrowed toward them, his wings bright indigo and purple jewels under the sunlight.

Catta was maybe a hundred yards away now and moving in fast toward the ground, her minions flying downward as well. But Dallas could see faint connecting lines between Catta and the others, dark tendrils of magic. Those witches were only in the air because of Catta.

Dallas called on a breaking spell, held up her hands and threw it not at Catta, but at the nearly invisible tendrils between her mother and the others.

Sparks of yellow burst in the air as the lines snapped free. One witch screamed as she started to fall, diving straight for Dallas's pond.

The others fell as well, tossing out their own spells so they wouldn't die or break bones when they collided with the ground.

Catta was still barreling toward Dallas and Rhys. He let out a stream of fire at Catta, but it arched around her, not touching her.

Dallas kept the fallen witches in her peripheral vision, but the majority of her focus was on Catta as she hurled a confusion spell at her mother. It was only one of many in her arsenal.

Catta laughed and lobbed it back at her, the ball of energy flying straight for Dallas. She dove out of the way even as Rhys breathed out another ball of fire at Catta, this one even brighter, hotter.

On a scream, Catta turned toward him and threw what looked like lightning at him. Bolt after bolt arched through the air, straight at Rhys.

No! Rage boiled up inside Dallas, hot lava spilling outward as the lightning went straight for his wing. He dodged at the last moment and breathed out a bright blue stream of fire, clipping Catta in the leg. She screamed but remained airborne.

Her attention split, Dallas sprinted for the nearest fallen witch, who was now maybe thirty yards away chanting something as she tried to break the protection spell on Willow.

Willow was screeching at her as her wings flapped angrily, her body language clear. She wanted this female gone.

"Pick on someone your own size!" Dallas hauled back and threw a distraction spell to the left of the woman instead of straight at her face. She wasn't sure why she did it, some intrinsic knowledge. The woman dodged as if expecting a direct hit and ran straight into the ball of pure white light.

Dallas's magic hit her in the throat, as if she'd thrown an actual grenade, nearly taking her head off. One down.

Willow screamed in rage, and to Dallas's surprise let out a small burst of flames at the fallen witch, incinerating her body.

Dallas didn't have time to appreciate it fully as she continued running across the field toward two other witches who were attempting to cast destruction spells of their own. Dallas's breaking spell had only slowed them down, but it wouldn't hold them off forever. She had to strike fast and hard.

Above her, Catta and Rhys were battling in the air, flames and destruction flying all around them.

The west side of Dallas's garden was in flames but she ignored it. Nothing mattered except surviving with Rhys and destroying all of these witches. She needed to tell him that she loved him, that she was sorry she hadn't told him the truth earlier.

"So this is the infamous Dallas." A blonde female with big eyes and a Jessica Rabbit-type body snarled as she strode toward her, her hands lifted out from her sides. Soft red flames glowed in her palms as she lifted them, tossing them straight at Dallas.

She ducked, narrowly avoiding being hit, and bent to yank out chunks of grass and soil. She cupped the rich earth in her hand and whispered a soft spell as the female lifted her hands again, ready to burn her. But Dallas was faster.

The grass and soil fell from her hands as she rolled to the ground, avoiding another hit. Roots sprung up from the earth where the soil had fallen, long talons reaching and grabbing, angry claws as they raced toward the enemy witch. Dallas's land might not be sentient, but it sensed that this interloper was trying to hurt it, had dared to bring black magic here.

The roots speared the witch straight through both her eyes and her heart as Dallas raced toward another witch. She heard the dying witch's brief scream, then nothing.

A scream above her almost tore her focus away but she had to trust that Rhys could handle himself with Catta. If he didn't... *No.* She refused to think that for even one moment. She had to take out the ones on the ground so he could take out the biggest threat.

Her leg muscles tightened as she ran and called on all of her internal magic now. Instead of being exhausted, she felt adrenaline pumping hard through her veins, making her feel as if she could do anything. Willow's wings flapped wildly next to her as she flew alongside Dallas.

The witch racing at them looked at her and Willow, raised both hands and— Willow let out a stream of fire. The fire dispersed around the witch's body, not touching her.

But the witch stumbled back, falling onto her knees, so the fire had affected her protection spell a little.

Dallas reached deep inside herself, called on a type of healing spell that would shatter the darkness inside the witch—and break her apart from the inside.

The female screamed as a dark smoke rose out of her mouth and arrowed straight for Dallas, its intent clear. *Kill.*

Closing her eyes, Dallas threw a blocking spell up, and a small shimmer of magic surrounded her and Willow. The blackness rammed into it, nearly knocked her back, but she held her ground. The problem with this kind of spell was that she couldn't fight back with her most powerful magic. Its sole purpose was to keep her contained, safe.

So she let it drop and threw a brilliant blue light at the witch. It hit her full in the chest and the female incinerated on the spot.

Above her, Rhys let out a stream of the most beautiful, brilliant blue fire she'd ever seen. She squinted against it and for the first time ever she saw Catta looking terrified.

Catta raced away from him, swooping downward and dive-bombing so that she was behind Dallas, about twenty yards away and closing fast. Her beautiful face was twisted into a snarl, her eyes sparking with rage and hatred.

From out of nowhere, another witch appeared in the air and threw a yellow ball of flames at Rhys from behind. It slammed into his tail and he screeched, his blue fire arching wild as he fell toward the earth.

Dallas's heart jumped in her throat as she watched him fall. She threw out a spell to break his fall before turning back to her mother. She never wanted to give Catta her back.

Catta was hobbling toward her now, clearly not able to fly anymore.

Dallas threw the blocking spell up, knowing her mother couldn't penetrate it even as Dallas raced for Rhys. She had to know that he was okay.

Her giant dragon softly landed on the earth, her spell saving him from a hard landing. Immediately he shifted to human form but looked dazed and confused as he stumbled toward her.

On a scream, Dallas allowed the blocking spell around her to ease down a fraction and turned toward the other advancing witch who had hurt Rhys. She threw the nastiest spell she'd ever created at the female, one she'd never tried before, but it poured out of her as if she'd done it a thousand times.

The witch stopped and started clawing at her face, screaming nonsensically as blood poured out of her eyes and ears. She wasn't long for this world and Dallas didn't care.

As Dallas reached Rhys, he stared at her as if he didn't recognize her. Then he looked past her and said his sister's name. "Eilidh."

Oh goddess, no. Catta had combined confusion and glamour spells, making him see what wasn't there.

Willow screeched in the air, breathing fire at Catta as she dive-bombed her. But Catta lifted a hand and tossed Willow back hundreds of yards with a burst of magic.

Her mother's malignant magic scraped against Dallas's senses, the sensation of hundreds, maybe thousands of screams raking against her skin. All of her mother's victims.

"What's going on?" Rhys murmured, wobbling on his feet.

"You stupid girl!" Catta screamed. "You just had to get involved." Moving slowly, she stalked across the ripped-up grass, still limping.

Next to Dallas, Rhys stumbled again and she knew he wasn't seeing her at all. His eyes were glazed over as he wobbled back and forth on his feet. "What did you do to him?" she screamed at the woman who had given her life.

Catta's beautiful face twisted into a sneer. "All he sees is his sister right now. I'm going to take him from you and then I'm going to take everyone you ever cared for. I gave you a chance to fight alongside me. You could have had everything! You're weak and pathetic and I should've killed you the day you were born."

Dallas resisted the urge to look for Willow, her heart breaking at the thought of her sweet dragon injured or worse. She had to break Rhys out of whatever Catta had done to him, then they had to kill Catta. There was no other way.

Sweat poured down her spine as she faced off with Catta. "I'm going to kill you if it's the last thing I do," she snarled, magic and resolve tingling along her fingertips.

Her mother threw her head back and laughed, looking insane, but the laughter itself made Dallas cover her ears as pain reverberated in her skull. Catta continued to laugh and laugh, the sound like glass scraping over glass. Dallas squinted at the pain, a deep ache spreading across the back of her head.

No! She reached for Rhys, grabbed his hand.

He looked at her and blinked. "Dallas?" he whispered, his dragon flickering in his gaze.

She slapped him across the face. Hard. "Catta spelled you. Wake up! Wake up now! I love you, you big, foolish dragon! Wake up!"

He shook his head then and seemed to come back to himself even as he winced at the laughs that sounded more like screams. Her mother's laughter was another spell, thousands and thousands of screams descending on them, threatening to burst their eardrums as they tried to fight the intense agony punching through them.

"Fight it. Call on your dragon," Dallas snarled. "I know he's in there!"

In that moment his beast looked back at her, all fire and rage and determination.

She fell to the ground under the weight of the pain, her knees slamming into the hard earth. Catta was still advancing on them. Still laughing that maniacal laugh. She thought it was over. That she had won.

You will never win. Not while I'm alive.

Dallas closed her eyes and reached deep for every ounce of magic she'd ever stored over the years. "Come to me. Obey me." She called on her power even as magic sparks of light burst next to her everywhere.

Rhys shifted to his dragon form even as her mother laughed, trying to destroy them with her evil.

Then Catta burst into red flames, fire dancing over her hair and body, her fingertips glowing black as she strode toward them. She looked like something straight out of Hell.

"You have broken far too many laws, man's laws, the supernatural laws," Dallas whispered as she commanded her magic to do her bidding. "And now you have trespassed onto my land. Onto another witch's sacred ground. And you tried to take the male I love." She screamed the last part, injecting all of her rage and hatred at her mother.

She took great pleasure when Catta stumbled back, her flames flickering out. But it wouldn't be enough. She and Rhys had to take her down together.

The earth rumbled beneath Dallas, all of her magic rising up and filling her. She lifted off the ground as her magic propelled her upward. There was too much inside her to contain as white-hot flames licked along her arms and legs without burning her. Instinctively she knew exactly what to do.

Rhys rose next to her, his dragon snarling as smoke poured out of his mouth.

Dallas called on all her magic and threw her white flames straight at Catta even as her dragon opened his mouth and screamed out a stream of raging blue fire.

Catta held up her hands, throwing back red fire. It pushed and pushed against both of them but deep in her bones Dallas felt it.

She felt Catta's power crack. Start to crumble.

Dallas's magic pushed her forward on the air without her order, the sensation of levitating exhilarating even as it was foreign. She shoved back harder with her magic, digging as deep as possible with all her strength.

Rhys's fire was crackling hot, a never-ending stream as it slammed into Catta's shield, cracking the dark web around her.

The sound of shattering glass rent the air and Catta's shield completely burst. As one, their combined flames slammed into her.

Catta screamed as the flames engulfed her, trying to fight it with her power, but she was no match for them. Finally the fire incinerated her into nothing, as if she'd never existed.

"Willow!" Dallas screamed the moment Catta disappeared. Catta was finally dead and she would deal with the fallout later. There was no time to feel relieved. No time for anything. She needed to get to Willow.

They flew together, sobs rising up in her throat as she landed next to Willow. *Oh goddess, no. No, no, no.* Willow was so still, her wings unmoving against the grass as she lay there like a statue.

Suddenly Rhys was in his human form, lifting Willow's head and tugging her close as Dallas cupped her dragonling's face.

"Wake up," she whispered, injecting healing magic into Willow's wings and body. *Please, please, be enough,* she silently prayed.

Suddenly Willow's eyes snapped open and she looked between the two of them, blinking. She made a burping sound and shook her head as if coming out of sleep. Then inside her head, Dallas heard the words, *You good fren* in a very stilted language. *Willow love.*

Dallas's eyes widened.

"Did you hear that?" Rhys whispered.

"I did," she whispered back.

Willow love Dallas. Willow love Rhys, she heard in her head again.

"I love you too," she choked out as she wrapped her arms around Willow's neck and held her close, sobbing against her girl. Emotion surged through her, a tidal wave she couldn't control as it all poured out. She couldn't stop shaking as she clutched onto Willow.

Rhys wrapped his own arms around both of them, holding them close. "I love you both," he rumbled, his grip tightening.

Raw emotion surged through her and she started crying even harder, pretty sure she would never stop.

"Don't cry," he murmured, tugging her into his arms. She buried her face against his neck and felt Willow patting her back with her wing.

"It's done. You're free of her. You can go home in peace," she sobbed out. His sister was dead because of Catta. And Rhys had almost died minutes ago.

"Did you not hear when I said I loved you?" he murmured quietly.

Her heart stilled. Leaning back, she swiped away her tears. "You really love me?"

"I love you more than life itself." He cupped her cheeks, looking down into her eyes.

She was still trembling from a mixture of shock, relief and exhaustion. "Even though I lied to you?"

"I don't care. You are *nothing* like her. Nothing at all. You are my Dallas. *Mine.* Now and forever. Nothing will change that."

All the tension that had balled tight inside her finally eased as she digested his words. Sharp relief slid through her. "Stay with me."

His lips kicked up. "You think I would leave now? You're never getting rid of me. And…I wasn't exactly truthful either. That glow from before, from when we were making love? It means that you're my mate. I just didn't want to scare you off. So you better be damn sure this is what you want, because I'm never letting you go once we mate. You're mine, Dallas."

She kissed him hard. That was her answer. Yes to now, and yes to forever.

CHAPTER 31

D allas sensed Rhys more than heard him as he approached her from behind. Then his big arms encircled her, pulling her back against his chest. Exactly where she wanted to be. She didn't think she'd ever get tired of him holding her like this.

"I can't believe you already fixed all this," he murmured against the top of her head as he joined her to watch Willow snoozing with a stray cat that had showed up an hour ago. The gray and white feline was currently lying on Willow's head without a care in the world.

"I'm bonded with my land." Something that happened with witches who stayed in one place for a long time. "My magic runs deep here." It had only taken a few hours to repair all of the damage Catta and those other witches had done. If anything, her land was stronger now and so was she. She wouldn't have the same rebound as before, wouldn't need all that rest.

"Well, it's incredible. *You* are incredible. And you're mine." He nuzzled her neck gently, his words and touch sending little waves of pleasure spiraling through her.

She reached behind her, moving her arm around his back at an odd angle just because she wanted to feel him even closer. Relief still hummed through her that he didn't care about Catta being her mother. "What did King say?" Rhys had offered to call the Alpha and she was glad. She hadn't wanted to deal with questions from King and hadn't wanted to lie.

"He discovered the identities of the witches killed in the city. The woman we thought was Catta was a female named Margaret. They had a very similar look. Apparently two different groups of their coven took turns torturing various groups of kidnap victims, so the ones they recently rescued had never seen Catta or the females we killed. I told him about the witches we killed, that we took care of the bodies. From his intel, he thinks their entire coven is gone now. He's going to do some digging to make sure though. I didn't tell him that Catta was your mother. I figured if you wanted, you could tell him later."

"Thank you." With Catta gone, even if there were any stragglers left, she wasn't worried about taking on another witch. But her mother wouldn't have come here without all the backup possible. Dallas didn't think anyone was left. She'd probably tell King later, but there didn't seem to be a point to it now—and she simply didn't want to talk about it anymore.

She turned in his arms, not wanting to think about Catta ever again. She simply wanted to move forward in this moment with Rhys, to create a life with him. To have a real future. He'd already explained to her about the mating process—how if one of them died, then the other did too. She was all in. "I want to be your mate. I don't know if that's the right phrase or—"

He crushed his mouth to hers, taking her off guard.

But she sank into him, laughing against his mouth. "Okay, then," she murmured, though it came out kind of garbled as he practically devoured her.

He lifted her into his arms so she wrapped her legs around his waist. She didn't care where they made love or even how the whole mating process happened. She simply couldn't get enough of him. He was the family she'd always wanted. And she would never let him go.

Moments later they were in her house, and she found herself flat on her back in bed.

"I'll bite you when we mate," he murmured as he started stripping off her pants, his fingers moving quickly.

Feeling frenzied, she tugged off her shirt, her nipples beading tight at the cool air and the hot look he gave her. "Kinky. I like it."

He paused once before his full mouth turned up into a wicked grin. Then he shucked the rest of his clothes and his big body covered hers once again.

Just like that, she heated up from the inside out, the feel of all that power dominating her, pinning her to the bed. And his beautiful indigo glow was everywhere, surrounding them like a warm embrace. He'd explained to her that once they mated, it would go away and she knew she would miss the beauty of it, the feel of his own magic.

But it was a fair exchange for getting to belong to him forever. To belong together.

They kissed each other everywhere, teasing and exploring until she was a panting, writhing mass of emotions and sensations.

He had two fingers buried inside her as he teased her clit with his tongue over and over. He kept bringing her right to the brink of orgasm, then stopping. And she thought she might die if he didn't finish what he'd started.

He must have sensed that she was close to her breaking point because he finally flipped her onto her knees, pulling her ass up against his cock. Her inner walls clenched, needing to be filled with something other than his fingers. She needed all of him, needed to be claimed by him.

"Mine," he growled against her shoulder, his canines raking against her skin.

She shuddered in anticipation as he reached between her legs from behind, rubbing the head of his cock against her slick folds.

All her muscles trembling, she had no more patience and pushed backward.

He groaned as he thrust forward, completely filling her. After all the buildup from that wicked mouth of his, she was so close to climaxing already. And as he pushed into her, by the fourth thrust her orgasm started, her inner walls tightening faster and faster around his thick length. The male was absolute perfection and was hitting the right spot with each thrust.

He bent forward then, his canines breaking the skin between her neck and shoulder.

She cried out at the sudden bite of pain but it quickly turned to pleasure, sending sparks of energy shooting to all her nerve endings. Her orgasm burst through her, sharper than anything she'd ever experienced as she came around him.

He palmed her stomach, slid his hand lower and tweaked her clit, sending off another burst of pleasure before he joined her. He withdrew his canines as he came, calling out her name as he spent himself inside her.

By the time they finally collapsed against the bed every part of her was sensitive and sated.

He rolled onto his back, tugging her so that she was splayed on top of him. Right where she wanted to be.

His arms tightened around her fiercely. "I love you, Dallas. Never imagined I would get a chance at love. Hell, I never imagined I deserved someone as wonderful as you."

She smiled at her mate. "I love you too. And I never imagined I would meet someone like you either."

Then he kissed her again and she lost herself in the sensation of her mate. Her forever.

CHAPTER 32

King rubbed his temples as he looked at his corkboard. As they rebuilt the city, the power structure had to be clear and concise for everyone. Right now they were sitting on a powder keg. This was where he kept all of his information in one place. It was a running list of all the territories and powers in charge of different sects. Some he'd sanctioned, others that were a problem. Any key power player.

Ace, his friend and one of his lieutenants, stood next to him, his arms crossed over his chest as he eyed the information as well. "At least Ingrid's coven is now firmly in your corner. It's progress."

"Yes." It was progress, but it had cost a lot of lives. He would have rather gained Ingrid's loyalty a different way. "There are still a lot of vampires in the city who haven't given me full allegiance."

"You haven't been in charge that long, even if it feels like it. It will take time."

He knew that. He was just worried that they didn't *have* time.

"If you take a strong mate, it will go a long way in solidifying everything," Ace said mildly.

"Maybe." He turned away from the board, immediately thinking of Aurora.

Things were currently in his favor and he was allied with packs and clans around the globe. But he had to keep his own territory in order if he wanted to remain in control, and that was a tricky thing.

"No maybe about it," Ace said as King went to sit behind his desk.

"How so?" King leaned back in his chair, not wanting to discuss mating. He wanted Aurora, that wasn't the problem. If she'd shown even a fraction of interest in him, he'd have made his move. But she'd been in captivity for a year, and though she'd never told him what happened...he could guess there were things she didn't want to discuss. He was pretty sure she just needed a friend.

Ace strode to the window that overlooked the massive yard of their compound. "You need someone who is likable, but also strong. Someone to balance out all of your rough edges. Someone most beings trust. Because you'll never make everyone happy. That's impossible."

Yeah, he'd thought about that. "I'm not mating with a vampire." And he wasn't going to mate with someone he didn't love. He would make almost any sacrifice but that. His wolf wouldn't allow him to anyway. There were simply some things he couldn't force.

Ace snorted and turned back to look at him. "I know." Then he gave him a long, knowing look.

King glanced away, not wanting to have this conversation because he knew exactly where his childhood friend was heading with this. *Aurora.* And King wasn't discussing her with anyone.

"No response?"

"Nope."

"She would make a good mate," he said quietly. "Everybody likes her. Hell, loves her. And she's an Alpha. A young one, but her powers..." Ace let out a low whistle. "She's just coming into them. She'll be a true force one day."

"I know. We're just friends."

Ace had opened his mouth to say something when a sharp knock came at the door. King scented Delphine before she called out, "It's me."

"It's open," King said.

The door swung open and she strode in, her jaw tense. "It's probably nothing, but we're getting reports of some human gang activity near the college housing. I'm headed over there with a team to check things out."

"Keep me updated." He shoved up from his chair. He wasn't sure why he'd thought he would get any rest right now. He had way too much to do, like meeting with a small pride of jaguars who were dealing with harassment from humans. He trusted Delphine and his team to take care of whatever was going on at the college.

She nodded once and strode out, her movements brisk.

"Just think about what I said," Ace said.

King knew he would think about his choice of mate far too much but he simply nodded. "Come on, I'm sure we both have work to do."

Ace started out with him. Another day, another problem to deal with.

At least one problem was gone and done with—those treacherous witches. Now he just needed to figure out if there were more like them lurking in his city.

CHAPTER 33

"I'm nervous," Dallas whispered, clenching Rhys's fingers in hers. Her other hand was stretched out, holding on to Willow for support.

"I'm nervous too," he whispered back, squeezing her hand. She shot him a look that said he was crazy. And maybe he was.

They'd just transported to his brother's castle in Scotland via demigod transportation. Which was basically the most terrifying thing he'd ever done—not that he'd admit it out loud. It had been like being in a tornado and hurricane at the same time.

Weeks ago, Dallas had mentioned to Cynara that they planned to go to Scotland to visit Rhys's family but were waiting until they felt comfortable leaving Willow. Or until she was strong enough to make the entire flight with them.

Cynara had told them that her sister-in-law was a demigod who specialized in transportation. He'd never even heard of such a thing before but here they were. It was hard to believe that five minutes ago they'd been in New Orleans and now they were in the Highlands, an icy wind whipping around them. The trip itself had been a cacophony of noise and wind. And now the rich scent of heather filled his senses.

He hadn't seen his family in thousands of years and he'd been an angry, raging dragon constantly on the warpath back then. He'd hated everything, everyone. Hated the whole world for taking his baby sister. He'd let that consume him to the point that he'd pushed his whole family away. So yeah, he actually *was* nervous to see them even if he'd spoken to his brothers on the phone in the last few weeks.

Now they were standing in a large, colorful garden and just waiting outside Lachlan's castle. It was a mammoth stone structure with multiple turrets jutting up into the sky, as if it had always been part of the landscape. Nyx—the demigod—and her mate, Bo, had walked off into the huge hedge of yew mazes and told them they'd return later.

Suddenly two heavy doors burst open from the back of the castle and Lachlan and Cody raced across the thick, lush lawn to greet them.

Dallas squeezed his hand once and then let go, pushing him forward not so gently.

Heart in his throat, he raced for his brothers, colliding with both of them, wrapping his arms around their necks as they embraced him in turn, gripping tight. They were as large as him, cut from the same cloth.

Rhys wasn't ashamed as tears welled up in his eyes, as emotion clogged his throat to the point that he couldn't speak.

"My brother has come home," Lachlan rasped out, tears in his eyes as well as he slightly loosened his grip. "I have missed you so much," he said as he pulled Rhys back in for another bone-crunching hug.

"I've missed you too, brother." He gripped the back of Lachlan's neck and did the same to Cody, looking fully at his brothers, memorizing their faces again. Gods, it had been too long. "Eilidh has finally been avenged."

"Aye," Lachlan rasped out.

Cody broke away first, wiping at his own cheeks. "Let's meet the lass who is likely too good for you."

Laughing, he turned to find Willow hiding behind Dallas, her big head peeking around Dallas's long, lithe body. He shook with laughter as he strode toward his waiting mate and their Willow. "This is Dallas Kinley, my much too good for me mate," he said, wrapping his arm around her shoulders. "And this is Willow."

He'd told his brothers that he had a pet dragon, but he wasn't sure they'd actually believed him until now.

They both stared, smiles on their faces as they approached. Then Lachlan pulled Dallas into a big hug, lifting her off her feet.

Rhys only snarled a little, which made Cody howl with laughter and mutter about possessive mates before Cody picked her up into a tight hug as well.

"Welcome to the family," Cody said.

Then Star, who he only recognized from TV, raced out. "I couldn't wait any longer, I'm sorry," she said as she joined them. "I wanted to give you guys a brother moment but... You have a real dragon!"

Lachlan looked adoringly at his mate and it warmed Rhys to see his big brother so completely smitten. "Star, this is Rhys, Dallas and Willow."

She rushed Rhys, pulling him into a tight embrace before she hugged Dallas as well, who let out a yelp of surprise at the intense hold.

"I'm going to say this probably more than once, but I'm a huge fan," Dallas said as she stepped back, her smile brilliant.

Star gave her a genuine smile. "Well I'm a fan of your pet. She's the cutest thing I've ever seen."

As the two women talked, Lachlan grabbed him by the shoulder and pulled him close. He wrapped his fingers around the back of Rhys's neck and pressed his forehead to Rhys's. "Brother mine," he murmured, emotion clogging his throat.

Rhys swallowed hard once. "Your Star has the faint scent of..." He cleared his throat, not wanting to say the name of Lachlan's long-dead human love. He never wanted to remind his brother of his loss, his pain, but that scent was there, lingering, and the familiarity startled Rhys.

Lachlan grinned once as he stepped back, though he didn't give him much room. "She does smell like her. And it seems we have much to talk about." He cleared his throat once, his expression turning serious again. "I know your home is with your mate now. I'm just so damn happy that you've found peace."

"More than peace. Happiness and love."

And he had. With the incredible female who had stolen his heart from practically the beginning. Even if he hadn't realized it at the time.

It was always going to be Dallas for him. Always.

ACKNOWLEDGMENTS

Once again, I owe a lot of thanks to Kaylea Cross for helping me to plot out this book during our Saint Augustine getaway (ha, and for listening to me start talking about these Ancients even longer ago). I'm also grateful to Julia Ganis for her editing skills, Sarah for her beta reading, and Jaycee for another fabulous cover. And I know I've said this before, but thank you dear readers for asking for more of this world once I ended the Darkness series. It's been a joy to continue writing in this world.

BOOKLIST

ABOUT THE AUTHOR

Katie Reus is the *New York Times* and *USA Today* bestselling author of the Red Stone Security series, the Darkness series and the Deadly Ops series. She fell in love with romance at a young age thanks to books she pilfered from her mom's stash. Years later she loves reading romance almost as much as she loves writing it.

However, she didn't always know she wanted to be a writer. After changing majors many times, she finally graduated summa cum laude with a degree in psychology. Not long after that she discovered a new love. Writing. She now spends her days writing dark paranormal romance and sexy romantic suspense. For more information on Katie please visit her website: https://katiereus.com

Made in United States
Orlando, FL
25 May 2023

33405355R00150